Christina Lauren is the combined pen name of longtime writing partners/besties/soulmates and brain-twins Christina Hobbs and Lauren Billings, the *New York Times*, *USA Today* and #1 international bestselling authors of the Beautiful and Wild Seasons series, *Sublime*, *The House* and *Autoboyography*.

You can find them online at:

ChristinaLaurenBooks.com

Facebook.com/ChristinaLaurenBooks

@ChristinaLauren

love
and
other words

CHRISTINA LAUREN

piatkus

PIATKUS

First published in the US in 2018 by Gallery Books,
an imprint of Simon & Schuster, Inc.
First published in Great Britain in 2018 by Piatkus
This paperback edition published in 2018 by Piatkus

22

A CIP catalogue record for this book is available from the British Library.

ISBN 978-0-349-41756-1

Printed and bound in Great Britain by Clays Ltd, Elcograf S.p.A.

Papers used by Piatkus are from well-managed forests
and other responsible sources.

Piatkus
An imprint of
Little, Brown Book Group
Carmelite House
50 Victoria Embankment
London EC4Y 0DZ

An Hachette UK Company
www.hachette.co.uk

www.littlebrown.co.uk

For Erin and Marcia,
and the house near the creek in the woods.

love
and
other words

prologue

My dad was a lot taller than my mother—I mean a *lot*. He was six foot five and my mom was just over five foot three. Danish big and Brazilian petite. When they met, she didn't speak a word of English. But by the time she died, when I was ten, it was almost as if they'd created their own language.

I remember the way he would hug her when he got home from work. He would wrap his arms all the way around her shoulders, press his face into her hair while his body curved over hers. His arms became a set of parentheses bracketing the sweetest secret phrase.

I would disappear into the background when they touched like this, feeling like I was witnessing something sacred.

It never occurred to me that love could be anything other than all-consuming. Even as a child, I knew I never wanted anything less.

But then what began as a cluster of malignant cells killed my mother, and I didn't want any of it, ever again. When I lost her, it felt like I was drowning in all the love I still had that could never be given. It filled me up, choked me like a rag doused in kerosene, spilled out in tears and screams and in heavy, pulsing silence. And somehow, as much as I hurt, I knew it was even worse for Dad.

I always knew that he would never fall in love again after Mom. In that way, my dad was always easy to understand. He was straightforward and quiet: he walked quietly, spoke quietly; even his anger was quiet. It was his love that was booming. His love was a roaring, vociferous bellow. And after he loved Mom with the strength of the sun, and after the cancer killed her with a gentle gasp, I figured he would be hoarse for the rest of his life and wouldn't ever want another woman the way he'd wanted her.

Before Mom died, she left Dad a list of things she wanted him to remember as he saw me into adulthood:

1. Don't spoil her with toys; spoil her with books.

2. Tell her you love her. Girls need the words.

3. When she's quiet, you do the talking.

4. Give Macy ten dollars a week. Make her save two. Teach her the value of money.

5. Until she's sixteen, her curfew should be ten o'clock, no exceptions.

The list went on and on, deep into the fifties. It wasn't so much that she didn't trust him; she just wanted me to feel her influence even after she was gone. Dad reread it frequently, making notes in pencil, highlighting certain things, making sure he wasn't missing a milestone or getting something wrong. As I grew older, the list became a bible of sorts. Not necessarily a rule book, but more a reassurance that all these things Dad and I struggled with were normal.

One rule in particular loomed large for Dad.

25. When Macy looks so tired after school that she can't even form a sentence, take her away from the stress of her life. Find a weekend getaway that is

3

easy and close that lets her breathe a little.

And although Mom likely never intended that we actually *buy* a weekend home, my dad—a literal type—saved, and planned, and researched all the small towns north of San Francisco, preparing for the day when he would need to invest in our retreat.

In the first couple of years after Mom died, he watched me, his ice-blue eyes somehow both soft and probing. He would ask questions that required long answers, or at least longer than "yes," "no," or "I don't care." The first time I answered one of these detailed questions with a vacant moan, too tired from swim practice, and homework, and the dull tedium of dealing with persistently dramatic friends, Dad called a real estate agent and demanded she find us the perfect weekend home in Healdsburg, California.

We first saw it at an open house, shown by the local Realtor, who let us in with a wide smile and a tiny, judgmental slant of her eyes toward our big-city San Francisco agent. It was a four-bedroom wood-shingled and sharply angled cabin, chronically damp and potentially moldy, tucked back into the shade of the woods and near a creek that would continually bubble outside my window. It was bigger than we needed, with more land than we could possibly maintain, and neither Dad nor I would realize at the time that the most important room in the house would be the library he would make for me inside my expansive closet.

Nor could Dad have known that my whole world would end up next door, held in the palm of a skinny nerd named Elliot Lewis Petropoulos.

now

tuesday, october 3

If you drew a straight line from my apartment in San Francisco to Berkeley, it would only be ten and a half miles, but even in the best commuting window it takes more than an hour without a car.

"I caught a bus at six this morning," I say. "Two BART lines, and another bus." I look down at my watch. "Seven thirty. Not too bad."

Sabrina wipes a smudge of foamy milk from her upper lip. As much as she understands my avoidance of cars, I know there's a part of her that thinks I should just power through it and get a Prius or Subaru, like any other self-respecting Bay Area resident. "Don't let anyone tell you you're not a saint."

"I really am. You made me leave my bubble." But I say it with a smile, and look down at her tiny daughter on my lap. I've only ever seen the princess Vivienne twice, and she seems to have doubled in size. "Good thing *you're* worth it."

I hold babies every day, but it never feels like this. Sabrina and I used to live across a dorm room from each other at Tufts. Then we moved into an apartment off-campus before quasi-upgrading to a crumbling house during our respective graduate programs. By some magic we both ended up on the West Coast, in the Bay Area, and now Sabrina has a *baby*. That we are old enough now to be doing this—birthing children, *breeding*—is the weirdest feeling ever.

"I was up at eleven last night with this one," Sabrina says, looking at us fondly. Her smile turns wry at the edges. "And two. And four. And six . . ."

"Okay, you win. But to be fair, she smells better than most of the people on the bus." I plant a small kiss on Viv's head and tuck her more securely into the crook of my arm before carefully reaching for my coffee.

The cup feels strange in my hand. It's ceramic, not a paper throwaway or the enormous stainless steel travel mug Sean fills to the brim for me each morning, assuming—not incorrectly—that it takes a hulking dose of caffeine to get me ready to tackle the day. It's been forever since I had time to sit down with an actual mug and sip anything.

"You already look like a mama," Sabrina says, watching us from across the small café table.

"The benefit of working with babies all day."

Sabrina is quiet for a breath, and I realize my mistake. Ground rule number one: never reference my job around mothers, especially *new* mothers. I can practically hear her heart stutter across the table from me.

"I don't know how you do it," she whispers.

The sentence is a repeating chorus to my life right now. It seems to boggle my friends over and over again that I made the decision to go into pediatrics at UCSF—in the critical-care track. Without fail, I catch a flash of suspicion that maybe I'm missing an important, tender bone, some maternal brake that should prevent me from being able to routinely witness the suffering of sick kids.

I give Sabrina my usual refrain of "Someone needs to," then add, "And I'm good at it."

"I bet you are."

"Now pediatric neuro? *That* I couldn't do," I say, and then pull my lips between my teeth, physically restraining myself from saying more.

Shut up, Macy. Shut your crazy babble mouth.

Sabrina offers a small nod, staring at her baby. Viv smiles up at me and kicks her legs excitedly.

"Not all the stories are sad." I tickle her tummy. "Tiny miracles happen every day, don't they, cutie?"

The subject change rolls out of Sabrina, loud enough to be a little jarring: "How's wedding planning coming?"

I groan, pressing my face into the sweet baby smell of Viv's neck.

"That good, huh?" Laughing, Sabrina reaches for her daughter, as if she's unable to share her any longer. I can't blame her. She's such a warm and shapable little bundle in my arms.

"She's perfect, honey," I say quietly, handing her over. "Such a solid little girl."

And, as if everything I do is somehow hardwired to my memories of *them*—the raucous life next door, the giant, chaotic family I never had—I am hit with nostalgia, of the last non-work-related baby I spent any real time with. It's a memory of me as a teenager, staring down at baby Alex as she slept in her bouncy chair.

My brain leapfrogs through a hundred images: Miss Dina cooking dinner with the swaddled bundle of Alex slung against her chest. Mr. Nick holding Alex in his beefy, hairy arms, staring down at her with the tenderness of an entire village. Sixteen-year-old George trying—and failing—to change a diaper without incident on the family couch. The protective lean of Nick Jr., George, and Andreas as they stared down at their new, most beloved sibling. And then, invariably, my mind shifts to Elliot just beyond or behind, waiting quietly for his older brothers to move on to their fighting or running or mess making, leaving him to pick up Alex, read to her, give her his undivided attention.

I ache, missing them all so much, but especially him.

"Mace," Sabrina prompts.

I blink. "What?"

"The wedding?"

"Right." My mood droops; the prospect of planning a wedding while juggling a hundred hours a week at the hospital never fails to exhaust me. "We haven't moved on it yet. We still need to pick a date, a place, a . . . everything. Sean doesn't care about the details, which, I guess, is good?"

"Of course," she says with false brightness, shifting Viv to covertly nurse her at the table. "And besides, what's the rush?"

In her question, the twin thought is very shallowly buried: *I'm your best friend and I've only met the man twice, for fuck's sake. What* is *the rush?*

And she's right. There is no rush. We've only been together for a few months. It's just that Sean is the first man I've met in more than ten years who I can be with and not feel like I'm holding back somehow. He's easy, and calm, and when his six-year-old daughter Phoebe asked when we were getting married, it seemed to switch something over in him, propelling him to ask me himself, later.

"I swear," I tell her, "I have no interesting updates. Wait—no. I have a dentist appointment next week." Sabrina laughs. "That's what we've come to, that's the only thing other than you that will break up the monotony for the foreseeable future. Work, sleep, repeat."

Sabrina sees this as the invitation it is to talk freely about her new family of three, and she unrolls a list of accomplishments: the first smile, the first belly laugh, and just yesterday, a tiny fist shooting out with accuracy and firmly grabbing her mama's finger.

I listen, loving each normal detail acknowledged for what it really is: a miracle. I wish I got to hear all of her "normal details" every day. I love what I do, but I miss just . . . talking.

I'm scheduled today for noon, and will probably be on the unit until the middle of the night. I'll come home and sleep for a few hours, and do it all over again tomorrow. Even after coffee with Sabrina and Viv, the rest of this day will bleed into the next and—unless something truly awful happens on the unit—I won't remember a single thing about it.

So as she talks, I try to absorb as much of this outside world as I can. I pull in the scent of coffee and toast, the sound of music rumbling beneath the bustle of the customers. When Sabrina bends down to pull a pacifier out of her diaper bag, I glance up to the counter, scanning the woman with the pink dreadlocks, the shorter man with a neck tattoo taking coffee orders, and, in front of them, the long masculine torso that slaps me into acute awareness.

His hair is nearly black. It's thick and messy, falling over the tops of his ears. His collar is folded under on one side, his shirttails untucked from a pair of worn black jeans. His Vans are slip-on and faded old-school check print. A well-used messenger bag is slung across one shoulder and rests against the opposite hip.

With his back to me, he looks like a thousand other men in Berkeley, but I know exactly which man this is.

It's the heavy, dog-eared book tucked under his arm that gives it away: there's only one person I know who rereads *Ivanhoe* every October. Ritually, and with absolute adoration.

Unable to look away, I'm locked in anticipation of the moment he turns and I can see what nearly eleven years have done to him. I barely give thought to my own appearance: mint-green scrubs, practical sneakers, hair in a messy ponytail. Then again, it never occurred to either of us to consider our own faces or degree of put-togetherness before. We were always too busy memorizing each other.

Sabrina pulls my attention away while the ghost of my past is paying for his order.

"Mace?"

I blink to her. "Sorry. I. Sorry. The . . . what?"

"I was just babbling about diaper rash. I'm more interested in what's got you so . . ." She turns to follow where I'd been looking. "*Oh.*"

Her "oh" doesn't contain understanding yet. Her "oh" is purely about how the man looks from behind. He's tall—that happened suddenly, when he turned fifteen. And his shoulders are broad—that happened suddenly, too, but later. I remember noticing it the first time he hovered above me in the closet, his jeans at his knees, his broad form blocking out the weak overhead light. His hair is thick—but that's always been true. His jeans rest low on his hips and his ass looks amazing. I . . . have no idea when *that* happened.

Basically, he looks exactly like the kind of guy we would ogle silently before turning to each other to share the wordless *I know, right?* face. It's one of the most surreal realizations of my life: he's grown into the kind of stranger I would dreamily admire.

It's strange enough to see him from the back, and I'm watching him with such intensity that for a second, I convince myself that it's not him after all.

Maybe it could be anyone—and after a decade apart, how well do I really know his body, anyway?

But then he turns, and I feel all the air get sucked out of the room. It's if I've been punched in the solar plexus, my diaphragm momentarily paralyzed.

Sabrina hears the creaking, dusty sound coming from me and turns back around. I sense her starting to rise from her chair. "Mace?"

I pull in a breath, but it's shallow and sour somehow, making my eyes burn.

His face is narrower, jaw sharper, morning stubble thicker. He's still wearing the same style of thick-rimmed glasses, but they no longer dwarf his face. His bright hazel eyes are still magnified by the thick lenses. His nose is the same—but it's no longer too big for his face. And his mouth is the same, too—straight, smooth, capable of the world's most perfectly sardonic grin.

I can't even imagine what expression he would make if he saw me here. It might be one I've never seen him make before.

"Mace?" Sabrina reaches with a free hand, grabbing my forearm. "Honey, you okay?"

I swallow, and close my eyes to break my own trance. "Yeah."

She sounds unconvinced: "You sure?"

"I mean . . ." Swallowing again, I open my eyes and intend to look at her, but my gaze is drawn back over her shoulder again. "That guy over there . . . It's Elliot."

This time, her "*Oh*" is meaningful.

then

friday, august 9
fifteen years ago

I first saw Elliot at the open house.

The cabin was empty; unlike the meticulously staged real estate "products" in the Bay Area, this funky house for sale in Healdsburg was left completely unfurnished. Although as an adult I would learn to appreciate the potential in undecorated spaces, to my adolescent eyes, the emptiness felt cold and hollow. Our house in Berkeley was unselfconsciously cluttered. While she was alive, Mom's sentimental tendencies overrode Dad's Danish minimalism, and after she died he clearly couldn't find it in himself to dial back the decor.

Here, the walls had darker patches where old paintings had hung for years. A path was worn into the carpet, revealing the preferred route of the previous inhabitants: from the front door to the kitchen. The upstairs was open to the entryway, the hallway looking over the first floor with only an old wooden railing at the edge. Upstairs, the doors to the rooms were all closed, giving the long hallway a mildly haunted feeling.

"At the end," Dad said, lifting his chin to indicate where he meant for me to go. He had looked at the house online, and knew a bit more than I did what to expect. "Your room could be that one down there."

I climbed the dark stairs, passing the master bedroom and bath, and continued on to the end of the deep, narrow hallway. I could see a pale green light coming from beneath the door—what I would soon know to be the result of spring-green paint illuminated by late-afternoon sun. The crystal knob was cold but unclouded, and it turned with a rusty whine. The door stuck, edges misshapen from the chronic dampness. I pushed with my shoulder, determined to get in, and nearly tumbled into the warm, bright room.

It was longer than it was wide, maybe even doubled. A huge window took up most of the long wall, looking out onto a hillside dense with moss-covered trees. Like a patient butler, a tall, skinny window sat at the far end, on the narrow wall, overlooking the Russian River in the distance.

If the downstairs was unimpressive, the bedrooms, at least, held promise.

Feeling uplifted, I turned back to go find Dad.

"Did you see the closet in there, Mace?" he asked just as I stepped out. "I thought we could make it into a library for you." He was emerging from the master suite. I heard one of the agents call for him, and instead of coming to me, he made his way back downstairs.

I returned to the bedroom, walked to the back. The door to the closet opened without any protest. The knob was even warm in my hand.

Like every other space in the house, it was undecorated. But it wasn't empty.

Confusion and mild panic set my heart pounding.

Sitting in the deep space was a boy. He had been reading, tucked into the far corner, back and neck curled into a C to fit himself into the lowest point beneath the sloped ceiling.

He couldn't have been much older than thirteen, same as me. Skinny, with thick dark hair that badly needed to see scissors, enormous hazel eyes behind substantial glasses. His nose was too big for his face, teeth too big for his mouth, and presence entirely too big for a room that was meant to be empty.

The question erupted from me, edged with unease: "Who are you?"

He stared at me, wide-eyed in surprise. "I didn't realize anyone would actually come see this place."

19

My heart was still hammering. And something about his gaze—so unblinking, eyes huge behind the lenses—made me feel oddly exposed. "We're thinking of buying it."

The boy stood, dusting off his clothes, revealing that the widest part of each leg was at the knee. His shoes were brown polished leather, his shirt ironed and tucked into khaki shorts. He looked completely harmless . . . but as soon as he took a step forward, my heart tripped in panic, and I blurted: "My dad has a black belt."

He looked a mixture of scared and skeptical. "Really?"

"Yeah."

His brows drew together. "In what?"

I dropped my fists from where they'd rested at my hips. "Okay, no black belt. But he's huge."

This he seemed to believe, and he looked past me anxiously.

"What are you doing in here anyway?" I asked, glancing around. The space was enormous for a closet. A perfect square, at least twelve feet on each side, with a high ceiling that sloped dramatically at the back of the room, where it was probably only three feet high. I could imagine sitting in here, on a couch, with pillows and books, and spending the perfect Saturday afternoon.

"I like to read in here." He shrugged, and something dormant woke inside me at the mental symmetry, a buzz I hadn't felt in years. "My mom had a key when the Hanson family owned the place, and they were never here."

"Are your parents going to buy this house?"

He looked confused. "No. I live next door."

"So aren't you trespassing?"

He shook his head. "It's an *open* house, remember?"

I looked him over again. His book was thick, with a dragon on the cover. He was tall, and angled at every possible location—all sharp elbows and pointy shoulders. Hair was shaggy but combed. Fingernails were trimmed.

"So you just hang out here?"

"Sometimes," he said. "It's been empty for a couple years."

I narrowed my eyes. "Are you *sure* you're supposed to be in here? You look out of breath, like you're nervous."

He shrugged, one pointy shoulder lifted to the sky. "Maybe I just came back from running a marathon."

"You don't look like you could run to the corner."

He paused for a breath, and then burst out laughing. It sounded like a laugh that wasn't given freely very often, and something inside me bloomed.

"What's your name?" I asked.

"Elliot. What's yours?"

"Macy."

Elliot stared at me, pushing his glasses up with his finger, but they immediately slid down again. "You know, if you buy this house I won't just come over and read in here."

There was a challenge there, some choice offered. *Friend or foe?*

I could really use a friend.

I exhaled, giving him a begrudging smile. "If we buy this house you can come over and read if you want."

He grinned, so wide I could count his teeth. "Maybe all this time I was just getting it warmed up for you."

now

tuesday, october 3

Elliot still hasn't seen me.

He waits near the espresso bar for his drink with his head ducked as he looks down. In a sea of people connecting to the world via the isolation of their smartphones, Elliot is reading a book.

Does he even *have* a phone? For anyone else, it would be an absurd question. Not for him. Eleven years ago he did, but it was a hand-me-down from his father and the kind of flip-phone that required him to hit the 5 key three times if he wanted to type an *L*. He rarely used it as anything other than a paperweight.

"When was the last time you saw him?" Sabrina asks.

I blink over to her, brows drawn. I *know* she knows the answer to this question, at least generally. But my expression relaxes when I understand there's nothing else she can do right now but make conversation; I've turned into a mute maniac.

"My senior year in high school. New Year's."

She gives a full, bared-teeth wince. *"Right."*

Some instinct kicks in, some self-preservationist energy propelling me up and out of my chair.

"I'm sorry," I say, looking down at Sabrina and Viv. "I'm going to head out."

"Of course. Yeah. Totally."

"I'll call this weekend? Maybe we can do Golden Gate Park."

She's still nodding as if my robotic suggestion is even a remote possibility. We both know I haven't had a weekend off since before I started my residency in July.

Trying to move as inconspicuously as possible, I pull my bag over my shoulder and bend to kiss Sabrina's cheek.

"I love you," I say, standing, and wishing I could take her with me. She smells like baby, too.

Sabrina nods, returning the sentiment, and then, while I gaze at Viv and her chubby little fist, she glances back over her shoulder and freezes.

From her posture, I know Elliot has seen me.

"Um . . ." she says, turning back and lifting her chin as if I should probably take a look. "He's coming."

I dig into my bag, working to appear extremely busy and distracted. "I'm gonna jet," I mumble.

"Mace?"

I freeze, one hand on the strap of my bag, my eyes on the floor. A nostalgic pang resonates through me as soon as I hear his voice. It had been high and squeaky until it broke. He got endless shit about how nasal and whiny he was, and then, one day, the universe had the last laugh, giving Elliot a voice like warm, rich honey.

He says my name again—no nickname, this time, but quieter: "Macy Lea?"

I look up, and—in an impulse I'm sure I will be laughing about until I die—I lift my hand and wave limply, offering a bright "Elliot! Hey!"

As if we're casual acquaintances from freshman orientation.

You know, as if we met once on the train from Santa Barbara.

Just as he pushes his thick hair out of his eyes in a gesture of disbelief I've seen him make a million times, I turn and press through the crowd and out onto the sidewalk. I'm jogging in the wrong direction before catching my mistake halfway down the block and whipping around. Two long strides back the other way, with my head down, heart hammering, and I slam right into a broad chest.

"Oh! I'm sorry!" I blurt before I look up and realize what I've done.

Elliot's hands come around my upper arms, holding me steady only a few inches away from him. I know he's looking at my face, waiting for me to meet his gaze, but my eyes are stuck on the sight of his Adam's apple, and my thoughts are stuck remembering how I used to stare at his neck, covertly, on and off for hours while we were reading together in the closet.

"Macy. Seriously?" he says quietly, meaning a thousand things.

Seriously, is it you?

Seriously, why did you just run off?

Seriously, where have you been for the past decade?

Part of me wishes I could be the kind of person to just push past and run away and pretend this never happened. I could get back on BART, hop on the Muni to the hospital, and delve into a busy workday managing emotions that, honestly, are much bigger and more deserving than these.

But another part of me has been expecting this exact moment for the past eleven years. Relief and anguish pulse heavily in my blood. I've wanted to see him every day. But also, I never wanted to see him again.

"Hi." I finally look up at him. I'm trying to figure out what to say here; my head is full of senseless words. It's a storm of black and white.

"Are you . . . ?" he starts breathlessly. He still hasn't let go of me. "Did you move back here?"

"San Francisco."

I watch as he takes in my scrubs, my ugly sneakers. "Physician?"

"Yeah. Resident."

I am a robot.

His dark brows lift. "So what are you doing here *today*?"

God, what a weird place to begin. But when there's a mountain ahead of you, I guess you start with a single step to the straightest point ahead. "I was meeting Sabrina for coffee."

He scrunches his nose in a painfully familiar expression of incomprehension.

"My college roommate," I clarify. "She lives in Berkeley."

Elliot deflates a tiny bit, reminding me that he doesn't know Sabrina. It used to bother us when we would have a month in between updates. Now there are years and entire lives unknown to each other.

"I called you," he says. "Like a million times. And then that number changed."

He runs his hand through his hair and shrugs helplessly. And I get it. This whole fucking moment is so surreal. Even now it's incomprehensible that we let this distance happen. That *I* let this happen.

"I know. I, um, got a new phone," I say lamely.

He laughs, but it isn't a particularly happy sound. "Yeah, I figured."

"Elliot," I say, pushing past the clog in my throat at the feel of his name there, "I'm sorry. I really have to run. I need to be at work soon."

He bends so that he's level with my face. "Are you kidding?" His eyes go wide. "I can't just run into you at Saul's and be like, 'Hey, Macy, what's up,' and then you go to work, and I go to work, and we don't talk for another *ten fucking years*."

And there it is. Elliot was never able to play the surface game.

"I'm not prepared for this," I admit quietly.

"Do you have to *prepare* for me?"

"If there's anyone I have to prepare for, it's you."

This hits him where I meant it to—straight in the bull's-eye of some vulnerable nucleus—but as soon as he winces I regret it.

Goddammit.

"Just give me a minute," he urges, pulling me to the edge of the sidewalk so we aren't obstructing the steady stream of commuters. "How are you? How long have you been back? How is Duncan?"

All around us, the world seems to go still.

"I'm good," I say mechanically. "I moved back in May." I am obliterated by his third question, and my answer comes out trembling: "And, um . . . Dad died."

Elliot lurches slightly backward. "*What?*"

"Yeah," I say, voice garbled. I am struck dumb by this,

struggling to rewrite history, to rewire a thousand synapses in my brain.

Somehow, I'm managing to have this conversation without completely losing my shit, but if I stand here for two more minutes, all bets are off. With Elliot right here asking about Dad, and going on two hours of sleep and the prospect of an eighteen-hour day ahead of me . . . I need to get out of here before I melt down.

But when I look up at him, I see Elliot's face is a mirror to what's happening in my chest. He looks devastated. He's the only one who would look that way after hearing that Dad died, because he's the only one who would have understood what it did to me.

"Duncan *died*?" His voice comes out thick with emotion. "Macy, why didn't you tell me?"

Holy shit, *that* is an enormous question.

"I . . ." I start, and shake my head. "We weren't in touch when it happened."

Nausea rolls up from my stomach to my throat. What a cop-out. What an unbelievable evasion.

He shakes his head. "I didn't know. I'm so sorry, Mace."

I give myself three more seconds to look at him, and it's like another punch to the gut. He's my person. He's always been my person. My best friend, my confidant, probably the love of my life. And I've spent the last eleven years being angry and self-righteous. But at the end of the day, he tore a hole in us, and fate ripped it wide open.

29

"I'm going to go," I say in an abrupt burst of awkward. "Okay?"

Before he can answer, I split, booking it down the street toward the BART station. The entire time I'm speed walking, and for the full rumbling trip back under the bay, I feel like he's right there, behind me or in a seat in the next car down.

then

friday, october 11

fifteen years ago

The entire Petropoulos family was in their front yard when we pulled up in a moving van two months later. The van was only half-full because Dad and I had both thought at the rental counter that we'd have more to bring with us. But in the end, we'd bought only enough furniture from the consignment store to have somewhere to sleep, eat, and read, and not much else.

Dad called it "furniture kindling." I didn't get it.

Maybe I would have if I'd let myself think about it for a few seconds, but the only thought I had during the entire ninety-minute drive was that we were going to a house that

31

Mom had never seen. Yes, she wanted us to do this, but she hadn't actually picked it out, she hadn't seen it. There was something so horribly sour about that reality. Dad still drove his rumbling old green Volvo. We still lived in the same house on Rose Street. Every piece of furniture inside had been there when Mom was alive. I had new clothes, but I always felt a little like Mom picked them out through some divine intervention when we shopped, because Dad had a way of bringing me the biggest, baggiest things, and invariably some sympathetic saleswoman would swoop in with an armload of more suitable clothing and a reassurance that, yes, this is what all the girls are wearing now, and, no, don't worry, Mr. Sorensen.

Climbing from the van, I straightened my shirt over the waistband of my shorts and stared up at the crew now assembling on our gravelly driveway. I spotted Elliot first—the familiar face in the crowd. But around him were three other boys, and two smiling parents.

The vision of the bursting-at-the-seams family there, waiting to help, only magnified the ache clawing its way up my throat from my chest.

The man—so clearly Elliot's father, with the thick black hair and telltale nose—jogged forward, reaching to shake Dad's hand. He was shorter than Dad by only a couple of inches, a rarity.

"Nick Petropoulos," he said, turning to shake my hand next. "You must be Macy."

"Yes, sir."

"Call me Nick."

"Okay, Mr. . . . Nick." I had never in my life imagined calling a parent by their first name.

With a laugh, he looked back to Dad. "Thought you could use a hand unloading all this."

Dad smiled and spoke with his trademark simplicity: "That's nice of you. Thanks."

"Also thought my boys could use some exercise so they don't wallop each other all day." Mr. Nick extended a thick, hairy arm and pointed. "Over there you'll see my wife, Dina. My boys: Nick Jr., George, Andreas, and Elliot."

Three strapping guys—and Elliot—stood at the base of our front steps, watching us. I was guessing they were all around fifteen to seventeen, save Elliot, who was so physically different from his brothers that I wasn't sure how old he was. Their mother, Dina, was formidable—tall and curvy, but with a smile that brought deep, friendly dimples to her cheeks. Other than Elliot—who was the stick-figure version of his father—all of her sons looked just like her. Sleepy-eyed, dimpled, tall.

Cute.

Dad's arm came around my shoulders, pulling me close. I wondered if it was a protective gesture or if he, too, was feeling how listless our tiny family seemed in comparison.

"I didn't realize you had four sons. I think Macy already met Elliot?" Dad looked down to me for confirmation.

In my peripheral vision, I could see Elliot shifting on his feet in discomfort. I gave him a sly grin. "Yeah," I said, adding in my best *who does this?* tone: "He was reading in my closet."

Mr. Nick waved this away. "The day of the open house, I know, I know. I'll be honest, that kid loves a book, and that closet was his favorite spot. His buddy Tucker used to come here on the weekends, but he's gone now." Looking to Dad, he added, "The family up and moved to Cincinnati. Wine country to Ohio? The shits, right? But don't worry, Macy. Won't happen again." With a smile, he followed Dad's stoic march up the steps. "We've lived right next door the past seventeen years. Been in this house a thousand times." A stair creaked beneath his work boot, and he toed it with a frown. "That one's always been a problem."

Even at my age I saw what this did to Dad's posture. He was an easygoing metro guy, but Mr. Nick's casual familiarity with the property immediately pushed some macho rigidity into his spine.

"I can fix that," Dad said, voice uncharacteristically deep as he leaned on the creaky step. Eager to reassure me that every tiny problem would be corrected, he added quietly, "I'm not wild about the front door, either, but that's easy enough to replace. And anything else you see, tell me. I want it to be perfect."

"Dad," I said, nudging him gently, "it's already perfect. Okay?"

While the Petropoulos boys wandered down to the moving truck, Dad fumbled with his keys, finding the right one on a ring heavy with keys for other doors, for our other life seventy-three miles away from here.

"I'm not sure what we'll need for the kitchen," Dad mumbled to me. "And there's probably some renovations to come . . ."

He looked at me with an unsure smile and propped the front door open. I was still evaluating the wide porch that wrapped around to the side, hiding some unknown view of the thick trees beyond the side yard. My mind had drifted to goblins and tromping through the woods looking for arrowheads. Maybe a boy would kiss me in those woods someday.

Maybe it would be one of the Petropoulos boys.

My skin flamed with a blush that I hid by ducking my head and letting my hair fall forward. To date, my only crush had been Jason Lee in seventh grade. After having known each other since kindergarten, we'd danced stiffly to one song at the Spring Fling and then awkwardly burst apart, never to speak again. Apparently I was fine on a friend level with nearly everyone, but add in some mild romantic chemistry and I turned into a spastic robot.

We created an efficient line of arms passing boxes, and quickly emptied the truck, leaving the furniture to the bigger bodies. Elliot and I each grabbed a box labeled *Macy* to carry upstairs. I followed him down the long hallway and into the bright emptiness of my bedroom.

"You can just put that in the corner," I said. "And thanks."

He looked over at me, nodding as he set the box down. "Are these books?"

"Yeah."

With a tiny look toward me to make sure it was okay, Elliot lifted the flap on the box and peered inside. He pulled out the book on top. *Pay It Forward*.

"You've read this?" he asked dubiously.

I nodded and took the beloved book from him and placed it on the empty shelf just inside the closet.

"It's good," he said.

Surprised, I looked up at him, asking, "You read it, too?"

He nodded, saying unselfconsciously, "It made me cry."

Reaching in, he grabbed another book and dragged a finger across the cover. "This one's good, too." His large eyes blinked up at me. "You have good taste."

I stared at him. "You read a lot."

"Usually a book a day."

My eyes went wide. "Are you serious?"

He shrugged. "People come to the Russian River on vacation and a lot of times they leave their holiday reads here when they go. The library gets a ton, and I have a deal with Sue down there: I get first crack at the new donations as long as I pick them up on Monday and bring them back on Wednesday." He nudged his glasses up the bridge of his nose. "One time, she got six new books in from a family that was visiting for the week, and I read them all."

"You read them all in three days?" I asked. "That's insane."

Elliot frowned, narrowing his eyes. "You think I'm lying?"

"I don't think you're lying. How old are you?"

"Fourteen, last week."

"You look younger."

"Thanks," he said flatly. "I was going for that." He blew his breath out, puffing his hair off his forehead.

A laugh burst free of my throat. "I didn't mean it like that."

"How old are *you*?" he asked.

"Thirteen. My birthday is March eighteenth."

He nudged his glasses up. "You're in eighth grade?"

"Yeah. You?"

Elliot nodded. "Same." He looked around the empty space, surveying. "What do your parents do? They work in the city?"

I shook my head, chewing my lip. Without realizing it, I had really enjoyed talking to someone who didn't know that I was motherless, hadn't seen me broken and raw after I lost her. "My dad owns a company in Berkeley that imports and sells handmade ceramics and art and stuff." I didn't add that it all started when he began importing his father's beautiful pottery and it sold like crazy.

"Cool. What about your—"

"What do *your* parents do?"

37

He narrowed his eyes at my outburst but answered anyway. "My mom works part-time in the tasting room at Toad Hollow. My dad is the town dentist . . ."

The town dentist. The *one* dentist? I guess I hadn't realized how small Healdsburg was until he said that. In Berkeley, there were three dentists' offices on my four-block walk to school.

"But he only works three days a week, and you can probably tell he doesn't like to stay still. He does everything around town," Elliot said. "Helps at the farmers' market. Helps with operations at a few wineries."

"Yeah, wine's a big deal around here, isn't it?" I realized as he spoke about it how many wineries we passed on the drive here.

"Wine: it's what's for dinner," Elliot said with a laugh.

And there, right there in that second, it felt like we had something easy.

I hadn't had easy in three years. I had friends who stopped knowing how to talk to me, or got tired of me being mopey, or were so focused on boys that we no longer had anything in common.

But then he ruined it: "Are your parents divorced?"

I sucked in a breath, oddly offended. "No."

He tilted his head and watched me, unspeaking. He didn't need to point out that both times I'd visited this town, I'd come without a mother.

I released my breath what felt like an hour later. "My mom died three years ago."

This truth reverberated around the room, and I knew my admission irrevocably changed something between us. The simple things I was no longer: his new neighbor, a girl, potentially interesting, also potentially uninteresting. Now I was a girl who had been permanently damaged by life. I was someone to be handled carefully.

His eyes had gone wide behind his thick lenses. "Seriously?"

I nodded.

Did I wish I hadn't told him? A little. What was the point of a weekend retreat if I couldn't actually retreat from the one truth that seemed to stall my heartbeat every few minutes?

He looked down at his feet, toyed with a stray thread on his shorts. "I don't know what I would do."

"I still don't know what to do."

He fell quiet. I never knew how to reel a conversation back after the Dead Mother topic. And which was worse: having it with a relative stranger like this, or having it back home with someone who had known me my entire life and no longer knew how to speak to me without false brightness or syrupy sympathy?

"What's your favorite word?"

Startled, I looked up at him, unsure I'd heard him right. "My favorite word?"

He nodded, slipping his glasses up his nose with a quick, practiced scrunch of his face that made him look angry and then surprised within a single second. "You have seven boxes of books up here. A wild guess tells me you like words."

I suppose I had never thought about having a favorite word, but now that he asked, I kind of liked the idea. I let my eyes lose focus as I thought.

"*Ranunculus,*" I said after a moment.

"What?"

"Ranunculus. It's a kind of flower. It's such a weird word but the flowers are so pretty, I like how unexpected that is."

They were my Mom's favorite, I didn't say.

"That's a pretty girly answer."

"Well, I am a girl."

He kept his eyes on his feet but I knew I wasn't imagining the gleam of interest I'd seen when I said *ranunculus*. I bet he had expected me to say *unicorn* or *daisy* or *vampire*.

"What about you? What's your favorite word? I bet it's *tungsten*. Or, like, *amphibian*."

He quirked a smile, answering, "*Regurgitate.*"

Scrunching my nose, I stared at him. "That is a gross word."

This made him smile even wider. "I like the hard consonant sounds in it. It kinda sounds like exactly what it means."

"An onomatopoeia?"

I half expected trumpets to blast revelatory music from an invisible speaker in the wall from the way Elliot stared at me, lips parted and glasses slowly sliding down his nose.

"Yeah," he said.

"I'm not a complete idiot, you know. You don't have to look so surprised that I know some big words."

"I never thought you were an idiot," he said quietly, looking toward the box and pulling out another book to hand to me.

For a long time after we returned to our slow, inefficient method of unpacking the books, I could feel him looking up and watching me, tiny flashes of stolen glances.

I pretended I didn't notice.

now

wednesday, october 4

I feel like I've torn open some stitches overnight. Everything inside is raw—as if I've bruised an emotional organ. Above me, the ceiling looks drab; water stains crawl along the spidery cracks in the plaster that radiate from the light fixture in the ceiling. The fan circles lazily around and around and around the frosted globe. As they turn, the blades cut through the air, mimicking Sean's rhythmic exhale while he sleeps beside me.

Chh.

Chh.

Chh.

He was asleep when I got home around two this morning. For once, I'm thankful for the long hours; I don't know how I would have sat through dinner with him and Phoebe when all I could think about was Elliot showing up at Saul's yesterday.

I had this momentary clench of guilt last night on the bus home, when the chaos of my shift was slowly ebbing from my thoughts and the run-in with Elliot pushed its way back in. In a panicked burst, I wondered how rude it was of me to not introduce Elliot to Sabrina.

So fucking quickly he comes back, front and center.

Sean wakes when I move to rub my face, rolling to me, pulling me close with his hand curled around my hip, but for the first time since he kissed me last May, I feel like I'm betraying something.

Groaning, I push away and sit up, propping my elbows on my knees at the side of the bed.

"You okay, babe?" he asks, moving close behind me and resting his chin on my shoulder.

Sean doesn't even know about Elliot. Which is crazy, when I think about it, because if I'm marrying him, he should know every part of me, right? Even if we haven't been together that long, the big things should be placed right up front, and for most of my adolescence, it doesn't get much bigger than Elliot. Sean knows I grew up in Berkeley, spent many weekends up in the wine country of Healdsburg, and had some good friends there. But he has no idea that I met Elliot when I was thirteen, fell in love with him when I was fourteen, and pushed him out of my life only a few years later.

I nod. "I'm good. Just tired."

I feel him turn his head beside me and glance at the clock, and I mimic his action. It's only 6:40, and I don't need to start rounds until 9:00. Sleep is a precious commodity. *Why, brain, why?*

He runs a hand through his salt-and-pepper hair.

"Of course you're tired. Come back to bed."

When he says this, I know he really means *Lie back down and let's have some of the sex before Phoebs is up.*

The problem is, I can't risk the chance that doing that with him will feel wrong now.

Fucking Elliot.

I just need a couple of days of distance from it, that's all.

then

thursday, december 20

fifteen years ago

'd never spent Christmas away from home before, but early December that first year at the cabin, Dad said we were going to have an adventure. To some parents, this might have meant a trip to Paris or a cruise to somewhere exotic. To my dad, it meant an old-fashioned holiday in our new house, lighting the Danish *kalenderlys*—a Christmas candle—and enjoying roast duck, cabbage, beetroot, and potatoes for Christmas dinner.

We arrived around dinnertime on the twentieth, our car bursting with packages and newly purchased decorations, followed closely by a man from town with a gold tooth, a wooden leg, and a trailer carrying our freshly cut Christmas tree.

I watched as they wrestled with the mammoth tree, wondering briefly if it would even fit through our front door. It was cold outside, and I shuffled my feet on the ground to keep warm. Without thinking, I looked over my shoulder at the Petropoulos house.

The windows glowed, some of them foggy with condensation. A steady stream of smoke rose from a crooked chimney, curling like ribbon before disappearing into blackness.

We'd been to the cabin three times since October, and during each visit Elliot had come to the door, knocked, and Dad let him upstairs. We would lie on the floor of my closet—slowly being converted into a tiny library—and read for hours.

But I'd yet to visit his house. I tried to guess which room was his, to imagine what he might be doing. I wondered what Christmas was like for them, in a house with a dad and a mom, four kids, and a dog who looked more horse than canine. I bet it smelled like cookies and freshly cut pine. I decided it was probably hard to find someplace quiet to read.

We had been there barely an hour when the old chiming doorbell rang. I opened it to find Elliot and Miss Dina, holding a paper plate laden with something heavy and covered in foil.

"We brought you cookies," Elliot said, pushing his glasses up the bridge of his nose. His mouth was newly crammed with braces. His face was covered by a metallic network of headgear.

I stared wide-eyed at him, and he glowered at me, cheeks growing pink. "Focus on the cookies, Macy."

"Do we have guests, *min lille blomst*?" Dad asked from the kitchen. In his voice I heard the mild disapproval; the unspoken *Can't the boy wait until tomorrow?*

"I'm not staying, Duncan," Miss Dina called. "Just walked these cookies over, but you send Elliot home whenever you two are ready to eat, okay?"

"Dinner is almost ready," Dad said in reply, his calm voice hiding any outward reaction to anyone who didn't know him as well as I did.

I walked to the kitchen and slid the plate of cookies beside him on the island. A peace offering.

"We're going to read," I told him. "Okay?"

Dad looked at me, and then down at the cookies, and relented. "Thirty minutes."

Elliot came willingly, following me past the hulking tree and up the stairs.

Christmas music filtered up the open landing from the kitchen, but it vanished as we stepped into the closet. In the time since we'd bought the house, Dad had lined the walls with shelves and added a beanbag chair in the corner, facing the small futon couch against the front wall. Pillows from home were scattered around, and it was starting to feel cozy, like the inside of a genie's bottle.

I closed the door behind us.

"So what's with the new hardware?" I asked, motioning to his face. He shrugged but said nothing. "Do you have to wear the mask all the time?"

"It's headgear, Macy. Usually only when I sleep, but I decided I want these braces off sooner."

"Why?"

He stared back blankly at me, and, yeah, I got it.

"Are they annoying?" I asked.

His face twisted into a sardonic grin. "Do they look comfortable?"

"No. They look painful and nerdy."

"*You're* painful and nerdy," he teased.

I flopped down onto the beanbag chair with a book and watched him peruse the shelves.

"You've got all of the *Anne of Green Gables* books," he said.

"Yeah."

"I've never read them." He pulled one from the lineup and curled onto the futon. "Favorite word?"

Already this ritual seemed to roll out of him and into the room. It didn't even catch me off guard this time. Looking down at my book, I thought for a second before offering, "*Hushed*. You?"

"*Persimmon*."

Without further conversation, we began to read.

"Is it hard?" Elliot asked suddenly, and I looked up to

meet his eyes: amber and deep and anxious. He cleared his throat awkwardly, clarifying, "Holidays without your mom?"

I was so startled by the question that I quickly blinked away. Inside, I begged him not to ask more. Even three years after her death, my mom's face swam continuously in my thoughts: dancing gray eyes, thick black hair, deep brown skin, her lopsided smile waking me up every morning until that first one she missed. Every time I looked in the mirror I saw her reflected back at me. So yeah, *hard* didn't cover it. *Hard* was like describing a mountain as a lump, like describing the ocean as a puddle.

And neither of those things could contain my feelings about Christmas without her.

He watched me in the careful way he had. "If my mom died, holidays would be rough."

I felt my stomach clench, my throat burn, asking, "Why?" even though I didn't need to.

"Because she makes a big deal out of them. Isn't that what moms do?"

I swallowed back a sob and nodded tightly.

"What would your mom do?"

"You can't just ask stuff like that." I flipped onto my back and stared up at the ceiling.

His apology came out in an immediate burst: "I'm sorry!"

Now I felt like the jerk. "Besides, you know I'm okay." Even just saying it backed up the emotional eighteen-wheeler.

I felt the tears retreat down my throat. "It's been almost four years. We don't have to talk about it."

"But we *can*."

I swallowed again and then stared at the wall, hard. "She started Christmas the same every year. She made blueberry muffins and fresh orange juice." The words came out in a woodpecker staccato. "We would eat in front of the fireplace, opening stockings while she and Dad told me stories from their childhood until eventually we started making up crazy stories together. We would all start cooking the duck, and then open gifts. And after dinner, we would curl up in front of the fireplace and read."

His voice was barely audible. "Sounds perfect."

"It was," I agreed, more softly now, lost in the memory. "Mom loved books, too. Every gift was a book, or a journal, or cool pens, or paper. And she read *everything*. Like, every book I saw on the tables at the bookstore, she had already read."

"It sounds like I would really like your mom."

"Everyone loved her," I told him. "She didn't have much family—her parents died when she was young, too—but I swear everyone she met claimed her as their own."

And they all floundered like fish out of water now without her, unsure what to do for us, unsure how to navigate Dad's quiet reserve.

"Did she work?" Elliot asked.

"She was a buyer for Books Inc."

"Wow. Really?" He sounded impressed that she was part of such a large Bay Area retailer, but inside I knew she'd grown tired of it. She always wanted her own store. It was only when she started getting sick that she and Dad were in a position to afford it. "Is that why your dad is building this closet for you?"

I shook my head, but the idea hadn't even occurred to me until he said it. "I don't think so. Maybe."

"Maybe he wanted a place you could feel close to her."

I was still shaking my head. Dad knew I couldn't possibly think of Mom *more*. And he wouldn't try to help me think of her less, either. It wouldn't help. Just like holding your breath doesn't change your body's need for oxygen.

And as if I'd said that aloud, he asked, "But do you think of her more when you're in here?"

Of course, I thought, but I ignored him, fidgeting instead with the edge of the quilt hanging over the side of the bean-bag. *I think of her everywhere. She* is *everywhere, in every moment, and also she's in no one moment. She misses every single one of my moments and I'm not sure who that is harder for: me surviving here without her, or her without me, existing wherever she is.*

"Macy?"

"What."

"Do you think of her in here? Is that why you love this room?"

"I love the room because I love reading."

And because when I find that book that makes me lose myself for just one hour, maybe more, I forget.

And because my dad thinks of Mom every time he buys me a book.

And because you're here and I feel about a thousand times less lonely with you.

"But—"

"Please stop." I squeezed my eyes shut, feeling my palms sweat, heart race, stomach curl into a knot around itself and all the feelings that sometimes felt too big for my body.

"Do you ever cry about her?"

"Are you kidding?" I gasped, and his eyes widened but he didn't back down.

"It's just that it's Christmas," he said quietly. "And when my mom was baking cookies earlier, I realized how familiar it was. It must be weird for you, that's all."

"Yeah."

He leaned in, trying to get me to look at him. "I just want you to know you can talk to me."

"I don't need to talk about it."

He sat up, watching me for a few more breaths of silence, and then returned to his book.

now

wednesday, october 4

I leave the warm comfort of bed and shuffle into the kitchen, kissing the top of a head of brown tangles. Sean should know by now that we can't be sneaky in the morning: Phoebe is always up before us anyway.

Phoebs is a dream kid. She's six, clever and affectionate, and boisterous in a way that tells me a little bit about her mom, because her dad is all mellow containment. Who the hell knows where Ashley, her deadbeat mother, is, but it stabs something in me to see Phoebe growing up without her. At least I had ten years with Mom, and her disappearance from my life doesn't feel like a betrayal. Phoebe only got three be-

55

fore Ashley went to a weekend retreat for her investment banking job and came home with a taste for cocaine that turned into a hankering for crack, which eventually led to her giving up everything for speedballs. At what point will Sean be forced to tell his perfect kid that her mom loved drugs more than she loved them?

I remember walking out of his bedroom the morning after our first tipsy hookup to find Phoebe sitting at the kitchen table eating Rice Chex, hair already in crooked pigtails, wearing mismatched socks, puppy-dog leggings, and a polka-dot sweater. In his haze of flirtation, Sean hadn't mentioned he had a kid. I try to see it more as a testament to how great my boobs looked in that blue sweater than a huge, dickish omission on his part.

That morning, she looked up at me, eyes wide enough to easily confirm what he'd said the night before—that he hadn't brought a woman home with him in three years—and asked if I was a new roommate.

How could I say no to puppy-dog leggings and crooked ponytails? I've been there every night since.

It's not really a sacrifice. Sean is a dream in bed, easygoing, and makes a mean cup of coffee. At forty-two, he's also financially secure, which goes a long way when you're staring down the barrel at med school loans. And maybe it was initially the alcohol, but sex with him was only the second sex of my life that didn't feel immediately afterward like I'd sent something priceless crashing to the floor.

"Chex?" I ask her, blindly reaching for the coffee filters above the sink.

"Yes, please."

"Sleep good?"

She gives a small grunt of affirmation and then, after a minute, mumbles, "It was hot."

So it wasn't just my body's claustrophobic response to seeing Elliot and waking up beside Sean; her dad's been futzing with the thermostat again. That man was born for central Texas weather, not Bay Area. I move across the room, turning the heat down. "I thought you were on Daddy Heater Duty last night."

Phoebe giggles. "He snuck away from me."

The sound of the shower turning on drifts into the kitchen, and I feel like I've just been given a game-show challenge with a buzzer counting down: *Get out of the house in the next two minutes!*

I pour Phoebe's cereal, jog into the bedroom, pull on a clean set of scrubs, pour my coffee, yank my shoes on, and plant one more kiss on Phoebe's head before I'm out the door.

It's crazy—at least it makes me *sound* crazy—but if Sean asked me about my day yesterday, I know without a doubt it would all come tumbling out.

I saw Elliot Petropoulos yesterday for the first time in almost exactly eleven years and I realized that I'm still in love with him and probably always will be.

Still want to marry me?

57

Unfortunately, *a couple of days of distance* doesn't appear to be in the cards: Elliot is waiting outside the hospital when I walk up the hill from the bus stop.

It isn't accurate to say that my heart stops, because really I feel its existence intensely, a phantom limb. My heart pinches in, and then roars to life, brutally punching me from the inside out. I slow my steps and try to figure out what to say. Irritation flares in me. He can't be faulted for showing up at Saul's when I happened to be there yesterday, but today is all him.

"Elliot."

He turns when I call his name, and his posture deflates a little in relief. "I was hoping you'd show up early today."

Early?

I look at him as I approach, eyes narrowed. Stopping a few feet from where he stands, hands deep in the pockets of his black jeans, I ask, "How did you know where and what time I was supposed to work?"

Guilt drains the color from his cheeks. "George's wife works in reception there." He lifts his chin, indicating the woman who is sitting just inside the sliding doors, and whom I've seen every morning for the past few months.

"Her name is Liz," I confirm flatly, remembering the three letters etched into her blue plastic name tag.

"Yeah," he says quietly. "Liz Petropoulos."

I laugh incredulously. Under no other circumstances can I imagine a hospital administrative employee giving out information about a physician's work schedule. People turn pretty unreasonable when a loved one gets sick. Make that loved one a child and forget about it. Even in the short time I've been working here, I've seen parents go after doctors who failed to cure their kid.

Elliot stares at me, unblinking. "Liz knows I'm not dangerous, Macy."

"She could be fired. I'm a physician in critical pediatrics. She can't just give out my information, not even if it's her own family."

"Okay, shit. I shouldn't have done that," he says, genuinely contrite. "Look. I work at ten. I . . ." Squinting past me down Mariposa, he says, "I was hoping we would have time to talk a little before then." When I don't say anything in reply, he bends to meet my gaze, pressing, "*Do* you have time?"

I look up at him, and our eyes hook, tunneling me back to every other time we shared an intense, silent exchange. Even this many years later, I think we can read each other pretty fucking well.

Breaking the connection, I glance down at my watch. It's just after seven thirty. And although no one upstairs would complain if I showed up to work an hour and a half before I was scheduled, Elliot would know that if I said I had to get inside, I'd be lying.

"Yeah," I tell him. "I have about an hour."

He tilts his head, slowly leans to the right, and, as a smile curves his mouth, he takes one shuffle-step, then another, as if luring me with his cuteness.

"Coffee?" His smile grows, and I notice his teeth, how even they are. A flash of Elliot at fourteen, wearing headgear, pulses through my thoughts. "Bakery? Greasy spoon?"

I point to the next block and the tiny four-table café that has yet to be overrun with residents and family members anxiously waiting for news postsurgery.

Inside it's warm—bordering on too warm, the theme of my morning—and there are still two tables empty up front. Seating ourselves, we pick up the menus and peruse in tight silence.

"What's good?" he asks.

I laugh. "I've never had breakfast here."

Elliot looks up at me, blinks leisurely, and something in my stomach melts into a liquid heat that spreads lower. What's weird, I realize, is that Elliot and I ate out together only a handful of times, and never alone.

"I usually scarf a muffin or bagel from the cafeteria." I break eye contact, and decide on the yogurt and granola parfait before putting my menu down. "I bet everything is pretty tasty."

Covertly, I watch him read, his eyes scanning quickly across the words. Elliot and words. Peanut butter and chocolate. Coffee and biscotti. Love matches made in heaven.

He reaches up, idly scratching his neck as he hums. "Eggs or pancakes? Eggs or pancakes?"

As he leans forward on an elbow, his shoulder muscle bunches beneath his cotton T-shirt. He rubs a finger back and forth just below his bottom lip. His phone buzzes near his arm, but he ignores it.

Have mercy. The only thought I have—bewildering and breathless—is that Elliot has become a man who knows how to use his body. I didn't notice it yesterday, couldn't have.

As he grins in his decision,

as he slides the menu gently back into the holder,

as he reaches for his napkin and lays it carefully across his lap,

as he looks up at me, pursing his lips slightly in happiness,

I suddenly feel grateful for the eleven intervening years, because would I have noticed all these little things otherwise? Or would they have blended together, blurring, known as the constellation of tiny mannerisms that slowly becomes Just Elliot?

I blink away when our waitress comes to the table and takes our order.

When she leaves, he leans in again. "Is it possible to catch me up on a decade over breakfast?"

Memories reel through my thoughts: Leaving for college in a fog. Living in the dorm with Sabrina and, later, in a small apartment off-campus that always seemed to be full of books and beer bottles and clouds of weed smoke. Moving with her to Baltimore for med school and the long nights I spent pseudo-praying that I would be matched at UCSF so I could live close to home again, even if home was empty. How does one condense a lifetime into the time it takes to share a cup of coffee?

"Looking back, it doesn't feel all that busy," I say. "College. Med school."

"Well, and friends and lovers, joy and loss, I assume," he says, hitting the nail directly on the head. His expression straightens with awareness.

An awkward silence grows like a canyon between us. "I didn't mean *us*," he says, adding in a mumble, "necessarily."

With a dry laugh, I lean back in my seat. "I haven't been marinating in bad feelings, Ell."

Wow, that's a lie.

When his phone buzzes again beside him, he pushes it away. "Then why not call?"

"A lot happened." I shift back a little in my seat as our drinks arrive.

His eyebrows slant down in justifiable confusion. I've just told him my life was essentially rote and straightforward, but then too much happened to bother calling.

My mind cycles through a calendar of years gone by, and another sour awareness rolls over me. Elliot turns twenty nine *tomorrow*. I've missed nearly all of his twenties.

"Happy early birthday, by the way," I say quietly.

His eyes go soft, mouth curving at the edges. "Thanks, Mace."

October 5 has always been a tough day for me. What will it feel like this year, now that I've laid eyes on him? I cup my hands around my warm mug, changing the subject. "What about you? What have you been doing?"

He shrugs and sips his cappuccino, wiping a casual finger across his upper lip when it comes away foamy. Obvious comfort in his own body causes renewed heat to ripple through mine. Never have I known someone so wholly himself as Elliot.

"I graduated early from Cal," he says, "and moved to Manhattan for a couple years."

This hits the *stall* button in my brain. Elliot personifies Northern California, with all its shaggy chaos. I can't imagine him in New York.

"*Manhattan?*" I repeat.

He laughs. "I know. Total insanity. But it's the kind of place I could only stomach in my twenties. After a few years there, I interned at a literary agency for a while, but didn't love it. I came back here almost two years ago and started working for a nonprofit literacy group. I'm still there a couple days a week, but . . . I started writing a novel. It's going really well."

"Writing a *book*." I grin. "Who would have guessed?"

He laughs harder this time, and the sound is warm, and growling. "Everyone?"

I find myself biting both of my lips to rein in my smile, and his expression slowly straightens. "Can I ask you something?" he asks.

"Sure."

"What made you decide to come here with me this morning?"

I don't really need to point out that he pushed his way into my schedule, because I know that's not really what he means. What he said about Liz is true; we all know Elliot isn't dangerous. I could have told him to go home and not contact me again, and he would have listened.

So why didn't I?

"I have no idea. I don't think I would have been able to say no to you twice."

He likes that answer. A small smile arcs his mouth and nostalgia floods my veins.

"You went to med school at Hopkins," he says with quiet wonder in his voice. "Undergrad at Tufts. I'm so proud of you, Mace."

My eyes go wide in understanding. "You rat. You *Googled* me?"

"You didn't Google *me*?" he shoots back. "Come on, that's step one post-run-in."

"I got home from work at two in the morning. I fell face-first into the pillow. I don't know if I've brushed my teeth since this weekend."

His grin is so genuinely happy, it works a creaky hinge

open inside me. "Was it always your plan to move back here, or was it just where you matched?"

"This was my first choice."

"You wanted to be close to Duncan." He's nodding as if this makes perfect sense and it stabs me. "When did he die?"

"Was it always *your* plan to move back here?"

I can see him working through my deflection, but he takes a deep breath and lets it out slowly. "It was always my plan to live wherever you were. That plan failed, but I figured my odds of seeing you again were pretty good back in Berkeley."

This throws me. As in I am a brick, and have been hurled at the glass window. "Oh."

"You knew that. You had to have known that I'd be here, waiting."

I swallow a sip of water quickly to reply. "I don't think I knew that you were still hoping I'd—"

"I *loved* you."

I nod quickly at this bombshell interruption, looking for the rescue of our waitress bringing food. But she isn't there.

"You loved me, too, you know," he says quietly. "It was everything."

I feel as though I've been shoved, and push away from the table a little, but he leans in. "Sorry. This is too intense. I'm just terrified of not getting a chance to say it."

His phone hops across the table again, buzzing.

"Do you need to get that?" I ask.

Elliot rubs his face and then leans his chair back, eyes closed, face tilted to the ceiling. It's only now that I realize how stubbly he is, how tired he looks.

I lean back in. "Elliot, is everything okay?"

He nods, straightening. "Yeah, I'm fine." Eyeing me for a lingering moment, he seems to decide to tell me what's on his mind: "I broke up with my girlfriend last night. She's calling. She thinks she wants to talk, but really I think she just wants to yell at me. She won't feel great afterward, so I'm sparing us both for now."

I swallow past an enormous lump in my throat. "You broke up with her *last night*?"

He nods, toying with a straw wrapper and thanking the waitress quietly as she deposits our food in front of us. When she leaves, he admits in a low voice, "You're the love of my life. I assumed I would get over you eventually, but seeing you yesterday?" He shakes his head. "I couldn't go home to someone else and pretend to love her with everything I have."

Nausea rolls through me. I honestly don't even know how to translate this heavy emotion in my chest. Is it that I relate so intensely to what he's saying, but am far more of a coward? Or is it the opposite—that I *have* moved on, have found someone, and don't want the intrusion of Elliot into my easy, simple life?

"Macy," he says, more urgently now, and opens his mouth to continue, but another trigger has been pulled, another game-show challenge. I dig for my wallet—racing the buzzer—

but this time Elliot stops me, catching my arm in his gentle grip, his cheeks pink with anger. "You can't do this. You can't just continually run from this conversation. It's been eleven years in the making." Leaning in, he clenches his jaw as he adds, "I know I messed up, but was it that bad? So bad you just *vanished*?"

No, it wasn't. Not at first.

"This," I say, looking around us, "is a terrible idea. And not because of our past. Okay, yes, it's partly that, but it's also the intervening years." I meet his eyes. "You broke up with your girlfriend last night after seeing me for two minutes. Elliot, I'm getting *married*."

He drops my arm, blinking a few times, and seeming— for the first time I've ever witnessed—to be lost for words.

"I'm getting married . . . and there's so much you don't know," I say. "And a lot of that isn't your fault, but *this*," I wave a finger back and forth in the narrow space separating us across the table, "between us? It sucks that it's over, and it hurts me, too. But it's done, Ell."

then

As if Dad knew that I was delicate after the conversation about *Christmas Sans Mom* with Elliot, he was even quieter than usual at dinner Thursday night.

"Do you want to go to Goat Rock tomorrow?" he asked when he finished his chicken.

Goat Rock, the windy beach where the Russian River collides with the Pacific Ocean. It is notoriously cold, with a dangerous rip current rendering the beach unsafe for even wading into the water, and so much sand blustering in the air that it's nearly impossible to grill hot dogs.

I loved it.

Sometimes, sea lions and elephant seals lazed at the mouth of the river. Dark, rich seaweed washed up on shore, heavy with salt and nearly unreal to me in its otherworldly, translucent oddness. Sand dunes dotted the shoreline, and in the center of the beach and out a narrow isthmus was the lonely giant rock jutting straight up more than a hundred feet as if it had been dropped there.

"You could invite Elliot, if you wanted," he added.

I looked up at him and nodded.

The entire drive there, Elliot was fidgety. He shifted in his seat, tugged at his seat belt, ran his hand through his hair, futzed with his headgear. After about ten minutes, I gave up on trying to focus on my book.

"What's with you?" I hissed across the back seat.

He glanced at Dad in the driver's seat, and then back at me. "Nothing."

I felt more than saw Dad looking in the rearview mirror at what was going on in the back seat.

I stared at Elliot's hands, reaching now to toy with the strap of his backpack. They looked different. Bigger. He was still so skinny, but also so at home in his gawkiness that I didn't notice it anymore unless I really looked.

Dad pulled into the parking lot and we stepped out,

shocked at how the wind nearly knocked us over. We jerked our coats on, pulled our hats over our ears.

"No farther down the beach than the rock," Dad said, pulling his own treat—a pack of Danish cigarettes—out of his pocket. He never smoked near me; he'd officially quit as soon as Mom found out she was pregnant. The wind pushed his fair hair across his face and he shook it away, squinting at me, saying without words, *You okay with this?*, and I nodded. He tucked a cigarette between his lips, adding, "And at least fifty feet back from the seals."

Elliot and I trudged over a sand dune, standing at the top and staring out at the ocean. "Your dad intimidates the hell out of me."

I laughed. "Because he's tall?"

"Tall," he agreed, "and quiet. He has the commanding-presence thing down."

"He just says a lot more with his eyes than with his mouth."

"Unfortunately for me, I don't speak Danish Eyeball."

I laughed again and looked at Elliot's profile as he stared out at the crashing waves.

"I didn't know he smoked," he said.

"Only a couple times a year. It's his private luxury, I guess."

Elliot nodded, blurting, "Okay, look. I got you a Christmas present."

I groaned.

"Ever-gracious Macy." With a smile, he began walking back down the other side of the sand dune toward the beach, and only now did I notice a small wrapped package tucked beneath his arm. We navigated through thick sand, driftwood, and small hills of seaweed before reaching a tiny alcove, mostly guarded from the wind.

Sitting, he shifted the package into both hands, staring down at it. From the shape, I could tell it was a book. "I didn't expect you to get me anything," he said, nervously. "I'm always hanging out at your place on the weekends you're here, so I feel like I owe you."

"You don't owe me anything." I worked to tamp down the emotion I felt that he got me a book. Not just because it's what we did together—read—but because of what I'd told him last night, about Mom, and gifts. "You know you can always come over. I don't have siblings. It's just me and Dad."

"Well," he said, handing me the package, "maybe that's sort of why I got this."

Curious, I tore open the paper and looked down. I nearly lost the wrapping paper to a brutal gust of wind.

Bridge to Terabithia.

"Have you read it?" Elliot asked.

I shook my head, pulling my windblown hair out of my face. "I've heard of it." I saw him exhale quietly in relief. "I think."

72

He nodded, and seeming to be more settled, bent to pick up a stone to throw into the surf.

"Thank you," I told him, though I wasn't sure he heard me over the roar of the ocean.

Elliot looked up and smiled at me. "I hope you like it as much as I did. I sort of feel like I could be your May Belle."

now

thursday, october 5

M y phone vibrates in my messenger bag on the bus, conveniently waking me only a block from my stop.

I pull it out, realizing that it's nearly two in the morning again and I'm staring down at Viv's little face on the screen.

"Viv, you've learned technology so quickly!" I say, standing to pull my bag over my shoulder and make my way unsteadily down the narrow bus aisle.

Sabrina laughs on the other end. "I totally ganked your phone when you went to order food, and changed my profile pic. Your passcodes are so adorably predictable."

I growl, trying to be annoyed, but really, only two people

would know the four-digit pin I use for nearly everything: Sabrina and Elliot. It's my lucky number, fifteen, repeated.

"I'll change it," I tell her, thanking the bus driver with a smile he ignores as I step down and onto my street.

"Don't," Sabrina cautions. "You'll forget it."

"I'll have you know I'm great with numbers."

Silence greets me on the other end of the line, and I amend, "At least, the math kind of numbers, when they're right in front of me and I have a pencil." I stare up the steep hill I still need to climb before I can be in bed. "Did you call just to harass me? What are you even doing up?"

"I'm feeding the baby, obviously. I assumed you'd be on your way home. I called to check up on you. You *fled* yesterday."

Nodding, I begin my slow trudge uphill. The air is dense with moisture, and the incline, after the day I had, feels nearly vertical. "Elliot caught me on the sidewalk."

"Figured that when he sprinted out of there."

"He wasn't super happy with me for, you know, losing touch."

I hear her quiet scoff. "'Losing touch'?" she repeats. "Is that what we're calling it?"

Ignoring this, I say, "He tracked me down again today. He broke up with his girlfriend last night after seeing me."

Sabrina coos through the line, and I stop walking.

"What is that noise you're making?" I ask.

"It's *sweet*, that's all."

"You're on *his* side?"

Her tiny beat of silence communicates the magnitude of her disbelief. "You're telling me there was absolutely no swooning when he told *you* that?"

"You just don't like Sean."

"Don't be ridiculous. He's the first guy who's managed to last beyond three dates; of course I *like* him. He deserves my esteem for beating that record."

I am so tired, I can feel the unreasonable coming out. Tight defensiveness rises up in my chest, kick-starting my pulse. "Okay, let me clarify: you don't want me to *marry* Sean."

"Macy, honey, I *don't* want you to marry Sean—*yet*—that's true. But that's unrelated to me also wanting you to reconnect with Elliot. I adore you, you know this, but you've told me what it was like when your mom died. How hard you worked to keep everyone out or at arm's length—a can of worms we could totally open up, if you have the time—"

"Sabrina."

"My point is that you could never shut out Elliot. He's your soul mate. You think I don't know that?"

I nod, walking again. I've been on my feet for so long that my toes are numb in my shoes. I'm essentially just shuffling slowly uphill. "I'm so tired."

"Oh, honey," she says gently.

"And there's something else," I say, hesitating.

"Yeah?"

"He didn't know about my dad." The truth of that one still stings.

Sabrina gasps. *"What?"*

"I know. That part's all my fault, I get that." I rub my face. "I just assumed he would have heard about it . . . through the grapevine."

She's gone quiet, and it's the quiet that nearly breaks me because, holy hell, I am a monster. Sabrina must be thinking for the thousandth time that I am dead inside.

"You'd be fine if his parents died," she begins slowly, "and he didn't at least try to get in touch with you?"

Miss Dina's warm eyes and soft face with deep dimples flicker through my thoughts, sending a spike of pain through me. "I know, I see your point."

Sabrina's silent again; I hate having this conversation over the phone. I want the reassuring presence of her on the couch next to me.

"I'm not sure Elliot and I could just be friends."

She huffs out a breath. "I think it's worth a try."

Would I even be able to stay away? If I'm honest, wasn't part of the appeal of moving back here to be closer to what he and I once had, somehow?

"You really think it's a good idea for me to reconnect with him?" I ask.

"I've *always* thought that."

"How?" I hear how small my voice seems and pull out my keys, propping my phone between my ear and shoulder when

I drop them to the dark porch. "We had breakfast and I bolted. I don't have his number or address. No way does he have Facebook or Twitter or anything. Normal modes of stalking are out."

I can hear Sabrina's pensive hum as I search blindly for my house key. "You'll think of something."

then

fourteen years ago

From: Macy Lea Sorensen <minlilleblomst@hotmail.com>
Date: January 1, 11:00 PM
To: Elliot P. <elliverstravels@yahoo.com>
Subject: book

Hi Elliot,

Thanks again for Bridge to Terabithia and sorry for getting snot all over your shirt when I was trying to talk about it. Maybe now on the computer I can explain what I was trying to say.

I get why you gave me this book, and I just want you to know how thoughtful it was. I keep thinking about the first day I saw you in the closet, and how it's sort of how Jesse hated Leslie for beating him in a race. I didn't hate you, but

I wasn't sure I liked you, either. I guess it doesn't matter because now it feels like you're the person who understands me the best. Jesse and Leslie made up Terabithia as their sanctuary and when she died he brought May Belle there to be the new princess. Mom created this world of books with me, but without her I can bring you to the closet to share them instead.

I read it again on the drive home and started crying all over again and I thought my dad was going to totally lose it. He probably had no idea what was going on. He was all *What is with you, weirdo*? So he just pulled over and kept breathing all deep and asking me what happened. I told him you gave me this sad book. I told him how much it made me miss Mom. And then he cried when we got home, at least I think he did. He's always so quiet so I'm never sure.

I hate being sad in front of him because it's like he has this giant vault of sadness already and then he has to lock that all up just to take care of me. And when I think about it, I still have him, but he lost his whole world. Mom was the person he chose out of everyone and she's gone. I don't know. I think he doesn't like to see me cry. But it was good to talk about her. I'm scared I'll forget her. I miss her so much I need a new language for it.

There I go again. Anyway, did you finish Ivanhoed? That book was ginormous I would be asleep in about five minutes. I read the first page when you went to the bathroom and was all what? I understood about a millionth of it. What's it even about?

Anyway, school tomorrow. Thanks again for the book. And for just letting me talk about it I guess.

xo

Macy

PS No one here understands that I just want to be another girl at school not the kid whose mom died and who needs to be treated like she can break. Thanks for just saying stuff and not acting like it's all taboo.

From: Elliot P. <elliverstravels@yahoo.com>
Date: January 2, 07:02 AM
To: Macy Lea Sorensen <minlilleblomst@hotmail.com>
Subject: re: book

Hi Macy,

You're welcome for the book. It made me cry the first time I read it, too. I know I didn't tell you that, but I guess I should have.

I'm sure your dad figured out why you were crying. Also, I think it probably makes your dad happy that you're crying about it even if he's sad that you're sad. But I hope he's not mad at me for making you cry. I mean it was the book . . . I wouldn't want to make you cry because of me.

I don't think you're weird or different because your mom died. I think you're actually pretty cool, but it has nothing to do with whether or not you have a mom. You're cool because you're you. As an aside: you're handling it pretty well as far as I can tell.

Ivanhoe (no d) is pretty good. It's set in the 12th century after the Third Crusade. (Some of the current idea of Robin Hood is based on a character, Locksley. But he's not the main character.) I like the action and the style. I used to role-play a little with my friend Brandon in seventh grade so I guess that's where the interest in 12th century England came in. If you're still into Nicholas Sparks you probably won't like Ivanhoe.

See you,
Elliot

PS I didn't mean that to sound condescending. Dad told me I can be like that and so I'm not sure if that was. I'm sure Nicholas Sparks is really good, just different than Sir Walter Scott.

From: Macy Lea Sorensen <minlilleblomst@hotmail.com>
Date: January 2, 8:32 PM
To: Elliot P. <elliverstravels@yahoo.com>
Subject: re: book

Hi Elliot,

Nicholas Sparks is really *really* good. My friend Elena's mom met him at a book conference and said he was super nice and way smart, too. I bet he's read Ivanhoe (no d).

What do you mean you and Brandon role-played? Like the dork guys at the park with swords and flags?

xo
Macy

From: Elliot P. <elliverstravels@yahoo.com>
Date: January 2, 08:54 PM
To: Macy Lea Sorensen <minlilleblomst@hotmail.com>
Subject: re: book

Hi Macy,

Yes. Exactly like that. And also helmets and cardboard horses.

Elliot

love and other words

From: Macy Lea Sorensen <minlilleblomst@hotmail.com>
Date: January 2, 9:06 PM
To: Elliot P. <elliverstravels@yahoo.com>
Subject: re: book

I swear you make me laugh so hard. I know you're kidding but I can totally picture you on a cardboard horse all "On guard!" and "Ivanhoe!"

Macy

_____

From: Elliot P. <elliverstravels@yahoo.com>
Date: January 2, 09:15 PM
To: Macy Lea Sorensen <minlilleblomst@hotmail.com>
Subject: re: book

I was serious. We really did role-play like that. It's actually a very well organized community called The Nobles and there are battles and royalty and it's really fun. But I'm sure you wouldn't like it because there's no soft focus kiss at the end.

Elliot

From: Macy Lea Sorensen <minlilleblomst@hotmail.com>
Date: January 3, 6:53 PM
To: Elliot P. <elliverstravels@yahoo.com>
Subject: Crazy!

Hi Elliot,

I'm pretty sure that was you being condescending last night, so here is me being mature and ignoring it.

Want to hear something crazy? My friend Nikki got suspended for making out with a guy in the cafeteria today! I was all oh my god what is *happening*? I told Dad and he asked if I had kissed any boys and I was all no way! Who would I kiss at school they're all losers!

Anyway that was crazy!
Macy

_____

From: Elliot P. <elliverstravels@yahoo.com>
Date: January 3, 08:27 PM
To: Macy Lea Sorensen <minlilleblomst@hotmail.com>
Subject: re: Crazy!

My friend Christian got suspended last year for building a rocket in shop. I'm not even sure where he got the fuel but it totally flew through the window and hit a car in the parking lot. It was awesome.

So you don't hang out with guys at your school?

Elliot

From: Macy Lea Sorensen <minlilleblomst@hotmail.com>
Date: January 4, 7:32 AM
To: Elliot P. <elliverstravels@yahoo.com>
Subject: re: Crazy!

I do Doug and Cody have been in school with me since first grade so we are
sorta close but kissing close? Uh no they're nice but I think I'll probably meet
a college guy at some point because the guys at my school are all into video
games and skateboards and Danny (another friend) totally tried to touch my
butt once at a dance but I was all I don't think so.

Macy

_____

From: Elliot P. <elliverstravels@yahoo.com>
Date: January 4, 07:34 AM
To: Macy Lea Sorensen <minlilleblomst@hotmail.com>
Subject: re: Crazy!

Macy,

Punctuation is your friend.

Elliot

now

thursday, october 5

Liz *Petropoulos*, what a trip.

She's medium height, curvy, and has the most amazing skin. Also, no fewer than four times have I told her how much I covet her cheekbones. She's a smiler, saying hello to everyone who walks in the doors to the Mission Bay building and stopping anyone without a badge, beckoning them to sign in.

I raise my badge as I do every morning. Thankfully she was on break yesterday when I burst in, frazzled after my non-breakfast with Elliot, but today she smiles with a little glimmer in her eyes, like she knows more now than she did the last time I saw her.

"Well, hello, Liz *Petropoulos*," I say, approaching her, dropping any pretense.

She hesitates only a beat before saying, "Hi, Macy *Sorensen*," without having to check my badge. As I get closer, she smiles again. "Boy, have I heard a lot about this Macy person over the past seven years. And to think she's been the nice, new Dr. Sorensen complimenting my cheek-bones."

"Guess Elliot and George should give up and let *us* get married," I say, and she laughs. It's a round, delighted sound.

Her expression straightens pretty quickly. "I'm sorry I told him when you'd be in." She holds up a hand when I start to speak, and adds in a quieter voice, "He told me about running into you, and we put two and two together. You can't know what it means to him that he's seen you. I know it's not my business, but—"

"About that." I lean my elbows on the broad marble reception desk and smile down at her so she knows I'm not about to get her fired. "What do you say you do me one favor, and then we halt all nonapproved information sharing?"

"No question," Liz says, eyes wide. "What can I do for you?"

"His cell number would be fantastic."

Friends call friends, I tell myself. The first step to fixing things is to talk, to clear the air once and for all, and then we can move on with life.

Liz pulls out her phone, opens her Favorites list, and bends, scribbling his phone number.

Elliot's on her speed-dial.

But I get it: Attentive, considerate, emotionally mature Elliot would be the dream brother-in-law. Of *course* she's in regular contact with him.

"But don't tell him I have it," I tell her as she tears it off and hands it to me. "I'm not sure how long it will be before I figure out what to say."

Who am I kidding; this is such a bad idea. Elliot has a story to tell. I have a story to tell, too. We both have so many secrets, I'm not even sure we can backtrack that far.

The entire walk down the hall to the residents' break room, I keep checking the pocket in my scrubs pants to make sure that I haven't lost the small Post-it folded inside. Not that I really needed it in the first place. I stared at the numbers the whole ride up to the fourth floor. I guess it never occurred to me that he would have the same phone number all this time. His number used to be a rhythm that would get stuck in my head like a song.

I drop my bag in a locker in the break room and stare down at my phone. My rounds start in five minutes, and where I'm going, I need to be levelheaded. If I don't do this now, it will be a stone in my shoe the entire shift. My heart is a thunder-drum in my ear.

Without overthinking it, I text,

> I work 9-6 today. Do you want to meet for dinner? To talk.

Only a few seconds later, a reply bubble appears. He's typing. Inexplicably, my palms begin to sweat. It hadn't occurred to me until now that he could say, *No, you're too big a dick, forget it.*

> Is this Macy?

Or that he wouldn't have this number. I am an idiot.

> Yeah, sorry. I should have said.

> Not at all.

> Tell me where, and I'll be there.

then

thursday, march 13
fourteen years ago

As my fourteenth birthday approached, I could tell that Dad wasn't sure what to do. For as long as I could remember, we'd always done the same thing: he would make aebleskivers for breakfast, we'd all see a movie in the afternoon, and then I would pig out on a giant sundae for dinner and go to bed swearing I would never do that again.

After Mom died, the routine didn't change. The constancy was important to me, a small reminder that she'd really been here. But this was the first year we'd had the weekend house, and the first year I had a close friend like Elliot.

"Can we go to the house this weekend?"

Dad's coffee cup paused in mid-air, his eyes meeting mine over the thread of steam. He blew over the top before taking a sip, swallowing, and setting it back on the table. Picking up his fork, he speared a piece of scrambled egg, doing his best to act casual, as if there was nothing that particularly thrilled or disappointed him about my request.

It was the first time I'd asked to go up there, and I knew him well enough to know how relieved he was to be able to continually rely on the perfect predictions in Mom's list.

"Is that what you'd like to do this year? For your birthday?"

I looked down at my own eggs before nodding. "Yeah."

"Would you also like a party? We could bring a few friends up to the house? You could show them your library?"

"No . . . my friends here wouldn't get it."

"Not like Elliot."

I took a bite and shrugged casually. "Yeah."

"He's a good friend?"

I nodded, staring at my plate as I speared another bite.

"You know you're too young to date," Dad said.

My head shot up, eyes wide in horror. *"Dad!"*

He laughed. "Just making sure you understand the rules."

Blinking back down to my food, I mumbled, "Don't be gross. I just like it up there, okay?"

My dad wasn't a big smiler, not one of those people you

think of and immediately picture with a big grin on his face, but right now, when I looked back up, he was smiling. Really smiling.

"Of course we can go to the house, Macy."

We drove up early Saturday morning, the first day of my spring break. There were two things Dad wanted to check off the list this week, including items forty-four and fifty-three: planting a tree that I could watch grow for many years, and teaching me to chop firewood.

Before I could run off into my book wonderland, Dad pulled a tiny sapling from the back of the car and hauled it into the side yard.

"Grab the shovel from the back," he said, kneeling to cut the plastic container away from the apple tree using a razor blade. "Bring the work gloves."

In some ways I always assumed I was my mother's child: I liked the color and clutter of our Berkeley house. I liked lively music and warm days, and danced when I washed dishes. But up at the cabin, I realized I was my dad's kid, too. In the chill of the March wind snaking through the trees, we dug a deep pit in easy silence, communicating with the point of a finger or the tilt of a chin. When we'd finished, and a proud little Gravenstein tree was firmly planted in our side yard, instead of enthusiastically wrapping his arms around me and gushing his love in my ear, Dad cupped my face and bent, pressing a kiss to my forehead.

"Good work, *min lille blomst*." He smiled down at me. "I'm going to town for groceries."

With this permission, I took off. My shoes pounded on the ground as I moved in a straight path from the end of our driveway to the top of Elliot's. The doorbell rang throughout the house, carrying back to me from the open windows overhead. A loud bark reached my ears, followed by the clumsy scratch of a dog's nails against wooden floors.

"Shut it, Darcy," a sleepy voice said, and the dog fell silent, only to release a few small apologetic whines.

It occurred to me that in the nearly six months we'd had the cabin, I hadn't been inside Elliot's house. Miss Dina had invited us, of course, but Dad seemed to feel it was wrong to intrude. I think he also liked the solitude of our house on the weekends—Elliot's presence excepted, of course. Dad liked not having to come out of his shell.

I took a step back, nerves rising, when the door opened and a yawning, shaggy-haired Andreas stood in front of me.

The second-oldest Petropoulos brother had clearly just climbed out of bed—messy brown hair, sleep lines on his face, no shirt, and basketball shorts that defied gravity by barely clinging low on his hips. He had the kind of body I hadn't been entirely sure until that moment actually existed.

Is this what Elliot would look like in a couple of years? My mind could barely handle the idea.

"Hey, Macy," he said. It sounded like a growl, like a sin. He stood back, holding open the door and waiting for me to follow. "You coming in or not?"

I willed my eyebrows to inch back down my forehead. "Oh, sure."

It *did* smell like cookies inside. Cookies and boy. Andreas smiled and lazily scratched his stomach. "You guys are up for the weekend?"

I nodded and his smile widened. "And very talkative, I see."

"Sorry," I said, and then stood there, arms at my sides, fingers pulling at the hem of my shorts, still not sure what to say. "Is Elliot home?"

"I'll grab him." Andreas grinned and walked toward the staircase. "Hey, Ell! Your girlfriend is here!" His voice echoed in the wooden entryway as my body exploded into a scorching blush.

Before I could answer, there was the sound of feet pounding on the floor above us.

"You're such a douche!" Elliot said, barreling down the stairs and into his brother. Andreas grunted with the blow and grabbed Elliot, putting him in a headlock. Andreas was taller and pretty muscular, but Elliot seemed to have the desire to avoid public humiliation on his side.

The two boys wrestled, came dangerously close to knocking over a lamp, said a bunch of words I wasn't even supposed to think, and then finally broke apart, panting.

"Sorry," Elliot said to me, still glaring at Andreas. He adjusted his glasses and straightened his clothes. "My brother thinks he's funny and apparently can't dress himself." He motioned to Andreas's bare chest.

Andreas messed up Elliot's hair even more and rolled his eyes. "It's barely noon, prick."

"I think Mom should have you tested for narcolepsy."

With a dull punch to Elliot's shoulder, Andreas turned toward the stairs. "I'm heading to Amie's. Nice seeing you, Macy."

"You, too," I said lamely.

Andreas winked over his shoulder. "Oh, and Elliot?" he called.

"Yeah?"

"Door open."

His booming laugh filled the upstairs hall before finally disappearing behind the click of a closed door.

Elliot started toward the stairs but then stopped, turning around to frown at me. "Let's go to your house."

"You don't want to show me around?"

With a groan, he turned and pointed around us. "Living room, dining room, kitchen through there." He pivoted in place, indicating each room with a jab of his index finger. He walked up the stairs and I followed him as he mumbled, "Stairs," and "Hallway," and "Bathroom," and "Parents' room," and a list of other monotone labels until we stood in front of a closed white door with a periodic table taped to it.

"This one's mine."

"Wow, that's . . . expected," I said with a laugh. I was so happy to see his space, I felt a little dizzy.

"I didn't put that there, Andreas did." His voice took on an edge of defensiveness, as if he could only stand to be seen as ninety-eight percent nerd.

"But you haven't taken it down," I pointed out.

"It's a good poster. He got it at a science fair." He turned to me and shrugged, dropping his eyes. "It would be a waste to get rid of it, and he'd give me endless crap if I put it *inside* my room."

He opened the door and said nothing, only stepping back to let me move past him into his bedroom. Anxiety and thrill hit me in a blast: I was entering a boy's bedroom.

I was entering *Elliot's* bedroom.

It was sparse and immaculate: bed made, only a few dirty laundry items in a basket in the corner, drawers of his dresser neatly closed. The only disorder was in a pile of books stacked on his desk, and a box of books in the corner.

I sensed Elliot's tense presence behind me, could hear the jerky cadence of his breathing. I knew he wanted to get away from the chaos of his house and into the solitude of the closet, but I couldn't tear myself away. Behind his desk was a bulletin board, with a few ribbons pinned there, a photograph, and a postcard with a picture of Maui.

Moving closer, I leaned in, studying.

"Just some science fairs," he mumbled behind me, explaining the ribbons.

First place in his category at the Sonoma County science fair, three years in a row.

"Wow." I looked over my shoulder at him. "You're *smart*."

His smile came out crooked, his cheeks popped with color. "Nah."

I turned back, examining the photograph tacked in the corner. In it were three boys, including Elliot, and a girl on the far left. It looked like it had been taken a few years ago.

Discomfort itched in my chest. "Who're they?"

Elliot cleared his throat and then leaned in, pointing. He brought with him a burst of deodorant—mildly acidic and piney—and something else, a scent that was completely *boy* and made my stomach drop. "Um, that's Christian, me, Brandon, and Emma."

I'd heard these names in passing: casual stories about a class or a bike ride in the woods. With a sharp pang of jealousy, I realized that although Elliot was becoming my person, my safe place, and the only human other than Dad who I could truly trust, I didn't know his life very well at all. What side of him did these friends see? Did they get the smile that started out as a raised eyebrow and slowly spread to an amused twist of his lips? Did they get the laugh that overrode his tendency to be self-conscious and shot out in a loud *haha-haha-haha*?

"They look nice." I leaned back, and felt him quickly step away behind me.

"Yeah." He went quiet and the silence seemed to grow into a shimmering bubble around us. My ears started to ring, heart thudding as I imagined this Emma sitting on the floor in the corner, reading with him. His voice came in a whisper from behind me: "But you're nicer."

I turned and met his eyes as he did his quick wince-nose scrunch maneuver to get his glasses up higher.

"You don't have to say that just because—"

"My mom's pregnant," he blurted.

And the bubble popped. I heard the stomping of feet along the hallway, the barking of the dog.

My eyes went wide as his words sank in. "*What?*"

"Yeah, they told us last night." He shoved his hair off his forehead. "Apparently she's due in August."

"Holy crap. You're fourteen. It's going to be, like, fifteen years younger than you."

"I know."

"Elliot, that's crazy."

"I *know*." He bent down, retying his shoe. "Seriously though, I don't really want to talk about it. Can we go to your place? Mom has been queasy for a few weeks, Dad is acting insane. My brothers are dicks." Nodding to the box of books, he added, "And I have some classics to add to your library."

Dad gave us a knowing glance as we tromped inside and up the stairs.

"Isn't your birthday on Tuesday?" Elliot asked, following me down the hallway. His shoes were falling apart—his favorite pair of checkered Vans—and one sole made a flapping sound every step.

I looked back over my shoulder at him. "I told you that once, like, five months ago."

"Shouldn't you only *have* to tell me once?"

I turned back, leading us into my room and all the way back into the closet. Since we'd moved in, the space had slowly taken on a life of its own, and was now complete: of course there were the shelves along one entire wall, the beanbag chair in the far corner, and the futon couch on the wall opposite the bookcase. But only a couple of weeks before, Dad had painted the walls and ceiling a midnight blue, with silver and yellow stars dotted in constellations overhead. Two small lamps illuminated the space—one near each of the seating options. In the middle of the floor were blankets and more pillows. It was the perfect fort.

Elliot curled up on the floor, pulling a fleece blanket onto his lap. "And you're on spring break?"

I chewed my lip, nodding. "Yeah."

He fell quiet, and then asked, "Are you bummed you won't be with friends?"

"I *am* with a friend." I looked at him, widening my eyes meaningfully.

"I mean your girlfriends," he said, but I didn't miss the way he blushed.

"Oh," I said. "No, it's okay. Nikki is going to Peru to visit family."

Elliot didn't say anything. He watched me choose a book and rearrange my own pillows before getting comfortable. Thinking of how I felt looking at a picture of him with his friends—and how much more I wanted to know about *his* life outside of this closet—I considered my next words, letting them tumble around in my head before speaking. "I stopped hanging out with most of my friends for a while when Mom got sick, so I could spend time with her."

He nodded, and though his eyes stayed fixed on the notebook in front of him, I could tell his attention was solely on me.

I scanned the first page, turning to the chapter I'd just started. "And then when she was gone, I didn't really feel like going to sleepovers and talking about boys. It's kind of like they all grew up while I put myself back together. Nikki and I are still good, but I think it's because she doesn't really hang out outside of school, either. She has an enormous family she sees a lot."

I could feel him watching me now, but I didn't turn, knowing I'd never be able to finish if I did. The words seemed to bubble up in my chest, things I'd never talked about with anyone.

"Dad tried to get me to hang out more," I continued. "He even arranged for me to go to this kids' club thing down by his work?" I glanced quickly up at Elliot and then back down. "He said it was to socialize and make friends, but it wasn't. It was a group for grieving children."

"Oh."

"We all knew what we were doing there, though," I told him. "I remember walking into this huge white room. The walls were covered in things I think were supposed to be teen-related: boy band posters, pink and purple graffiti on bulletin boards, fuzzy beanbags and baskets of magazines." I picked at a stray thread on my jeans. "It was like someone's mom had come in and put up all this random stuff they thought teenage girls should have in their room.

"I remember looking around that first day," I continued, pulling my thick ponytail over my shoulder and fidgeting with the ends, "thinking how weird it was that we were all there to just hang out. After a few days I noticed that all the girls had almost the same haircut. Like seven girls, all around my age with these chin-length bobs. A few weeks later I found out that all those girls were like me, they had all lost their moms. Most of them just got these simple, easy haircuts." I paused and began twisting the ends of my hair around my finger.

"But my dad learned how to put my hair in ponytails, what kind of shampoo to buy, he even had someone teach him how to braid and use the curling iron for special occasions. He could have done what was easiest for him and just cut it all off. But he didn't."

For the first time I looked up to see Elliot watching me. His eyes were wide with understanding and he reached over and took one of my hands.

"Did I ever tell you that I have my mom's hair?" I said.

He shook his head but gave me a real smile. "I think you have the prettiest hair I've ever seen."

now

thursday, october 5

I stand outside the entrance to Nopalito on Ninth, and without having to look too deeply inside, I know Elliot is already in there. I know this because it's ten minutes past eight. We agreed to meet at eight, and Elliot never runs behind schedule. Something tells me that hasn't changed.

Pushing inside, I spot him immediately. His napkin slides to the floor and his thighs awkwardly collide with the table in his rush to stand. I notice two things: one, he's wearing a dress jacket, nice jeans, and a pair of black dress shoes that look newly polished. Two, he got a haircut.

It's still longish on top, but cut very short at the sides. It makes him somehow a little less highbrow literary hipster and more . . . skater hot. It's amazing that a look he would never have even attempted in adolescence is one he can absolutely rock at twenty-nine. That said, I'm sure he has only his stylist to thank. The boy I grew up with would give more thought to which type of pen he used to write a grocery list than what he looked like on any given day.

Fondness clutches me.

I make my way to him, trying to breathe through the hum of electricity surging in my bloodstream. Maybe it's the benefit of having had time to get ready tonight—and that I'm not in my scrubs—but this time, I feel the way his eyes move from my hair to my shoes and back up.

He's visibly shaken when I step closer and stretch to give him a quick hug. "Hi."

Swallowing, he lets out a strangled "Hi" and then pulls my chair out for me. "Your hair is . . . you look . . . beautiful."

"Thanks. Happy birthday, Elliot."

Friends. Not a date, I repeat, like a prayer. *I'm just here to make up for breakfast, and to clear the air.*

I attempt to brand it into my brain and my heart.

"Thank you." Elliot clears his throat, smiling without teeth, eyes tight. And really: where to start?

The waiter pours water into my glass and slides my napkin onto my lap for me. The entire time, Elliot is staring down at me as if I've come back from the grave. Is that what it feels like for him? At what point would he have given up on getting in touch with me, or would the answer be *never*?

"How was work today?" he asks, starting somewhere safe.

"It was busy."

He nods, sipping his water and then putting it down, letting his fingers trace drops of condensation as they flow from the lip to the base. "You're in pediatrics."

"Yes."

"And did you know as soon as you started med school that you wanted to work in that?"

I shrug. "Pretty much."

An exasperated smile quirks his mouth. "*Give* a little, Mace."

This makes me laugh. "I'm sorry. I'm not trying to be weird." After a deep inhale and long, shaking exhale, I admit, "I guess I'm nervous."

Not that it's a date.

I mean, of course it isn't. I told Sean I was meeting an old friend for dinner tonight, and promised myself I would give him the whole story when I got home—which I still intend to do. But he was preoccupied with setting up his new TV and didn't really seem to notice when I stepped out, anyway.

"I'm nervous, too," Elliot says.

"It's been a long time."

"It has," he says, "but I'm glad you called. Or texted, rather."

"You replied so quickly," I say, thinking of his old flip-phone again. "I wasn't prepared for that."

He beams with mock pride. "I have an iPhone now."

"Let me guess: Nick Jr.'s hand-me-down?"

Elliot scowls. "As if." He takes another sip of water and adds, "I mean, Andreas updates his phone *way* more often."

Our laughter dies down but the eye contact remains. "Well, in case you were wondering," I say, "the score is even at one–one. Liz gave me your number. Though I probably should have remembered it. It's the same one you always had."

He nods and my eyes flicker down reflexively when he lick-bites his bottom lip. "Liz is great."

"I can tell," I say. "I like her." Clearing my throat, I add quietly, "Speaking of . . . sorry about how I left at breakfast."

"I get it," he answers quickly. "It's a lot to process."

It's almost laughable; an ocean of information separates us, and there are an infinite number of places to begin. Start at the beginning and work forward. Start now, and work backward. Jump in somewhere in the middle.

"I honestly don't even know where to begin," I admit.

"Maybe," he says hesitantly, "maybe we check out the menu, order some wine, and then catch up? You know, like people do over dinner?"

I nod, relieved that he seems as mentally sturdy as ever, and lift the menu to scan it, but it feels like the words on the page are trumped by all the questions in my head.

Where does he live in Berkeley?

What is his novel about?

What about him has changed? What stayed the same?

But the petty, traitorous thought that lurks in the guilty shadows of my brain is the bravery it took him to end a relationship after seeing me for less than two minutes. I mean, unless it wasn't very established.

Or was already on its way out.

Is this the worst place to start? Am I a complete maniac? I mean, at the very least it was the last real thing we talked about yesterday, right?

"Is everything okay with . . . with . . . ?" I ask, wincing.

He looks up from his menu and maybe it's my slightly anxious expression that clues him in. "With Rachel?"

I nod, but her name triggers a defensive reaction in me: he *should* be with someone named *Rachel*, who reads with relish every issue of the *New Yorker*, and works in nonprofit, and composts all her eggshells and beet peelings so she can grow her own produce. Meanwhile, I'm a mess, with never-ending med school loans, mommy issues, daddy issues, Elliot issues, and a shameful subscription to *US Weekly*.

"Things are okay, actually," he says. "I think. I hope eventually we can be friends again. In hindsight, it couldn't ever have been more."

This sentiment slips into my bloodstream, warm and electric. "Elliot."

"I heard what you said," he says earnestly. "You're engaged, I get it. But it will be hard for me to *just* be your friend, Macy. It's not in my DNA." He meets my eyes and puts the menu back down near his arm. "I'll try, but I already know this about myself."

I feel his disarming honesty chipping away at the resilient shell around me. I wonder how many times he could tell me he loved me before I melted into a puddle at his feet.

"Then I think some ground rules are in order," I say.

"Ground rules," he repeats, nodding slowly. "As in, no expectations?" I nod. "And, maybe . . . anything you want to know, I'll tell you, and vice versa?"

If this is quid pro quo, I'm going to have to put on my big girl pants and get through it. Although everything inside me is rioting in panic, I agree.

"So," he says, easing into a smile, "I don't know what you'd like to know about Rachel. We were friends first. For years, in grad school and after."

The idea of him being friends with another female *for years* is a knife pushed slowly into my sternum. Taking a sip of water, I manage an easy follow-up. "Grad school?"

"MFA from NYU," he says, smiling. Rubbing a hand over his hair as if he's not quite used to the feel of it yet, he adds, "Looking back, it seems a little like when we hit twenty-eight, we defaulted into a relationship."

I know what he means. I turned twenty-eight and defaulted to Sean.

He's a mind reader: "Tell me about this guy you're going to marry."

This is a minefield, but I may as well put it all right up front and be honest, too.

"We met at a dinner welcoming all of the incoming residents," I say, and he doesn't need me to do the math for him, but I do: "in May."

His brows slowly inch up beneath his shaggy mop of hair. "Oh."

"We hit it off right away."

Elliot nods, watching me intensely. "I assume you'd have to."

I blink down to the table, clearing my throat and trying not to respond defensively. Elliot has always been brutally honest, but it never came out sharply at *me* before. To me, his words were always gentle and adoring. Now my heart is pounding so hard, I feel it swooshing between us, and it makes me wonder whether our individual heartaches are silently duking this out from inside our bodies.

"Sorry," Elliot mumbles, reaching across the table before thinking better of touching me. "I didn't mean it to come out like that. It's just fast, that's all."

I look up and give him a weak smile. "I know. It did move fast."

"What's he like?"

"Mellow. Nice." I twist my napkin in my lap, wishing I could come up with better adjectives to describe the man I plan to marry. "He has a daughter."

Elliot listens, nearly unblinking.

"He's a benefactor for the hospital," I say. "Well, in a sense. He's an artist. His work is . . ." I sense that I'm beginning to brag, and I don't know why it leaves me feeling unsettled. "It's pretty popular right now. He donates a lot of the newer art installations over at Benioff Mission Bay."

Elliot leans in. "*Sean Chen?*"

"Yeah. You've heard of him?"

"Books and art run in similar circles around here," he explains, nodding. "I've heard he's a good guy. His art is stunning."

Pride swells, warm in my chest. "He is. It is, yeah." And another truth rolls out of me before I can catch it: "And he's the first guy I've been with who . . ."

Shit.

I try to think of a better way to end this sentence than the bald truth, but my mind is completely blank but for Elliot's earnest expression and the gentle way his hands are cupping his water glass. He unravels me.

He waits, and finally asks, "Who what, Mace?"

Goddammit. "Who didn't feel like some sort of betrayal to . . ."

Elliot picks up my unfinished sentence with a gentle "Oh. Yeah."

I meet his eyes.

"I've never had one of those," he adds quietly.

Actually, *this* is a minefield. Blinking down to the table, with my heart in my windpipe, I barrel on: "So that's why I said yes when he proposed, impulsively. I'd always told myself the first man I was with and didn't feel wrong about, I would marry."

"That seems like . . . some sturdy criteria."

"It *felt* right."

"But really," Elliot says, drawing a finger through a drop of water that's made its way to the tabletop, "according to that criteria, technically wouldn't that person be me?"

The waiter is my new favorite human because he approaches, intent on taking our order just after Elliot says this, preventing me from the awkward dance of a non-answer.

Glancing at the menu, I say, "I'll have tacos dorados and the citrus salad." Looking up, I add, "I'll let him pick the wine."

As I probably could have guessed, Elliot orders the caldo tlalpeño—he always loved spicy food—and a bottle of the Horse & Plow sauvignon blanc before handing his menu to the waiter with quiet thanks.

Turning back to me, he says, "I knew exactly what you were going to order. Citrus salad? It's like Macy's food dream."

My thoughts trip over one another at this, at how easy it is, at how in sync we still are right out of the gate. It's too easy, really, and it feels unfaithful in a *really* surreal and backward way to the man who's a couple of miles away, installing a television in the small home we share. I sit up, working to infuse some emotional distance into my posture.

"And she retreats . . ." Elliot says, studying me.

"I'm sorry," I say. He reads every tiny move I make. I can't fault him for it; I do the same thing. "It started feeling a little too familiar."

"Because of the fiancé," he says, tilting his head back, indicating *elsewhere*. "When's the wedding?"

"My schedule is pretty nuts, so we haven't set a date yet." It's partly the truth.

Elliot's posture tells me he likes this answer—however disingenuous it may be—and it stirs the anxiety in my belly.

"But, we're thinking next fall," I add quickly, straying even further from the truth now. Sean and I haven't discussed dates at all. Elliot narrows his eyes. "Though if it's left to me, it will happen in whatever we're wearing at the courthouse. I am apparently really uninterested in planning a wedding."

Elliot doesn't say much for a few loaded seconds, just lets my words reverberate around us. Then he gives me a simple "Ah."

I clear my throat awkwardly. "So, tell me what you've been doing?"

He's interrupted only briefly when the waiter returns with our wine, displaying the label for Elliot, opening it tableside, and offering a taste. There are ways in which Elliot's confidence throws me, and this is one. He grew up in the heart of California wine country, so he must be comfortable with this, but I've never seen him taste wine at the table. We were so young . . .

"It's great," he tells the waiter, then turns back to me while he pours, clearly dismissing the man from his thoughts. "How far back should I go?"

"How about start with now?"

Elliot leans into his chair, thinking for a few moments before he seems to figure out where to begin. And then it all rolls out of him, easy and detailed. He tells me that his parents are still in Healdsburg ("We couldn't pay Dad to retire."); that Nick Jr. is the district attorney for Sonoma County ("The way he dresses is straight out of some bad crime show and I'd only say that in this safe space, but no one should wear sharkskin."); Alex is in high school and an avid dancer ("I can't even blame my gushing on brotherly pride, Mace. She's *really* good."); George—as I know—is married to Liz and living in San Francisco ("He's a suit, in an office. I honestly can never really remember what his job title is."); and Andreas is living in Santa Rosa, teaching fifth grade math, getting married later this year ("Of all of us to end up working with kids, he would have been the least likely, but turns out, he's the best at it.").

The whole time he updates me, all I can think is that I'm getting the cream, skimmed from the top. Beneath it is still so much. Volumes of tiny details I've missed.

The food comes, and it's so good but I eat it without giving it any attention, because I can't seem to get enough information, and neither can he. College years are outlined in the monochromatic ways of hindsight, graduate school horror stories are exchanged with the knowing laugh of someone who has also suffered and seen the other side. But we don't talk about falling in love with someone else and where that leaves us now, and no matter how much it's with us in every breath, and every word, we don't talk about what happened the last time I saw him, eleven years ago.

then

monday, july 28
fourteen years ago

Our first summer with the cabin, my dad and I were there nearly every day, with only one trip home, late July, for a visit from his brother, Kennet.

Kennet had two daughters, and a wife, Britt, whose idea of affection was a cupped hand around my shoulder. So when I came to her, whispering in mild horror that I thought I'd started my period, she handled me with the anticipated emotional sterility: buying me a box of pads and a box of tampons and having her younger daughter, Karin, awkwardly explain the basic application process.

Dad was better, but not by a very wide margin. Once we

returned to the cabin that weekend, he referred to Mom's list, where, at position twenty-three, she had written:

When Macy starts her period, make sure she doesn't have any questions about what is happening with her body. I know it's awkward, men amor, but she needs to know that she is amazing, and perfect, and if I were there I would tell her the story in the envelope marked 23.

Dad opened it, his cheeks pink. "When I—" He coughed, correcting, "Your mother first started her . . . ah . . . ."

I grabbed the letter from his hands and jogged upstairs, to the comfort of my library.

I used to have the worst cramps, it began, and the sight of her handwriting made my breastbone ache.

They would hit me at the most unexpected times. Shopping with my friends, or at a birthday party. Midol helped, when I discovered it, but what helped the most was visualizing the pain evaporating from my stomach.

I would imagine it again and again, until the pain subsided.

I don't know that it will work for you, or if

you will need this, but if you do, imagine my voice, helping. You will be tempted to hate this thing that your body does, but it's your body's way of telling you everything is working, and that is a miracle.

But most of all, meu docinha, imagine how proud I am to share this with you. You're growing up. Starting my period was the process that eventually let me get pregnant with you, when I was ready.

Treat your body carefully. Take care of it. Don't let anyone abuse it, and don't abuse it yourself. Every inch of your skin I made diligently; months I slaved over you. You are my masterpiece.

I miss you. I love you.
Mãe

I blinked up, startled. At some point while I'd been reading, Elliot had materialized in the doorway, but he didn't see my tears until I'd turned my face to him. His grin slowly melted away as he took one step, and then two, closer to me, kneeling on the floor beside where I sat on the futon.

His eyes searched mine. "What's wrong?"

"Nothing," I said, shifting in my seat as I folded the letter. He eyed it before looking back at me.

Nearly fifteen, and he was already too perceptive.

More and more it bothered me that our daily lives were these odd unknowns to each other. We gave updates whenever we met in here. Who we spent time with, what we were studying. We talked about who irritated us, who we admired. And, of course, we shared our favorite words. He knew my two closest friends' names—Nikki and Danny—but not their faces. Although I'd seen their faces in the photograph in his room, I had the same limited information about Elliot's friends at school. I knew Brandon was quiet and calm, and Christian was a criminal record waiting to be written. In here, we read, and we talked, and we learned about each other over time, but how could I tell him what was happening to me?

It wasn't just that I got my period so much later than all my friends had, or even that Dad was struggling to relate to me, or that my mom was dead, or any of it. Or maybe it was *all* of it. I loved my dad more than anything, but he was so ill-equipped for some of this. Without a doubt, I knew he was downstairs, pacing, listening for the sound of my voice to know whether he had been right to let Elliot upstairs, or whether his instincts were all wrong.

"I'm okay," I said, hoping I'd spoken loud enough for the words to reach downstairs. The last thing I wanted was both of them up here, worrying about me.

Frowning, Elliot took my face in his hands in a move that shocked me, and his eyes searched mine. "Please, tell me what's wrong. Is it your dad? School?"

"I really don't want to talk about it, Ell." I pulled back a little, wiping my face. My fingers came away wet, explaining Elliot's panic. I must have been really sobbing when he came in.

"We tell each other everything in here, remember?" Reluctantly he shifted back. "That's the deal."

"I don't think you want to know this."

He stared at me, unfazed. "I do want to know this."

Tempted to call his bluff, I looked him dead in the eye and said, "I started my period."

He blinked several times before straightening. Color spread from his neck to his cheekbones. "And you're upset about it?"

"Not upset." I bit my lip, thinking. "Relieved, mostly. And then I read a letter from my mom, and now I'm a little sad?"

He smiled. "That sounded an awful lot like a question."

"It's just that all your life you hear about periods." Talking about this with Elliot was . . . actually, not that bad. "You wonder when it's going to happen, what it will be like, if you'll feel any different after. When your girlfriends get theirs, you're like, 'What's wrong with me?' It's like a little biological time bomb sitting inside you."

He bit his lip, trying to stifle an uncomfortable laugh. "Until now?"

"Yeah."

"Well, do you? Feel any different?"

I shook my head. "Not really. Not like I thought I would, anyway. It sort of feels like something is trying to gnaw its way out of my stomach. And I'm a little testy."

Elliot lifted the blanket and scooted next to me, wrapping his arm around my shoulders. "I'm not going to be any help, but I think I'm supposed to be happy for you."

"You're being very mature and un-boy-like about this. I expected less compassion and more bumbling." I grew light-headed from the warmth of his body and the feeling of his arm around me.

He exhaled a laugh into my hair. "I have a baby sister on the way, and a mom who insists it's my job to show her the ropes, remember? So I need you to explain everything."

I curled into his side, closing my eyes against the sting of tears I felt there.

"Is there anything I can do?" he asked quietly.

A weight settled heavily in my chest. "Not unless you can bring my mom back."

Silence pulsed around us and I heard him inhaling in preparation a few times before speaking. Finally, he settled on a simple "I wish I could."

I nodded against him, breathing in the sharp smell of his deodorant, the lingering smell of his boy-sweat, the wet-cotton smell of his T-shirt from the fifteen-foot run through the summer rain from his porch to mine. So weird that just hearing him say that made me feel a million times better.

"Do you want to talk about it?" he whispered.

"No."

His hand made the gentle path up and down my arm. I knew, without having to look too far and wide, that there were no other boys like Elliot, anywhere.

"I'm sorry you're grumpy."

"Me too."

"Do you want me to get a warm water bottle? I do that for my mom."

I shook my head. I wanted Mom to be here, reading her letter to me.

He cleared his throat, asking quietly, "Because it would make it feel like I'm your boyfriend?"

I swallowed, and the mood shifted in an instant. Boyfriend didn't seem to cover it. Elliot was kind of my Everyfriend. "I guess?"

He sat up, still all skinny arms and long twisty legs, but he was becoming something new, something more . . . man than boy. At nearly fifteen, he had an Adam's apple and faint stubble on his chin, and his pants were too short. His voice had deepened. "I guess we're too young for that."

I nodded and tried to swallow, but my mouth had gone dry. "Yeah."

now

friday, october 6

Early-morning light filters in through the gauzy curtains, turning everything faintly blue. Outside on Elsie Street, garbage trucks rumble down the asphalt. The squealing of metal on metal, the crash of the bins against the truck, and the sound of garbage cascading into the compactor carries up from outside. Despite the way the world continues to move forward on the other side of the window, I'm not sure I'm ready to start the day.

My ears still ring with snippets of conversation from dinner last night. I want to hold on to them for just a little longer, to relish the joy of having my best friend back in my life before all the complications that come along with it make their way to the surface.

Sean turns to me, pulling me right up against him, pressing his face to my neck.

"Morning," he growls, hands already busy, mouth on my throat, my jaw. He works my pajama shorts down my hips, rolling over onto me. "Did you actually get a full night's sleep?"

"Miracle of miracles: I *did*." I run both hands into his hair, digging in the thick tangle of salt-and-pepper. Hunger flushes through me; we haven't had sex in over a week.

We're still so new, I'm not sure we've ever gone that long before.

When he reaches my mouth, I kiss him once before hesitation spikes in me, and I pull back a little. "Wait."

"Oh. Period?" he asks, brows lifted.

"What?" I say, and then shake my head. "No, I just wanted to tell you about last night."

"About last night?" he repeats, confused.

"About my dinner with Elliot."

Sean's dark brows pull down now. "It could wait until after . . . ?" He presses into me, meaningfully.

"Oh." I guess it could. But the reality is that it probably shouldn't.

Elliot and I didn't even touch again after I hugged him hello. It's not like anything *happened*. But it feels like I'm lying by not telling Sean who Elliot is. Or, rather, who he was.

"It's nothing bad," I say, but Sean rolls off me anyway. "I just . . . one of the challenges you and I face is that we have these enormous histories that we couldn't possibly have laid out in the amount of time we've been together."

He acknowledges this with a little nod.

"I told you I was having dinner with an old friend last night, and that's true."

"Okay?"

"But he was really like my old . . . *everything*."

I meet Sean's eyes and melt a little. They're the first thing I noticed about him because they're so deep, and soulful, and glimmering. His eyes are amazing: brown, thickly lashed, and the way they lift gently at the outer edges easily makes them the best flirty eyes I've ever known. Right now, though, they're more guarded than playful.

I shrug, amending, "He was my *first* everything."

"Your first . . ."

"My first true friend, my first love, my first . . ."

"Sex," he finishes for me.

"It's complicated."

"How complicated?" he asks, gently. "Everyone has exes. Did he . . . hurt you?"

Quickly, I shake my head. "See, after Mom died, Dad was my whole world, but he still didn't know how to nurture the same way Mom had. And then I met Elliot and it was like . . ." I search for the right words. "I had someone my age who really understood me and saw me for exactly who I was.

He was like a best girlfriend and a first boyfriend all rolled into one."

Sean's expression softens. "I'm glad, babe."

"We had a fight one night, and . . ." I realize now that I'm going to shut this down prematurely. I'm not sure I can finish the story. "I needed some time to think, and 'some time' turned into eleven years."

Sean's eyes widen a little. "Oh?"

"We ran into each other a few days ago."

"I see. And it's the first time you've spoken since."

I swallow thickly. "Right."

"So there's some baggage to unpack," he says, smiling a little.

I nod, repeating, "Right."

"And has this relationship been hanging over you all this time?"

I don't want to lie to him. "Yes."

Other than the deaths of my parents, nothing looms larger in my life than Elliot.

"Do you still love him?"

I blink away. "I don't know."

Sean uses a gentle finger to turn my face to his. "I don't mind if you love him, Mace. Even if you think you might always love him. But if it makes you wonder what you're doing here, with me, *then* we need to talk about it."

"It doesn't, really. It's just been emotional to see him."

"I get that," he says quietly. "It brings up old stuff. I'm sure if I saw Ashley again, I'd struggle with all of that. Anger, and hurt, and yeah—the love that I still have for her. I never got to fall out of love. I just had to move on when she walked out."

It's a perfect description. *I never got to fall out of love. I just had to move on.*

He kisses me, once. "We're not eighteen, babe. We're not coming into this without a few chinks in our armor. I don't expect you to have room in your heart for me only."

I'm so grateful to him right now I nearly want to cry.

"Well, work on the friendship. Do what you need to do," he says, his weight returning above me, his body pushing against mine, hard and ready. "But right now, come back to me."

I wrap my arms around him, and press my face to his neck, but as he moves over me, and then into me, I have a brief flash of bare honesty. It's good—the sex has always been good—but it isn't *right*.

It doesn't set off alarm bells in my head, sure, but it doesn't send goose bumps across my skin, either. It doesn't make my chest ache so deliciously I'm nearly breathless. I don't feel urgent, or desperate, or too hot in my own skin because I'm so hungry for him. And in a tight gasp that Sean reads as pleasure, I worry that Elliot is right and I'm wrong and—like always—he's taking care of both of our hearts while I flop around, trying to figure it all out.

I feel my thoughts circling something, the same thing over and over: how Elliot went home after seeing me and broke up with Rachel.

He only had to see me to know, whereas I can barely trust a single feeling I have.

then

wednesday, november 26
fourteen years ago

Dad pushed the cart down the aisle, coming to a stop in front of a freezer case full of enormous turkeys.

We stared down at them together. Although Dad and I carried on many traditions since Mom died, we'd never done Thanksgiving alone.

Then again, we never really did it *with* her, either. With two twenty-first-century, first-generation immigrants as parents, Thanksgiving wasn't really a holiday any of us had cared much about. But we had the cabin now, and nearly a week off with nothing else to do but capably chop firewood and read in front of the flames. It felt wasteful, in a totally illogi-cal way, to not at least attempt the holiday meal.

But standing here, faced with the prospect of making such an enormous production for two, cooking felt decidedly more wasteful.

"These are thirteen pounds," Dad said, "at minimum." With an expression of mild distaste, he hefted a bird out of the case and inspected it.

"Don't they just have the . . ." I waved my hand toward the butcher, to the breasts displayed there.

Dad stared at me, not getting it. "The what?"

"You know, just smaller parts?"

He guffawed. "The *breasts*?"

I groaned, walking past him to find a bone-in turkey breast we could roast in less than half a day.

Coming up behind me, Dad said, "These are a more ap-propriate size." Leaning in, he added with a repressed laugh, "Decent-sized breasts."

Mortified, I shoved him away and moved to the produce section to get potatoes. Standing there, with baby Alex in a sling, was Elliot's mom, Miss Dina.

She had a cart full of food, a phone to her ear as she chatted with someone, the sleeping baby against her chest, and she inspected yellow onions as if she had all the time in the world. She'd given birth three months ago and was here, preparing to cook a huge meal for her troop of ravenous boys.

I stared at her, feeling the twisting combination of admiration and defeat. Miss Dina made things look so easy; Dad and I could barely figure out how to make a holiday meal for two.

She did a tiny double take when she saw me, and for maybe the first time in my life I imagined myself through someone else's eyes: my swim team track pants, the baggy Yale sweatshirt Dad got for Mom years ago, flip-flops. And I stood, staring at the breadth of the produce, motherless and clearly overwhelmed.

Miss Dina ended her call and pushed her cart over to me.

She looked at my face, then let her eyes move all the way down to my toes and back up. "You and your dad are planning to cook tomorrow?"

I gave her what I hoped was a humorously confident grin. "We're going to try."

She winced, looking past me and pretending to fret. "Macy," she said, leaning in conspiratorially, "I have more food than I know what to do with, and with little Alex here . . . it would help me out a lot if you and your dad would come over. If you could help me peel potatoes and make the rolls, you'd be a lifesaver."

Not in a million years would I have said no.

It smelled like baking pie crust, melted butter, and turkey all day—even in our house. The wind carried the smells of cooking into our window, and my stomach gnawed at itself.

Miss Dina had told us to come over at three, and I couldn't even count on Elliot to entertain me until then because, no doubt, he'd been put to work.

I heard the lawn mower going, the vacuum running inside. And, of course, I heard the roar of football on the living room television, filtering from their house to ours. By the time we made our way over with wine and flowers at two minutes before three o'clock, I was nearly insane with anticipation.

Dad made a good living, and our house in Berkeley had every material possession we could possibly need or want. But what we could never buy was chaos and bustle. We lacked noise, and strife, and the joy of overstuffed plates because everyone insisted that their favorite dish be made.

Just inside their door we were pulled like metal to magnets into the madness. George and Andreas shouted at the television. In the easy chair in the corner, Mr. Nick blew exuberant raspberries on Alex's tummy. Nick Jr. was polishing the dining room table while Miss Dina poured melted butter into the crossed tops of rolls to put in the oven, and Elliot stood over the sink, peeling potatoes.

I ran to him, reaching to take the peeler out of his hand. "I told your mom I would peel those!"

He blinked at me in surprise, reaching with a potato skin–covered finger to push his glasses up. I knew that help-

ing her with dinner was just a ruse—after all, I'd been smell-
ing the food all day—but for whatever reason, I was unable to
give it up.

The thing is, at fourteen I was old enough to understand
that many of the people who had lived in Healdsburg for
many years would not have been able to afford to live in
Berkeley. Although Healdsburg had been taken over by Bay
Area money and the wine craze of the nineties, many people
who lived here still worked for hourly wages and lived in
older, mildly soggy houses.

The wealth here was what was *inside*: the Petropoulos
family and the warmth and the knowledge—passed down
through generations—of how to cook a meal like this for a
family of this size.

I watched as Miss Dina gave Elliot a different job—
washing and chopping lettuce for the salad—which he did
without complaint or instruction.

Meanwhile, I hacked at the potatoes until Miss Dina
came in and showed me how to peel them more slowly, in
long, smooth strips.

"Nice dress," Elliot said once she'd left, his voice laced
with delicate sarcasm.

I looked down at the frumpy denim jumper I wore.
"Thanks. It was my mom's."

His eyes went wide. "Oh, my God, Macy, I'm sor—"

I threw a piece of potato skin at him. "I'm kidding. Dad
got it for me. I felt like I needed to wear it sometime."

He looked scandalized, then he grinned.

"You're evil," he hissed.

"You mess with the bull," I said, holding up my index and pinkie fingers, "you get the horns."

I felt him watching me and hoped he saw my smile.

Mom always had a wicked sense of humor.

Dad sat, watching the Niners game with feigned interest with Mr. Nick and the boys until Miss Dina called us in to eat.

There was a ritual once we were at the table, a choreographed scene that Dad and I followed carefully: everyone sat in their chairs and linked hands. Mr. Nick said grace, and then everyone went around in turn and said something they were thankful for this year.

George was thankful for making varsity track.

Miss Dina was thankful for her healthy baby girl (who slept quietly in a vibrating baby chair near the table).

Nick Jr. was thankful that he was nearly done with his first semester of college, because, man, it sucked.

Dad was thankful for a good year in business and a wonderful daughter.

Andreas was thankful for his girlfriend, Amie.

Mr. Nick was thankful for his boys, and his—now two—girls. He winked at his wife.

Elliot was thankful for the Sorensen family, and especially for Macy, who he missed during the week when she was back home.

I sat, staring at him and trying to find something else to say, something as good as that.

I focused on a spot on the table as I spoke, my words wavering. "I'm thankful that high school isn't terrible so far. I'm thankful I didn't get Mr. Syne for math." I looked up at Elliot. "But mostly, I'm thankful we bought this house, and that I was able to make a friend who wouldn't make me feel weird for being sad about my mom, or wanting to be quiet, and who will always have to explain things to me twice because he's so much smarter than I am. I'm thankful that his family is so nice, and his mom makes such good dinners, and Dad and I didn't have to try to make a turkey all by ourselves."

The table fell quiet, and I heard Miss Dina swallow a few times before she said brightly, "Perfect! Let's eat!"

And the routine dissolved as frenzy took over, with four teenage boys diving into the food. Rolls were passed, turkey and gravy were slopped onto my plate, and I savored every single bite.

It wasn't as good as Mom's everyday cooking, and Mom was missing something she would have absolutely loved—a room full of boisterous family—but it was the best Thanksgiving I'd ever had. I didn't even feel guilty for feeling that way, because I know Mom would want me to have more, and better, forever.

Back home later, Dad walked me upstairs, standing behind me and brushing my hair like he used to do while I brushed my teeth.

"I'm sorry I was so quiet tonight," he said, haltingly.

I met his eyes in the mirror. "I like your kind of quiet. Your heart isn't quiet."

He bent, pressing his cheek to my temple, and smiled at me in the mirror. "You're an amazing girl, Macy Lea."

now

friday, october 13

More miraculous even than a full night's sleep is the prospect of a full day off on a weekend. Getting a free Saturday feels like being ten years old and holding a twenty-dollar bill in a candy store. I don't even know where to start.

Well, that's not entirely true. I know I don't want to spend a second of the day indoors. The Mission Bay site for UCSF Children's has windows everywhere, but when you're a pediatric resident, you don't notice anything but the child in front of you, or your chief telling you where you need to be next.

Friday afternoon, on a short break after rounds, I remind

Sean of our plans to picnic at Golden Gate Park. I call Sabrina, confirming that she, Dave, and Viv can all come. I invite a couple old friends from my Berkeley neighborhood who still live in the area—Nikki and Danny. And then I get back to work with the feeling of buzzing in my ears, static in my thoughts. I can't leave this unfinished all day.

After delivering an update on some bloodwork to my current favorite parents, whose daughter is an inpatient in oncology, I sprint to the break room, ducking behind the locker to grab my phone and text Elliot.

> A few of us are going to Golden Gate Park tomorrow for a picnic.

> Think you'd want to come along?

What time were you thinking?

Was going to head up to H-burg for the afternoon but could be persuaded.

> We're meeting at eleven outside the botanical garden.

> It's totally fine if you can't make it, I know it's last minute.

> Just a few of my friends, and Sean, etc.

I'll be there. I'd love to meet everyone.

then

wednesday, december 31
fourteen years ago

Boys suck."

The wind whipped across us where we were hunkered down at Goat Rock Beach again, preparing for a weenie roast with our families, flag football, and New Year's Eve fireworks over the ocean.

"Do I want to know?" Elliot asked, not even looking up from his book.

"Probably not."

In all fairness, I didn't have strong feelings for any boys at my school, but it seemed like—since we began high school four months ago—none of them had any feelings whatsoever for me. Danny, my best guy friend, told me that his friends Gabe and Tyler both thought I was cute but, as he put it, "A little too, like, into books."

I couldn't escape it; everyone was starting to "go out with" everyone else. I hadn't even so much as kissed a boy.

Guess I'd be going to the ninth-grade dance with Nikki.

Elliot glanced over at me. "Can you tell me more about how boys suck?"

"Boys don't want girls who are *interesting*," I complained. "They want girls with boobs and who wear slutty clothes, and flirt."

Elliot slowly put his book down on a patch of beach grass beside him. "I don't want that."

Ignoring this, I went on, "And girls *do* want boys who are interesting. Girls want the shy geeks who know everything and have big hands and good teeth and say sweet things." I bit my lips closed. I might have said too much.

Elliot beamed at me, metal finally gone, his teeth perfect. "Do you like *my* teeth?"

"You're weird." Changing the subject, I asked, "Favorite word?"

He stared out at the ocean for a few breaths before saying, "*Cynosure*."

"What does that even mean?"

"It's a focal point of admiration. What about you?"

I didn't even have to think: "*Castration*."

Elliot winced. He stared down at his hands in his lap,

turning them over and inspecting them carefully. "Well, for what it's worth," he whispered, "Andreas thinks you're cute."

"Andreas?" I heard the shock in my own voice. I narrowed my eyes as I stared down the beach at where Andreas and George wrestled, and tried to imagine kissing Andreas. His skin was good, but his hair was too shaggy for my taste and he was a little bit of a meathead.

"He said that? He's with Amie."

Elliot scowled, picking up a small rock and throwing it toward the thrashing surf. "They broke up. But I told him if he touched you I would kick his ass."

I barked out a loud laugh.

Elliot was too rational to be offended by my reaction: what Andreas lacked in brains he made up in serious muscle.

"Yeah, so, he tackled me. We wrestled. We broke Mom's vase, you know that ugly one in the hall?"

"Oh no!" My distress was convincing, but I was mostly elated they'd been fighting over me.

"She grounded us both."

I bit my lip, trying not to laugh. Instead, I stretched out on the sand, returning to my book, and lost myself in the words, reading over and over again the same phrase: *It seemed to travel with her, to sweep her aloft in the power of song, so that she was moving in glory among the stars, and for a moment she, too, felt that the words Darkness and Light had no meaning, and only this melody was real.*

Hours may have passed before I heard a throat clear behind us, saw Dad appear. His frame blocked out the sun, casting a cool shadow over where we lay.

I registered only once he was there that I had slowly shifted so I was lying with my head on Elliot's stomach, in our secluded stretch of sand. I pushed to sit up, awkwardly.

"What are you guys doing?"

"Nothing," we said in unison.

I could hear immediately how guilty our joined answer made us sound.

"Really?" Dad asked.

"Really," I answered, but he wasn't looking at me anymore. He and Elliot were having some kind of male Windtalker exchange that included prolonged eye contact, throat clearing, and probably some mysterious form of direct communication between their Y chromosomes.

"We were just reading," Elliot said finally, his voice shifting deeper midway through the sentence. I'm not sure if this sign of his impending manliness was reassuring or damning as far as my dad was concerned.

"Seriously, Dad," I said.

His eyes flickered to mine.

"Okay." Finally he seemed to relax and squatted down next to me. "What are you reading?"

"*A Wrinkle in Time*."

"Again?"

"It's so good."

He smiled at me, reaching out to swipe his thumb along my cheek. "Hungry?"

"Sure."

Dad nodded and stood, making his way toward where Mr. Nick was busy building a fire.

A few seconds passed before it seemed like Elliot was able to exhale.

"Seriously. I think his palms are the size of my entire face."

I imagined Dad's hand gripping Elliot's entire face, and for some reason the image was so comical it made me laugh out a sharp cackle.

"What?" Elliot asked.

"Just, that image is funny."

"Not if you're me and he's looking at you like he has a shovel with your name on it."

"Oh, please." I gaped at him.

"Trust me, Macy. I know dads and daughters."

"Speaking of my dad," I said, adjusting my head on his stomach to be more comfortable, "guess what I found last week?"

"What?"

"He has dirty magazines. A lot of them."

Elliot didn't respond, but I definitely felt him shift beneath me.

"They're in a basket on the top shelf in the far corner of his closet at the cabin. *Behind the nativity scene.*" This last part felt somehow very important.

"That was oddly specific." His voice vibrated along the back of my head, and goose bumps spread across my arms.

"Well, that's an oddly specific place to put something like that. Don't you think?"

"Why were you in his closet?" he asked.

"That's not the point, Elliot."

"It's precisely the point, Mace."

"How?"

He placed a bookmark between the pages and sat up to face me, forcing me to sit up, too.

"He's a man. A *single* man." Elliot used the tip of his index finger to push his glasses up and held my gaze sternly. "His bedroom is his fortress of solitude—his closet is his *vault.* You might as well have been looking in his nightstand drawer or under his mattress." My eyes widened. "What were you expecting to find on the top shelf in the far corner of his closet behind the nativity scene?"

"Photo albums? Cherished mementos of a lost youth? Winter sweaters? Things of a parental nature?" I paused, giving him a guilty smile. "My Christmas presents?"

Shaking his head, he turned back to his book. "Snooping will always end badly, Mace. *Always.*"

I considered this. Dad didn't date much . . . well, *ever,* that I could think of, spending most of his time at work or with me. I'd never given a moment of thought to this sort of thing where he was concerned. I found the bent corner in my copy of *A Wrinkle in Time* and settled back onto the patch of grass behind me. "It's just . . . gross. That's all."

Elliot laughed: a loud, abrupt snort, followed by a shake of his head.

Glaring at him, I asked, "Did you just shake your head at me?"

"I did." He used a finger to hold his place in the book. "Why is it gross? The fact that your dad has the magazines or that he uses them to—"

Reflexively, I covered my ears. "Nope. Nope. I swear if you finish that sentence I will kick you in the balls, Elliot Petropoulos. Not everyone does that."

Elliot didn't answer, just picked up his book and continued reading.

"*Do* they?" I asked weakly.

He turned his head to look at me. "Yes. They do."

I was silent for a moment while I digested that. "So . . . *you* do that, too?"

The flush crawling up his neck betrayed his embarrassment, but after a few seconds, he nodded.

"A lot?" I asked, genuinely curious.

"I suppose that depends on your definition of 'a lot.' I'm a fifteen-year-old guy with an awesome imagination. That should pretty much answer your question."

I felt like we'd discovered a new hallway door leading into

a new room, which contained a new *everything*. "What do you think about? When you do that, I mean."

My heart was a jackhammer beneath my ribs.

"Kissing. Touching. Sex. Parts I don't have and things people do with them," he added with a wiggle of his brows. I rolled my eyes. "Hands. Hair. Legs. Dragons. Books. Mouths. Words . . . lips . . ." He trailed off and buried his nose in his book again.

"Wow," I said. "Did you say *dragons*?"

He shrugged but didn't look at me again. I eyed him curiously. The mention of books and words and lips had not escaped my attention.

"Like I said," he mumbled into the pages, "I have an awesome imagination."

now

saturday, october 14

"Okay, is it possible I'm beginning to appreciate my scrubs?" I groan.

Sean pokes his head into the bedroom. "What's the problem, babe?"

"Nothing," I say, throwing another shirt onto the pile of rejects on the bed. "It's just—I haven't seen some of these people in forever. And we're having a picnic. I need to look all cute and frolicky because I never get to wear actual clothes. I think I've forgotten how to dress."

"I thought you got dressed up for your dinner last week with him?"

"I don't just mean *Elliot*."

Sean's playful smirk tells me he thinks I'm full of shit, and it makes me laugh but then immediately gives me pause. It actually *isn't* about looking cute and frolicky for Elliot; he's seen me in everything from formal wear to frumpy overalls to nothing at all. And maybe it's just a chick thing—and explaining it makes it sound absurd—but I want to look cute for my *girlfriends*. But if Sean thinks I'm agonizing over what to wear for Elliot, shouldn't that bother him, even a little?

Apparently not, because he ducks back out, returning to the basket of food he's packing for the day. I love how much he loves to cook, especially because it is in direct proportion to how much I hate it.

I hear him mumble something quietly, and then Phoebe comes in, taking a leap and soaring onto the pile of clothes in the middle of the comforter.

"When are we going to the Bojangles garden?"

I plant a kiss on her forehead. "Botanical. And we're leaving in . . ." I glance at the clock on the nightstand. "Oof, twenty minutes."

"I like what you're wearing," she says, waving vaguely in my direction. "Daddy says it's wasteful when I change clothes too often."

There are moments I feel it's my job to impart some sort of feminist wisdom to Phoebs, but, as usual, Sean's way ahead of me.

Having lost interest in my fashion dilemma, she flops over dramatically. "I'm hungry."

"Want me to get you something? There were some strawberries earlier."

She wrinkles her nose. "No thanks, I'll ask Daddy."

She stands, just as Sean calls from the other room, having heard us, "I've got a banana you can eat, Applejack. All the strawberries are already packed up for the picnic."

And before I get any more of her, Phoebe is already out the door and back in the other room. When I think about it, I've had maybe a half hour with her this entire week. I always tell myself that just having a Mom Presence is a big deal for her, but as we've just witnessed, am I even that? And does she need it? I half wonder whether what Sean mumbled to her before she came in was a reminder that she needs to make me feel welcome here, and to come say hi.

God, I'm being ridiculous. But really, Sean and Phoebe seem entirely self-sufficient as a little twosome. I never felt that way about me and Dad. We loved each other, of course, but without Mom we were both sort of lost, arms outstretched as we tried to fumble through each day.

For about the millionth time I wonder about Ashley, and what kind of wife she must have been to Sean, back during a time before he was the hot new artist in San Francisco, when he was still just a *starving* artist, marrying a woman on her way to MBA stardom in finance. I know Phoebe came before they'd planned to have kids, and when Ashley was still climbing the ladder. Was she ever home? Did Sean raise little Phoebe, hands-on every second until she started school, the way Mom raised me?

How would my life be different if Dad had been home more when I was little? How would it have been different if *he* died when I was ten, not Mom?

I feel sick at the thought, as if I've just wished for some alternate reality that would kill my father first. Guilt-stricken, I say a quiet "I didn't mean it" to the air around me, wanting to take back whatever bad thing I might have just thrown out. Even though he's already gone, too.

Sean and Phoebe entertain themselves with a game of I Spy during the short drive to the park. Sabrina and Dave are waiting for us with little Viv in a complicated stroller-ish contraption when we arrive. Sean, Dave, and the kids go into the park to find a good spot, while Sabrina waits for the others with me closer to the parking lot.

I watch the two men walk away, admiring them from behind.

"Those are some fine men," I say, and then turn to find Sabrina watching me intensely. "What?"

"How're you doing?" she says. "You look *sexy* today."

I glance down at what I finally settled on for the unseasonably warm day: a white tank, cute cuffed jeans, and a chunky gold necklace. Having pulled my long hair up into a very intentionally and artfully messy bun, I suddenly wonder if I look like I've tried way too hard—I knew the necklace was too much. Sabrina is wearing old cutoffs and a nursing shirt. "Did I try too hard? I always worry that I've forgotten how to dress myself."

"Nervous?"

I shake my head. "Excited."

"Me too. I've never met him."

"I meant I'm excited for a day off, you little enabler. But since you mention it, you've never met Nikki or Danny, either," I remind her.

Sabrina laughs, stepping closer so she can put her arm around my shoulders. "I know you've known them since grade school, but I think we both know who I'm most curious about."

I glance behind us, to where Sean and Dave have disappeared from view. "Sean seems zero percent weird about the Elliot thing."

"Isn't that good?"

I shrug. "Sure. But I still feel guilty for how much I'm thinking about Elliot and the past, then when I talk to Sean about it, he's like—'It's cool, babe, no big deal.' But maybe it's because I'm not being totally honest with him about how it feels to *see* Elliot? Though," I add, thinking out loud, "Sean assumed right away that it was more than just catching up with an old friend when I brought it up, but it didn't even really rankle him. Is *that* weird?"

Sabrina answers my babble with a helpless look. At least I'm not the only one who's confused.

I groan. "I'm probably just overthinking it."

"Oh, I'm sure you are." I hear the twist in her voice, the complete lack of conviction, but I don't have time to question it because I see Nikki and Danny walking down the path toward us. Taking off at a jog, I run to them, throwing my arms around Nikki first, and then Danny.

Although I've been back in the Bay Area for about six months, I haven't seen them yet, and it's wonderfully surreal to see how they've changed, and—even more so—how they haven't. Nikki I met in the third grade when we were tablemates, and her parents clearly did a better job than most at coaching her through having a friend who lost her mom the following year, because while Nikki didn't always know what to say, she never stopped trying, either. Danny moved to Berkeley from L.A. when we were in sixth grade, so he missed the worst of my heartbreak and subsequent social fumbles, but he's always been on the low-drama, oblivious end of things anyway.

And to eyes that haven't seen her in nearly seven years, Nikki looks amazing. We both have South American blood, but whereas I inherited my mom's small stature and dark skin over Dad's height and fair complexion, Nikki is light-skinned and green-eyed, and has owned her naturally curvy body type her whole life. Now she looks like the captain of some high-octane competitive sport.

By contrast, Danny looks like every other twenty-eight-year-old guy living in Berkeley: slightly underweight, smiling, mildly unshowered.

We're just starting our catch-up—turns out Nikki is coaching women's basketball at Berkeley High, and Danny is a programmer working from home—when my attention is caught over Sabrina's shoulder.

I see a figure climb out of a well-loved blue Honda Civic, grab a sweater from the back seat, and begin his even, long stride straight toward us. I know he's seen me, and wonder whether his limbs go all wobbly the way mine still do when I see him.

"Elliot's here," I say, catching the jittery waver to my words a little too late to stop them.

"Here we go," Sabrina sings to herself, and I can't even pull my eyes away long enough to glare at her.

"*Elliot*-Elliot?" Nikki asks, eyes wide. "As in secret Elliot?"

Danny turns and looks. "Who?"

"Oh, my God," Nikki whispers, "I am so excited right now."

"Same!" Sabrina claps, and I realize now Elliot is facing a wall of women—and Danny—all waiting with giant smiles for his arrival.

"Is Elliot Macy's boyfriend?" Danny asks out of the side of his mouth, and then turns to Sabrina of all people, adding, "Oh, wait, this is the guy from the vacation town."

"Elliot *was* her boyfriend," Sabrina confirms in a delighted, scandalized whisper.

"For about ten minutes," I remind her.

"For about *five years*," she corrects me. "And considering you're only twenty-eight, that's a big chunk of your dating life."

I groan, wondering for the first time whether this is all a terrible idea.

Sabrina has met Sean three times now, and while she insists that she likes him, she thinks he's "oddly shallow for an *artist*" and "doesn't give her *very warm* vibes." It doesn't help that she met Dave our freshman year at Tufts and they dated for seven years before getting married, so a two-month dating span pre-engagement is unfathomable to her. It just sets off her alarm bells.

Before Sean, I had a few relationships, but as Sabrina reminds me, I was "that annoying friend who could find fault with anyone." She's not wrong. To review: Julian was weirdly attached to his guitar. Ashton was a terrible kisser, and no matter how adorable or fun he was, it was impossible to move past that. Jaden had a drinking problem, Matt was too fratty, and Rob was too emotional.

After meeting Sean for the first time, Sabrina asked me what I thought I was going to find wrong with him. And of course, being only a couple of months into it and deep in the infatuation stage, my answer was a semi-tipsy "Nothing!"

But in the private space of my own thoughts, I can't really blame her for thinking Sean isn't very warm. He's great in social situations, but I do know there's something arm's-length about him. He answers questions using as few words as possible, shows limited interest in my friends, lets emotional conversations go for about three minutes before he changes the subject, and outwardly isn't very affectionate with anyone but Phoebe.

But, I don't know. There's an element of comfort in that reserve. It makes sense to me, because as much as I let Elliot into my emotional headspace, I was never able to let anyone else in afterward. It was too hard. Maybe it's the same for Sean with Ashley; we are broken in the same way. On the spectrum of progressive men, Sean and Elliot are about as different as they could possibly be.

I need a Sean in my life.

I need an Elliot about as much as I need a hole in the head.

Elliot comes up with a smile that mirrors ours, looking at each of us in turn. "I assume this is the welcoming committee?"

Sabrina steps forward, hand extended. Her words come out high and breathless. "I'm Sabrina. I was Macy's college roommate, and I have wanted to meet you *forrrevverrrrrr*."

He bursts out laughing, looking at me with raised brows.

I put my hand on her shoulder, stage-whispering, "Take it down a notch."

Elliot opts to give her a hug over a handshake. Sabrina is on the tall side, but Elliot dwarfs her, wrapping her in arms that are surprisingly muscular, running tan and toned beyond the short sleeves of his black T-shirt. He tucks his face close to her as they hug, and I realize, with that one movement, Elliot has just endeared himself to Sabrina for all eternity. No one loves a good hug more than she does.

"Well," he says, stepping back and smiling at her, "it's nice to finally meet you."

Sabrina looks like she is going to pass out from elation. Turning, Elliot gazes at me expectantly.

"Nikki," I prompt, pointing. "And this is Danny."

I see the reaction move across Elliot's expression, the response to names he's heard for so long but faces he's only ever seen in photos. "Ah, okay," he says, smiling and shaking Danny's hand before embracing Nikki. "I've heard a lot about you."

I laugh, because what he's heard is all from the drama of high school. I wonder if he's thinking what I am, about Nikki's wild side and Danny's awkward boners. Elliot catches my eyes, and the glimmer there tells me I'm right. He suppresses a smile, and I bite my lip to do the same.

"All right," I say, "let's go find the food."

Dave and Sean have a nice little spot set up in the shade. Phoebe is drawing quietly on a blanket, Viv is asleep in the stroller, and the two guys are talking, but I can see Dave throw Sabrina a *rescue me* look as we approach. It makes protectiveness for Sean flare inside me, but the feeling is drenched by a flush of adrenaline when he stands, wiping his hands on his jeans and moving toward us. Toward Elliot.

What am I even doing?

I introduce Sean to Nikki and Danny first—the easy ones. Danny is clearly bewildered about what the hell is going on when he hears me say the word *fiancé*, and glances to Elliot as if he's missed something important.

Sean turns to Elliot, and static hums all around me. The tension is clear in Elliot, too: in his shoulders, and across his brow. Sean is as relaxed as ever.

"Sean, this is Elliot," I say, adding inexplicably, "my oldest friend."

"Hey!" Nikki says, and Danny choruses the sentiment as soon as it sinks in what I said.

I laugh. "Sorry, I didn't mean it like that. I just—"

Elliot comes to my rescue, saying, "Nice to meet you, Sean," as he reaches to shake Sean's hand, and God, this is so awkward. On so many levels.

Sean smiles easily and winks at me. "I thought *I* was your oldest friend?"

Everyone laughs cordially at this, and Sean releases Elliot's hand, turning to lay an enormous kiss on my mouth. And seriously, what the hell? Is Sean jealous, or not? It catches me so off guard I don't even close my eyes, which fly to Elliot's face. His chest moves backward with the force of his shocked inhalation. He recovers by moving away quickly, sitting down beside Phoebe and Dave, introducing himself. As Sean steps away from me, I hear the deep tenor of Elliot's voice asking what Phoebe's drawing.

Nostalgia wipes over my thoughts, taking me back to when Elliot would sit with baby Alex like this, gently observing, quietly praising. Now he picks up a crayon, asking if she'll show him how to draw a flower like she does.

"Ovary explosion," Sabrina mumbles in my ear, pretending to be kissing my cheek.

"Something like that," I whisper, wiping my hands on my jeans. I think I'm actually sweating.

We unpack the food, handing out sandwiches, drinks, and fruit to everyone. Conversation eases as soon as Nikki starts talking basketball, because Dave is a former basketball player himself and thank God for the two of them being here, because they carry the enthusiasm required for any good picnic. When Viv wakes up, Phoebe gets to hold her, and the joy in her eyes turns us into cooing, adoring messes. All in all, it goes how a picnic should: eating, talking, a few minor insect battles, and the semi-discomfort of sitting on blankets in the grass.

But something irreparable has happened in my heart. This shaking of my conviction started with the sex I could barely have with Sean the other morning, and it continued ripping down the middle today with the two of them here. I know Sabrina notices the looks Elliot and I can't seem to stop sharing. Maybe she notices, too, the way Sean and I barely interact.

It's hitting me at such an odd time that Elliot is here, *he's here*. He's back in front of me, accessible. I could reach out and touch him. I could crawl over to him, into his lap, feel the warmth of his arms around me.

He could be mine, still.

Why didn't I have this reaction when I should have—two weeks ago?

I reel back through all the things that have happened to me since our falling-out, and other than Dad dying, nothing else feels all that significant. It's as if life was just on hold, I was moving along, getting things done, but not really *living*. Is that awful, or fantastic? I have no idea.

Sabrina's hand comes over mine on the picnic blanket, and I meet her eyes, wondering how much she reads on my face.

"Okay there?" she asks, and I nod, forcing a smile and wishing like hell I believed it.

then

twelve years ago

The only reason I made it through freshman and most of sophomore year was because of Elliot—and Dad's willingness to spend nearly every weekend up in Healdsburg. The weekends we were up there were spent reading, tromping through the forest, and on occasional outings to Santa Rosa. Once, Elliot and I even ventured together as far as a concert all the way down in Oakland. Elliot was more family than friend, but over time, he became more personal in some ways than family, too.

But what all of this closeness meant was that whenever we missed a weekend at the cabin, the intervening weeks seemed interminable. We both did well in school, but I hated the social posturing and politics of high school friendships. Nikki and Danny felt the same about it, and were always zero drama—we spent lunch together every day as a group of outcasts-by-choice, sitting on a sloping patch of grass and watching most of the chaos unfold.

But after school, Nikki went to spend time with her grandmother, Danny went home to skateboard with the kids on his street, and I carried out my weekday routine that felt nearly ritualistic: swim practice, homework, eat, shower, bed. That we did nothing together outside of school made it hard to form very tight emotional bonds with them, but all three of us seemed oddly fine with it.

As spring of sophomore year wound down, I grew acutely aware of Elliot becoming . . . more. Not only intellectually, but physically, too. Seeing him only on weekends and during the summers made it feel like I was watching a time-lapse video of a tree growing, a flower blooming, a field sprouting across the year.

"Favorite word." He shifted on the pile of pillows, eyes moving over me. They were doing their own catch-up, apparently.

It was May 14, and I hadn't seen Elliot since my sixteenth birthday weekend in March—the longest we'd gone in nearly two years. He was . . . different. Bigger, somehow darker. He had new frames, thick black ones. His hair was too long, his shirt stretched tight across his chest. His jeans skimmed the tops of his black sneakers. New jeans, then, too.

"*Tremble*," I said. "You?"

He swallowed and replied, "*Acerbic*."

"Ooh, good one. Update?" I settled in, picking up a book of Dickinson Dad had left on my bed.

"I'm considering learning to skate."

I glanced up at him, eyes wide. "Like ice skate?"

He glared at me. "No, Macy. Like skate*board*."

I laughed at the emphasis he put on the word, but stopped when I took in his expression. In a pulse I wondered whether he was learning because he knew it was something Danny did . . . "Sorry, it's just . . . maybe just say *skateboard*."

He nodded tightly. "Anyway. I saved up and am looking into boards."

I bit back a smile. The boy was so hopeless. "There has to be a website that has lingo or something."

He tilted his head and narrowed his eyes, annoyed.

"Sorry. Go ahead."

"Also," he said, staring down at his shirt as if engrossed with the hem, "I'm taking some of my classes next semester at Santa Rosa."

"What?" I gasped. "Santa Rosa as in college?"

He nodded.

"As a high school *junior*?" I knew Elliot was smart, but . . . he was still only a sophomore now, and already qualified for college courses?

"Yeah, I know. Biology and . . ." He blinked away, suddenly fascinated with something in the corner of the room.

"Biology and *what*, Elliot?"

"Some math."

"'*Some* math'?" I gaped at him. He'd finished advanced calc already? I mentally glared at my impending algebra course.

"So the skateboarding is maybe to help me bond with some of the students in my grade."

The vulnerability in his voice made me feel like an enormous jerk. "But you're with them every day at school. Right?"

He was quiet, watching me. "Yeah, after school. At lunch."

"Wait. You're not in classes with kids in your grade now?"

"Only homeroom." He swallowed and attempted a smile. "I've been working on my own at school but I'll start this semester at SRJC."

I glanced down at the book in his hand. *Franny and Zooey*. It was dog-eared because we'd each read it several times.

"Why didn't you tell me you were so special?"

He laughed quietly at my question and then it transitioned into a full-on laugh attack.

"Sorry," he said, slowly catching his breath. "I don't really think of it that way."

I stared at him, trying to figure out why he thought it was so funny.

"It's just been this semester," he explained. "And, I don't know." He looked up and suddenly seemed years older. I had a preemptive pang for our lives in the future, wondering whether we'd be close like this forever. The possibility that we wouldn't was revolting to me. "It didn't seem like the right thing to include in an email because it seems sort of braggy."

"Well, I'm super proud of you."

He bit his lip through a smile. "Super?"

"Yeah. *Super*." I lifted my head, shifting my pillow. "What else is new?"

"There's a new 'skate park'"—he made quotation marks with his fingers and a teasing little grin—"just past the Safeway, though I've been learning in the beat-up parking lot behind the laundromat. And, let's see . . . Brandon and Christian are going hiking in Yellowstone for a month this summer with Brandon's dad."

His two closest guy friends. "You're not going?"

He shook his head. "Nah. Christian is already talking about how much booze he's going to hide in his suitcase, and it sounds like a mess."

I didn't press. I couldn't really see Elliot hiking in Yellowstone anyway.

"Go on."

"Went to a prom," he mumbled.

The sound of tires screeching to a halt echoed through my head. Taking classes at a junior college seemed tiny compared to the magnitude of this omission.

"A *prom*? But you're a sophomore."

"I went with a junior."

"Was he cute?" I swallowed my more honest, bitter reaction.

"Ha ha. *She* is fine looking. Her name is Emma."

I made a face. He ignored it. "'Fine looking,'" I repeated. "What a roaring compliment."

"It was pretty boring. Dancing. Punch. Awkward silences."

I grinned. "Bummer."

He shrugged but grinned back. Not a half-hearted half smile—a full, eager one. But it slowly straightened as my expression darkened. I remembered the name Emma, and the cute, rosy-cheeked preteen in the photo on his bulletin board.

"You mean the same Emma from that picture?"

He gave a deliberately casual shrug. "Yeah. We've known each other forever."

Forever. My stomach twisted. "Did you get lucky?" I asked, keeping my tone light.

His eyes narrowed and he shook his head. "No . . . I'm not sure I like her like that."

Not sure?

"Does it matter for guys?"

He continued to stare at me, confused.

"Did you *kiss* her?"

His cheeks pinked, and I had my answer.

172

Elliot had *kissed* someone.

Maybe he had kissed a lot of someones.

I mean, of *course* he had. Not everyone was as picky and socially stunted at the romance game as I was. Elliot was turning seventeen in a matter of months. It seemed almost laughable that I imagined he was innocent in the way I was. I was sure he'd done a lot more than kissing. My blood seemed to sour inside my chest, and I let out a little growl at my lap.

"Why are you so mad all of a sudden?" he asked quietly.

I kept my head down. "I don't know."

After all, Elliot was just my friend.

My Everyfriend.

"What's *your* update?" he asked.

I looked back up, eyes flashing. "I had my first orgasm."

His brows lifted, his face grew red, and his mouth formed about a hundred different shapes before he spoke. "What?"

"Or. Gaz. Um."

"You're . . . sixteen." He seemed to realize at the same time I did that this wasn't actually all that scandalous an age.

"You mean it's shameful to be so old?"

He let out a nervous laugh.

"Besides," I said, looking up at him, "you've had one. Probably lots and lots, thinking about dragons."

His neck flushed bright red and he sat up, sliding his hands between his knees. "But . . . only by myself."

His words sent a cold flush of relief through me, but my

173

temper was already off and running. "Well, what did you think I meant?"

His eyes suddenly fixated on my hands. "Oh. So no one . . ."

"Touched me?" I lifted my chin, struggling to not look away. "No."

"Oh." He swallowed audibly. All around us, the blue walls seemed to close in.

"Is that a weird update?" I asked.

He shifted where he sat. "Sort of."

I felt mortified. The blush I'd been fighting seemed to explode beneath my skin, and I wanted to roll over, press my face back into my pillow. I'd been jealous, trying to get a rise out of him, and had basically just thrown his own honesty back in his face. "Sorry."

"No, it's . . ." Elliot scratched his eyebrow, pushed his glasses up his nose, rallying. "It's good you told me."

"You said you did it, too."

He cleared his throat, nodded sternly. "It's normal for guys my age."

"So it's not normal for *girls*?"

With a cough, he managed, "Of course it is. I just meant—"

"I'm joking." I closed my eyes for a breath, working to get my own craziness back under control. What was with me?

"What did you think about?" The last word of his came out sticky, caught in a slightly strangled voice.

I stared at him. "I thought, 'Holy hell, this is amazing.'"

He laughed, but it was awkward and high-pitched. "No. Before. During."

I shrugged. "Being touched by someone else like that. Do you still think about dragons?"

His eyes flickered over every part of me all at once. "No," he said, not laughing at my joke even a little. "I think about . . . wrists and ears, and skin and legs. Girl parts. Girls." His words all ran together and it took me a beat to separate them.

Girls? My blood heated with jealousy.

"Any *girls* in particular?"

He opened a book, thumbed a page. He held still like he did when he omitted information. "Sometimes."

That was the end of the conversation. He didn't ask me anything else and didn't offer more.

now

saturday, october 14

I'm conscious that Elliot and I are in a bit of a social fishbowl, with Sabrina and Nikki clearly tracking how much time we spend orbiting each other. So, despite feeling constantly aware of him, I don't really speak to Elliot much at the picnic and it makes me crazy, wondering what he's thinking about all of this. He spends most of his time talking to Danny, while Nikki, Sabrina, Dave, and I catch up. I get the distinct impression that once Sabrina and Dave get time alone in the car on the way back they're going to explode in exasperated agreement that Sean is Really The Most Boring.

Based on my own observations, though, I can't really

blame them. Sean is tuned in to Phoebe, but is otherwise fucking around on his phone, or jumping into conversations only to add his thoughts before ducking back out again. I have this weird, bubbling awareness that I've never been in this situation with him before—sitting with a group of my friends, rather than a group of art enthusiasts or benefactors dying to get Sean Chen's attention. And apparently, unless he's being courted, he retreats, socially. I have a niggling fear that he's always been this way, it's just never come up, because we've never hung out with friends.

Does Sean even *have* friends?

Around four, the clouds roll in and it looks like it might rain. Because California is turning into a dustbowl, we clean up happily, as if we are a bunch of busybody relatives getting out of the way for some newlyweds staying over.

Sean carries Phoebe on his shoulders toward the parking lot, and I follow just behind, with Sabrina, pushing Viv in the stroller.

"You have to admit that's pretty cute," I tell her, lifting my chin to the duo in front of us. The stab of protectiveness I felt for him earlier has morphed into a strange sense of desperation. Sean and I are a great fit; we were before Elliot, and we are now. I'm hunting for evidence. My fondness for the sight of him and Phoebe is proof.

My appreciation of his ass in those jeans is proof.

She laughs. "He seems like a really great *dad*."

Sigh. "Message received."

Keeping her voice down so others can't hear us, Sabrina says, "We need to have a serious conversation about this. An intervention."

"Don't start."

"When have I ever talked you *out* of a relationship?" she say, eyes wide. "Doesn't that carry some weight?"

I open my mouth to answer when out of the corner of my eye I realize that Elliot is only a few paces behind us, and has probably heard every word.

I give him a knowing look. "Hey."

He's been studying something on his phone, but it's all a ruse. Elliot is about as interested in dicking around on an iPhone as he is in sticking a spoon in his ear. He catches up with two long steps and comes between us, putting an arm around our shoulders. "Ladies."

"You heard every word of that, didn't you?" I ask.

He slants his eyes to me, shrugging. "Yes."

"Snooper."

This makes him laugh. "I was coming up to thank you for inviting me. It wasn't like I was hoping to catch you discussing Sean." In a quieter voice, laden with meaning, he mumbles, "Trust me."

"The honesty here is a little disarming," Sabrina interjects. "I'm not sure if I should make an awkward getaway or stay and hear more." She pauses. "I really want to hear more."

"It's always been that way with us," I tell her.

"It's true," Elliot says. "We've never been very good at

lying to each other. When I was fifteen, Macy told me to change my deodorant. She hinted that the old one might not be working anymore."

"Elliot pointed out the specific day he noticed I was getting boobs."

Sabrina stares at us.

"I made Elliot bring Imodium with us when we went to see the Backstreet Boys, because I was having tummy troubles."

"The embarrassing part of that," he says, "is that I went to see Backstreet Boys."

"No," I correct him, "the embarrassing part was that I caught you dancing."

He acknowledges this with a little flicker of his eyebrows. "I had moves."

I laugh. "Yes. *Movement* is the only way to describe what you were doing."

Sabrina snorts at us and, when Dave calls to her, jogs ahead, but Elliot stops me with a hand on my arm, and we get a few curious glances as the rest of the group passes us on their way to the parking lot. Luckily, Sean and Phoebe are still ahead of us.

"Hey. So." Elliot tucks his hands into his pockets. His shoulders rise, pressing into his neck. He is still so angular, so long.

"Hey. So," I repeat.

"Thanks for inviting me today." He gives me this smile

that I don't know I can describe. It's the smile that says, *I know we've known each other forever, but it still means the world to me that you included me here*. How he does that with a simple curve of his lips and some eye contact, I'll never know.

"Well," I tell him, "you should probably know that I hosted this entire thing so that I could invite you to meet my friends." Only when I say it out loud do I realize it's true. This is what Elliot does to me: he pulls honesty from those scrambled parts of my brain.

His eyes narrow, irises blooming as his pupils become pinpoints in the dim light beneath the clouds. "Is that true?"

"Why did you pull me back?" I ask him instead. I don't even know what I want him to say here. How will I feel if he says that he's come to his senses and realizes that I'm right, that we can only be friends? A treasonous part of me hopes I don't find out.

"I wanted to ask you something."

My chest is a jungle; my heart is the drum. Am I thrilled or terrified?

"Just wondering when we could get together next," he says.

"Oh." I blink over his shoulder to the towering eucalyptus trees swaying in the darkening sky. "I think I have some time off around Thanksgiving."

He nods, and my heart droops a little. Why did I say that? Thanksgiving feels really far away.

Clearing his throat, he says, "Andreas is getting married in December—"

"December?" It seems an odd month for a wedding. Also, much farther away than Thanksgiving, if that's when he's thinking we'll hang out next.

"New Year's Eve, actually," he clarifies, "and I was wondering if you wanted to come with me."

New Year's.

New Year's.

He's really asking me that.

And from the look in his eyes, I know that he's aware of the weight of that date.

But instead of addressing that beast, I ask, "You don't want to hang out until *December*?"

I watch the thrill of this pass through his hazel eyes. "Of course I do." He laughs. "I'm free pretty much anytime you want to hang out. But since it's a holiday I wanted to ask ahead of time if you'd come."

"I can't come as your date."

Elliot shakes his head. "I'm not asking you on a *date*, Macy, while your fiancé and future stepdaughter are climbing into the car right there."

"So, just . . ." I flail, searching for words, "to come with you?"

"Yeah," he says, "to come with me. To Healdsburg." Then he adds, "For the weekend."

His shoulders drop back down as if it's so simple.

Come along.

We'll carpool.

It'll be fun.

But the words settle between us, and I hear them in a different tone the longer I fail to reply.

Come away with me for the weekend.

Forty-eight hours with Elliot.

What will things be like between us in two and a half months, when they're already so muddled *now*?

I blink over his shoulder to where Sean is buckling Phoebe into the Prius.

"Everyone would love to see you, and I'm the best man so it'd be nice to have a friend there with me," he says, struggling to pull the conversation back from the brink of death. "Mom and Dad asked about you . . . they're going insane knowing we're back in touch."

"I need to ask Sean what the plans are," I say lamely. "He might have some art showing or event already in the books."

Elliot nods. "Of course."

"Can I let you know?"

"Of course," he says with a small smile, a rumble of thunder bringing his attention to the sky. When he looks back down at me, I feel about as stable as the billowing rain clouds overhead. For a brief moment I imagine hugging him. I would wrap my arms around his neck and press my face there, breathing him in. He would bend closer, letting out that tiny little grunt of relief he always made. I want it so intensely it makes my mouth water, and I have to force myself to take a step back.

"I better . . ." I say, motioning over my shoulder.

"I know," he says, watching me, expression tight.

Another rip of thunder.

"Have a good night, Elliot."

And I finally turn to go.

then

saturday, july 9

twelve years ago

We were lying on the flat roof over his garage, basking in the sun. It was a summer break routine we'd had for nearly two weeks now: meet on the roof at ten, lunch around noon, swimming in the river, home to our families for the rest of the evening.

For as much as he enjoyed my company, Dad liked the quiet of solitude. Or maybe a teenage daughter was exhaustingly alien to him. Either way, he seemed content to let me stay out doing whatever I wanted with the Petropoulos kids until the bugs grew louder and the sky grew dark.

Andreas was on one side of me, Elliot on the other. One

brother playing something on his PSP, the other reading Proust.

"You two cannot possibly be related," I mumbled, turning the page of my book.

"He's a loser." Andreas laughed. "No game to speak of."

"He's a meathead," Elliot said, and then grinned at me. "Ruled by his—"

A horn honked below in the driveway and we all sat up to see a rusty Pontiac come to a crunching stop on the gravel.

"Oh," Elliot said, glancing at me and then jumping up. "Shit. Shit." He spun in a half circle, fisting the front of his hair and looking like he was panicking, then climbed into the window to the family room. A minute later he appeared in the front yard. A girl climbed out of the car and handed Elliot a stack of papers.

She was medium height, with thick dark hair in a cute bob and an average, pretty face. Vaguely familiar. Sporty but not thick. With boobs.

I growled internally.

She said something to Elliot and he nodded and then looked up at where Andreas and I sat watching them.

"Who is that?" I asked Andreas.

"Some chick named Emma from his school."

"Emma? *Prom* Emma?" My insides froze. "Does he like her?"

Andreas looked at my face and laughed. "Oh, this is so good."

"No, Andreas, don't—" I hissed, frantic.

"Elliot," he called out, ignoring me. "Bring your girlfriend up here to meet your other girlfriend!"

I closed my eyes and groaned.

When I looked back down at the ground, Emma was looking up at me, inspecting, eyes narrowed. Elliot was watching me, too, with a wide, terrified expression, and then looked at her.

I waved. I wasn't going to play the petty game.

She waved back, calling out, "I'm Emma."

"Hi, I'm Macy."

"Did you just move here?"

"No," I called down, "we live next door on the weekends and some vacations."

"Elliot's never mentioned you."

Elliot looked at her in shock, and from the expression on his face I would have guessed he mentioned me plenty. Well. Apparently Emma *was* going to play the petty game.

"She's my best friend, remember?" I heard Elliot say stiffly. "She goes to Berkeley High."

Emma nodded and then looked back at him, putting her hand on his arm and laughing at something she whispered to him. He smiled, but it was his tight courteous expression.

I lay back down on my blanket, ignoring the nausea rising

in my stomach. His words from only a week before—when he'd been on the brink of sleep on the roof and admitted quietly that he was more himself with me than anyone else—cycled through my mind.

I'd told him I felt that way, too. During the school year, my weekdays were a blur, hours smoothed together in a mess of homework and swim and crawling into bed hoping whatever I'd packed into my brain that day didn't seep out onto my pillow at night. In a sense, my time away from him felt like going to work, and the weekends and summer were coming home—unwinding, being with Elliot and Dad, being *myself*. But then things like this happened—and I was reminded that most of Elliot's world existed without me.

Several minutes passed before I heard the car start and drive away. Moments later, Elliot was climbing through the window back onto the roof. I quickly pushed my nose into my book.

"Smooth, Ell," Andreas said.

"Shut up."

His feet came into view in front of my book and I pretended to be so engrossed that I didn't even notice.

"Hey," he said quietly. "Want to grab a snack?"

I continued pseudo-reading. "I'm good."

He kneeled down close to me, ducked lower to catch my eye. I could see his apology written all over his face. "Come inside, it's sweltering."

In the kitchen, he pulled out a pitcher of lemonade and

two glasses, and started making us sandwiches. Andreas hadn't followed us inside and the house was cool, dark, and quiet.

"Emma seems lovely," I said dryly, rolling a lemon across the countertop.

He shrugged.

"She's the one you kissed at prom, right?"

He looked up at me and scrunched his glasses up his nose. "Yeah."

"Do you still kiss her?"

Turning his attention back down to the sandwiches, he spread the peanut butter on the bread and added jelly before answering. "No."

"Is that a lie by omission?"

When he met my gaze again, his eyes were tight. "I have kissed her on a few occasions, yes. I don't *still* kiss her."

His words hit my ears like bricks dropped from an airplane. "You kissed her other times besides prom last spring?"

He cleared his throat, turning a brilliant scarlet.

Jerk.

"Yeah." He shifted his glasses up higher again. "Two other times."

I felt like I'd swallowed a jagged ice cube; something cold and hard lodged in my chest. "But she's not your girlfriend?"

He shook his head calmly. "No."

"Do you *have* a girlfriend?" I wondered why I even had to ask this. Wouldn't he tell me? Or spend time with her during the summer instead of me? He was always honest, but was he forthcoming?

He put down the knife and assembled the sandwiches before looking at me with a smirk. "No, Macy. I've been with you every day this summer. I wouldn't do that if I had a girl-friend."

I wanted to throw the lemon at his head. "Would you *tell* me if you had a girlfriend?"

Elliot gave this full consideration before answering, his eyes locked on mine. "I think so. But, I mean, to be honest, this is the one topic where I'm never sure how much to share with you."

Even though a significant part of me knew what he meant, I still hated this answer. "Have you *ever* had a girlfriend?"

Blinking away, he returned his attention to the sand-wiches. "No. Not technically."

I rolled the lemon again and it fell onto the floor. He bent to pick it up and handed it back to me.

"Look, Macy. I guess what I'm trying to say is that I wouldn't want to hear if you kissed someone if it didn't mean anything, and kissing Emma didn't mean anything to me. That's why I never told you."

"Did it mean anything to her?"

His shrug said everything his silence omitted.

"Maybe it isn't my business," I said, "but I *do* want to know those things. I feel weird that I didn't know you have a thing with her."

"We don't have a *thing*."

"You kissed her on three separate occasions!"

He accepted this with a nod. "Have *you* kissed anyone?"

"No."

He froze with his sandwich midway to his lips. "No one?"

I shook my head, taking a bite and breaking eye contact. "I would have *told* you."

"Really?" he said.

I nodded, face burning. I was sixteen and hadn't been kissed. His *No one?* echoed inside my head, and I felt completely pathetic.

"What about Donny? Or . . . what's his name?"

I looked up at him and stared meaningfully. He *knew* Danny's name.

"Danny?"

He smiled, busted. "Yeah, Danny."

"Nope. Not even Danny. Like I said, I would have told you. Because you're my *best friend*—jerk."

"Wow."

He took a ginormous bite of sandwich and stared at me as he chewed.

I thought back to all the weekends we'd spent together, all the stories he'd told me about Christian being a maniac or Brandon having zero game with girls at school. I thought about his updates about his brothers and their girlfriends, and wondered why Elliot was always so tight-lipped about his own escapades. It threw me. It made me feel like maybe we weren't as close as I thought we were.

"Have you kissed a lot of girls?"

He mumbled, "A couple."

Something inside me was rioting. "Have you done more than kiss?"

He turned a new shade of red and finally nodded, taking another big bite so he wouldn't have to elaborate.

My jaw slowly lowered to the floor. I waited until he was done chewing and had taken a sip of lemonade to ask, "How far?"

Countries were established, went to war, and split into smaller countries in the time it took for Elliot to answer.

"Elliot."

"Shirts off." He scratched his eyebrow and nudged his glasses up his nose again with the tip of his finger. Stalling. Avoiding eye contact. "Um . . . and with one girl—not Emma—hands in pants."

"You *have*?" I felt my eyes bug out. "Who?"

"Emma was just shirts off. The rest was this other girl, Jill."

I put my sandwich down, my appetite completely gone. The kitchen was on the darkest side of the house this time of day, and it suddenly felt too cold. I lifted my hands, rubbing my bare arms.

"Macy, don't be mad."

"I'm not mad! Why would I be mad?" I took a shaky sip

of lemonade, trying to calm down. "I'm not your girlfriend. I'm just your best friend who apparently knows *nothing* about you."

He took a step around the kitchen island, and stopped. "Macy."

"Am I overreacting?"

"No . . ." he said, and took another step closer. "I would definitely take issue if I knew some guy had his hand down *your* pants."

"I think you'd also take issue if it happened and *I never told you.*"

He seemed to give this fair consideration. "Like I said, it depends. It would bug me, yeah, so I wouldn't want to know about it unless you felt something more than . . . momentary attraction."

"Is that what it was for you with Emma?" I asked. "'Momentary attraction'?"

He nodded. "Absolutely."

"When was the last time you fooled around with someone?"

He sighed and leaned a hip against the counter where he stood.

"If the situation was reversed, you would be giving me the Spanish Inquisition," I pointed out. "Don't *sigh* at me."

"Emma and I fooled around in March, then went to prom in May, and kissed again the weekend after, but it was nothing. It was sort of . . ." He floundered a little, staring up at the ceiling. "If you haven't kissed anyone, then it's hard to say what I mean, but we were all at a park, and she came up to me, and it just sort of happened."

I pulled a face at this and he laughed uncomfortably, shrugging. "Jill is Christian's cousin. She was visiting last December and we made out once. I haven't talked to her since."

I dismissed Jill with a wave of my hand. "So you don't like Emma, then?"

"Not the way you mean."

I looked away, taking a minute to calm down. I realized it would have been dramatic, but I wanted to storm out and make him follow me and grovel for, like, an entire day.

"I fooled around with Emma because she's here," he said quietly. "You're in Berkeley and we're *not together* and I'm in this tiny Podunk town. Who else am I supposed to kiss?"

Something shifted in that exact moment, something that would never shift back.

Who else am I supposed to kiss?

I looked at his big hands and his Adam's apple. I let my eyes linger on the muscular arms that used to be so thin and stringy, on legs that stretched, defined, beneath his torn jeans. I looked at the button-fly on the front of said jeans. I blinked away, up at the cabinets. Look anywhere but at those buttons. I wanted to touch those buttons, press my hand to them, and for the first time I realized I didn't want anyone else touching them.

"I don't know," I mumbled.

"Then come over here," he said in that same quiet voice. "*You* kiss me."

My eyes flew to his. "What?"

"Kiss me."

I thought he was calling my bluff, but I was worked up from the Emma situation and the way he looked, leaning against the counter, watching me. I was warm from the way his hands seemed so big now, and his jaw so angular . . . and the buttons on his jeans.

I walked around the center island and stood right in front of him. "Okay."

He stared down at me, a smile playing on his lips, but it straightened when he realized I was serious.

I pressed my hands to his chest and moved closer. I was so close that I could hear every quickly accelerating inhale and exhale, could see his jaw twitch.

Fascinated, he moved a hand to my lips, pressing two fingers there and staring. Without thinking, I opened my mouth and let his index finger slip inside and against my teeth. When he grunted quietly, I ran my tongue over his fingertip. He tasted like jelly.

Elliot pulled it back sharply. He looked like he was going to devour me: eyes wild and searching, lips parted, pulse a hammering presence in his neck. And because I wanted to kiss him, I did. I stood on my toes, slid my hands into his hair, and pressed my mouth to his.

It was different than I would have guessed. Different

than—I could admit to myself—I had imagined it would be. It was both softer and firmer, and definitely bolder. A short kiss, another, and then he tilted his head, covering my mouth with his. His tongue traced my bottom lip and it felt like instinct to let him in, to taste me.

I think that was probably his undoing. It was certainly mine. After that the moment dissolved for me into only sensation; everything else fell away. All the forbidden images of him, flesh and fantasy, secrets I kept even from myself, tore through my mind and I knew, somehow, that he was thinking the same thing: how good it felt to be this close . . . and everything else that touching like this could lead to.

One of his hands moved up my back and into my hair, and it was the weight of that touch, I think, that kept me from floating off the floor. But when his other hand slid up my side to my ribs and higher, I stepped back.

"Sorry," he said immediately, instinctively. "Shit, Mace. That was too fast, I'm sorry."

"No, it's just . . ." I hesitated, my mouth suddenly crammed with words that I didn't want to be thinking, let alone say out loud. "Doing that might not mean anything to Emma," I said, touching my lips where they tingled. "But it means everything to me."

now

saturday, october 14

S ean drops his keys in the bowl near the door and kicks off his shoes, groaning happily.

"Hungry, Applejack?" he asks Phoebe, and the two of them disappear into the kitchen.

I put their shoes side by side on the little shelf near the door and hang our jackets up on the hooks. Their voices echo back to the hallway; Phoebe is doggedly working on her dad to get her a pet, any pet—frog, hamster, bird, fish.

I am honestly so unsure what to feel. Sean and I had such a whirlwind start, and we tumbled easily into a domestic routine, but that routine really only involves me sharing his bed and our schedules rotating around each other like well-oiled gears.

I moved whatever I needed over from the Berkeley house, but it's still mostly full, and entirely uninhabited, while I'm shacked up here. Sean tells me he loves having me in his bed. Phoebe always seems happy to see me. But I realize, watching him today, that I don't actually know him that well. He and Phoebe have their own thing going. But if I want to be a part of it, I need to *make* myself part of it.

"Want me to cook dinner?" I ask, coming in after them, and they both look up from where they're digging into the fridge, staring at me blankly. "*Pasta*," I say, feigning insult. "I think I can handle pasta."

"Are you sure?" Phoebe remains unconvinced.

"I'm sure, you knucklehead," I say, smooching her cheek.

She squeals, running from the room, and Sean moves to the pantry, grabbing a box of pasta and some jarred sauce for me. "Need help?"

"You can keep me company." I nod to the breakfast bar, silently urging him to take a chair and talk to me. To help me assuage this feeling gnawing at my chest that he and I are never going to make it. We've never really had downtime together on weekends, and I have a clawing suspicion that this is why we're essentially strangers outside of bed.

He sits, reading through emails on his phone while I get water boiling.

I want to marry this man; I want him to want to marry me.

I like being around him.

I like his ass in those jeans.

"Did you have fun today?" I ask, keeping my voice light.

"Sure."

Scroll, scroll.

The jar of sauce opens with a satisfying pop, and marinara slops into the saucepan I've put on the stove. Sean looks up at the sound, mildly repulsed.

"Did you like meeting everyone?" I ask. "They really liked you."

He blinks away from the stove and meets my eyes, smiling as if he knows I'm full of shit. "Sure, babe, they were great."

His tone is so offhand, so uninterested, I want to crack him in the forehead with the empty jar. I want to beg him to meet me halfway. Instead, I rinse it out briefly and drop it into the recycling bin. Irritation with him prickles at my skin like an itch. "Try not to sound so enthusiastic."

"What do you mean?" he asks, just the slightest bit sharp in defense. "It was fine, Mace, but they're your friends, not mine."

"Well, eventually they might become your friends, too," I tell him. "Isn't that what couples do? Share things? Blend their lives?"

I realize, in this moment, that we've never argued. I don't even know how it looks to disagree. We overlap for a total of maybe one waking hour a day. How disastrous would it be to calculate the total number of hours we've spent together? Do we even care enough to argue?

My phone buzzes on the counter, and I pick it up, reading the text there from Sabrina.

> Hey cutie, I'm sorry if I came off too harsh about you know what.

I realize I shouldn't be answering right now, but if I don't take this tiny breather, I'm liable to say something to Sean I might regret. I inhale deeply and type out a reply.

> It's okay.

> Maybe we can have lunch next week? I can bring Viv to the city?

> So you can stage the intervention?

She answers with a string of heart-eyed emojis and I realize her apology opener was really just a ruse to soften me up to more of the same conversation. Her timing is, as ever, impeccable. Putting my phone facedown on the counter, I look back at Sean, determined to salvage this, make plans, do *something*.

"How does your week look?" I ask.

"Pretty light. Might take Phoebs to the Exploratorium. Was thinking about camping a couple nights, maybe." He shrugs, lifting his chin to the stove. "Water's boiling."

"Don't backseat-drive here, sir," I say, trying to joke. "I got this."

"Do you want me to make a salad or something?" He turns his attention to the fridge, indicating there's stuff to be found there.

"Would it ease your mind to make it?"

"Either way," he says, looking down to his phone. "I don't just want noodles and plain sauce for dinner, that's all."

I stare at him for a few silent beats. I mean, a *thank you* would do wonders right now. "Of course not."

With that, I turn to get the lettuce and veggies out of the fridge.

In bed later, Sean snuggles closer, humming into my neck. "Mmm, babe, you smell good."

I stare at the ceiling, trying to figure out what I want to say. I organized a picnic on my day off, giving him a chance to get to know my friends, and he barely talked to any of them about their lives, their jobs, their interests. We came home, and I offered to cook—he ate it wordlessly, huddled at the other end of the table with Phoebe, helping her draw a unicorn.

Phoebe showed it to me, proudly, after dinner, but other than that, it was as if I wasn't even there.

Has it always been this way, and I didn't notice because I

was so happy to be included in their twosome, and I was so busy there was nothing else pressing on my mind? Was it such a relief to have something sorted, to not feel *anything*—not guilt or love or fear or uncertainty—that I just let this routine become my future?

Or has something changed since Elliot came back into the picture, and no matter how much Sean denies it, it's created a wrinkle in our easy, bland little life?

Sean kisses his way across my collarbone and then up my neck. He's hard, pushing off his boxers, ready to go, and we've said maybe three words to each other in the last two hours.

"Can I ask you something?" I say.

He nods but doesn't stop his progression up my chin, to my mouth. "Anything," he says, speaking into a kiss.

"Are you excited to get married again?"

He reaches between us, coaxing my legs apart as if he's planning to answer this question after he starts having sex with me. But I shift away and he sighs, leaning into my neck. "Sure, babe."

I balk a little at this. "'Sure, babe'?"

With a groan, Sean rolls to my side. "Isn't it what you want? I mean," he says, "I've been married. I know what's great about it, and what's not so great about it. But if you want it—"

I stop him, holding up a hand. "Do you remember how it happened?"

He thinks for a beat. "You mean, the night we talked about it?"

I nod, although "the night we talked about it" isn't the most apt description. After a fun night out at the movies with Phoebe, we'd tucked her in bed, then Sean took me to his room, made a satisfied woman out of me, and then mumbled, "Phoebe thinks we should get married," before he fell asleep between my boobs.

He remembered the next morning, and asked if I'd heard him.

Confused at first, I'd finally said, "I heard you."

"For Phoebe," he'd said. "If we're doing this, I want to do it full-on."

We didn't have time to talk about it then, because I had to leave for the hospital, but the words seemed to loop in my head like a song all day. *If we're doing this, I want to do it full-on.*

Looking back, all I can really remember is the overwhelming relief I felt at the prospect of having that bit of my life sorted with such *convenience*. There was nothing messy or turbulent about it. There were no manic highs with Sean, but there were no angst-ridden lows, either. Sean was easy, and he and Phoebe were a family I could just . . . join. But in hindsight and in the stark contrast to the intensity of emotions I feel around Elliot, it almost seems insane that I came home later that day and gave Sean an enthusiastic yes.

We certainly haven't done a lot more planning since then.

We still haven't picked out a ring, probably because we both realized that Phoebe doesn't seem to be that concerned after all about the woman in her house, and whether that woman is going to be her new mommy.

The only person who consistently asks where we are with the plan is Sabrina, and she is the one person who has said outright that she thinks this whole thing is a farce.

Sean runs a hand over my hip. "Babe, I think you need to figure out what you want."

I meet his eyes. "What *I* want?"

"Yeah," he says, nodding. "Me, Elliot, neither of us."

And who *does* this? Who is so unaffected by the potential loss of his fiancée that he can suggest I give this some good thought while casually stroking my hip, suggesting the relationship may end but the sex can still happen?

"Does it matter to you that things are obviously so weird between us?"

Sean moves his hand away, closing his eyes with another long sigh. "Of course it matters to me. But I've been through these ups and downs, and I just can't let them rule me. I can't control what you're feeling."

And I get that what he's saying is the ideal reaction to the situation we're in—it's the well-adjusted, textbook version of this difficult conversation—but is that really how the human heart *works*? You tell it to chill, and it chills?

I stare at him now, with his arm across his eyes, and I'm trying to find that flicker of something bigger, of an emotion

that consumes me. I do what I used to do with Elliot sometimes: I imagine Sean standing up, walking out the door, and
never coming back. With Elliot, my stomach would react as if
I'd been punched.

With Sean, I feel vague relief.

I think back to Elliot's face when I told him I was engaged. I think about his face now: the longing there, the tiny
sting of pain I see in his eyes when we turn to head our separate directions. Eleven years later, and he still aches for what
we had.

I'm terrified of what I'm feeling; I feel like I've just woken
up. I thought I didn't want intensity, but in fact, I'm desperate for it.

I look over at Sean and it feels like I'm in bed with a one-
night stand.

Pushing up, I climb out.

"Where are you going?" he asks.

"Couch."

He follows me out. "Are you mad?"

God, this is the weirdest situation in the history of weird
situations, and Sean is so . . . calm. How did I end up here?

"I just think you're right," I say. "Maybe I need to figure
out what I want."

then

saturday, september 10

twelve years ago

Elliot was stretched out on the floor, staring up at the ceiling. He'd been that way for a while now, his worn copy of *Gulliver's Travels* abandoned on the pillow next to him. He seemed so intent on what he was thinking he didn't even notice the way my eyes moved over his body whenever I turned a page.

I was beginning to wonder if he would ever stop growing. Almost seventeen, he had shorts on today and his long legs seemed to go on forever. They were hairier than I remembered. Not too hairy, just a light dusting of brown over his tanned skin. It was masculine, I decided. I liked it.

One of the strangest things about going stretches of time between seeing someone is all the changes you'd miss if you saw them every day. Like leg hair. Or biceps. Or big hands.

In his update he'd said his mom asked him about having laser surgery so he wouldn't have to wear glasses anymore. I tried to imagine him without his glasses, being able to look into his greenish-gold eyes without the benefit of black frames between us. I loved Elliot's glasses, but the thought of being so close to him without them did warm, weird things to my stomach. It made him feel somehow undressed in my head.

"What do you want for Christmas?" he asked.

I jumped slightly, startled. I was pretty sure I looked exactly like someone looks when they're caught staring at their best friend with less than innocent thoughts. We hadn't kissed again.

But I really wanted to.

His question echoed in my head. "*Christmas?*"

Dark eyebrows pulled together, serious. "Yeah. Christmas."

I tried to cover. "Is that what you've been thinking about all this time?"

"No."

I waited for him to elaborate, but he didn't.

"I don't really know," I told him. "Any particular reason you're asking me this in September?"

Elliot rolled to his side to face me, his head propped in

his hand. "I'd just like to get you something nice. Something you want."

I put my book down and rolled to face him, too. "You don't have to get me anything, Ell."

He made a frustrated sound and sat up. Pushing up off the carpet, he moved to stand. I reached out, wrapping my hand around his wrist. The light, lusty mood between us had been only on my end, apparently.

"Are you mad about something?"

Elliot and I didn't fight, really, and the idea that something between us was off tilted my internal balance, making me feel immediately anxious. I could feel his pulse like a steady drum beneath his skin.

"Do you think about me when you're back there?" His words came out sharp, exhaled roughly.

It took me a second to process what he meant. When I was back home. Away from him. "Of course I do."

"When?"

"All the time. You're my best friend."

"Your best *friend*," he repeated.

My heart dipped low in my chest, almost painfully. "Well, you're more, too. You're my best *everything*."

"You kissed me this summer and then acted like nothing happened."

This came at me like a blade to my lungs. I closed my eyes and covered my face with my hands. It *had* happened like that. After I kissed him in his kitchen, I'd made everything go back to how it was: reading on the roof in the morning, lunch in the shade, swimming in the river. I'd felt his eyes on me, the shaking restraint of his hands. I remembered how warm his lips had been, and the way I felt like a lit fuse when he growled into my mouth.

"I'm sorry," I said.

"Why are you *sorry*?" he asked carefully, crouching down beside me. "Are you sorry because you didn't like kissing me?"

I felt my hands flush cold, looking at him in shock. "Did it *feel* like I didn't like it?"

"I don't know," he said, shrugging helplessly. "It felt like you liked it. A *lot*. And I did, too. I can't stop thinking about it."

"Really?"

"*Yeah*, Mace, and then you just . . ." He scowled at me, face tight. "You got weird."

My thoughts got all tangled—the memory of Emma beside him in the driveway and the panic I always felt when I imagined him leaving my life for good. "I mean, there's Emma—"

"*Fuck* Emma," he said, voice rough, and it surprised me so much that I leaned back on my hands, tilting away from him.

Elliot looked immediately remorseful and reached to move a strand of hair out of my face. "Seriously, Mace. There's nothing going on with me and Emma. Is that really why you don't want to talk about what happened with us in the kitchen?"

"I think it's also that it scares me to think of messing this up." Looking down, I added, "I've never had a boyfriend—or anything. You're, like, the only person other than Dad who really matters to me, and I'm honestly not sure I could handle it if I didn't have you in my life."

When I closed my eyes at night, the only thing I could see was Elliot. Most nights I was desperate to call him just before I fell asleep, so I could hear his voice. I hated to think beyond the next weekend, because I wasn't sure how our futures were going to align. I imagined Elliot going away to Harvard, and me going somewhere in California, and we'd slowly turn into vague acquaintances. The idea was repellent.

When I met his eyes again, I noticed the hard line of his mouth had softened. He sat down in front of me, his knees touching mine.

"I'm not going anywhere, Mace." He picked up my hand. "I need you the same way you need me, okay?"

"Okay."

Elliot looked at my hand in his and moved our palms so they were pressed together, lacing our fingers.

"Do you think about *me*?" I asked. Now that he'd raised it, the question gnawed at me.

"Sometimes it feels like I think about you every minute," he whispered.

A bubble of emotion wedged tightly beneath my ribs, hitting a tender spot. I watched our clasped hands for a long time before he spoke again.

I struggled to keep my eyes from his body.

"Favorite word?" he whispered.

"*Zipper*," I answered without thinking, feeling rather than seeing his smile in response. "You?"

"*Crackle*."

"Do you have a girlfriend?" I asked, and the words sounded like an explosion of wind into the room, an awkward window opened.

He looked up from our hands, scowling. "Is that a serious question?"

"Just checking."

He let go of my hand and returned to his book. He wasn't reading it; he looked like he wanted to throw it at me.

I scooted a little closer to him. "You can't be surprised I asked."

He gaped at me, setting the book down. "Macy. I just asked you if you think about me. I asked why you got weird after we kissed. Do you really think I would push this subject if I had a girlfriend?"

I chewed my lip, feeling embarrassed. "No."

"Do you have a boyfriend?"

I gave him a grin. "A few here and there."

He let out a wry laugh, shaking his head as he picked his book back up.

Obviously, whenever I imagined kissing anyone, it was always Elliot. And we'd already covered that: perfect fantasy, sublime reality, potentially treacherous aftermath. Even the idea of kissing him led to thoughts of a nasty awkward breakup and that would cause my stomach to spasm painfully.

Still . . . I could never stop *looking* at him. When did he lose all his awkwardness and get so completely perfect? What would I do with him if I ever had the chance? Nearly-seventeen-year-old Elliot was a work of long lines and definition. I would have no idea how to touch his body. Knowing him, he would just tell me. Probably give me a guidebook to the male anatomy and draw me a few diagrams. While staring at my boobs.

I snorted. He looked up.

"Why are you staring at me?" he asked.

"I was . . . not."

He let out a short, dry sound of disbelief. "Okay." Stretching his neck, he looked back down. "You're still staring."

"I'm just wondering how it works," I asked.

"How *what* works?"

"When you . . ." I made a telling gesture with my hand. "With guys and the . . . you know."

He raised his eyebrows, waiting. I could see the moment he knew what I was talking about. His pupils dilated so fast his eyes looked black.

"You're asking me how *dicks* work?"

"Ell! I don't have sisters—I need someone to tell me these things."

"You can't even handle talking about kissing me, and you want me to tell you what it's like when I get myself off?"

213

I swallowed down the thrilled swell in my throat. "Okay, never mind."

"Macy," he said, more gently now, "why don't you ever go out with anyone back home?"

Gaping at him, I told him what I thought was obvious. "I'm not interested in other guys."

"*Other* guys?"

"I mean," I said, catching my slip, "anyone."

"'Other' implies there is one guy"—he held out the palm of one hand and then lifted the other—"and then, other guys. But in this case, you said you aren't interested in any others. So, there is just one guy you're interested in?"

"Stop debate-teaming me."

He grinned crookedly. "Who is the *one*?"

I watched him for a long beat. Inhaling deeply, I decided this didn't have to be so bad. "You know I compare every boy to you. We aren't in revelation territory."

The grin widened. "You do?"

"Of course I do. How could I not? Remember? You're my best everything."

"Your best everything you ask about wanking."

"Exactly."

"Your best everything who no other guy compares to and whose tongue you let touch your tongue."

"Right." I didn't like where this was heading. This was heading to admissions, and admissions changed things. Admissions make feelings intensify simply because they are given space to breathe. Admissions lead to love, and admitting love is like tying yourself to a train track.

"So maybe your best everything should be your boyfriend."

I stared at him and he stared at me.

I spoke without thinking. "Maybe."

"Maybe," he agreed in a whisper.

now

True to her promise, Sabrina brings Viv to the city to meet me for lunch. The first time that works for both of us is nearly two weeks after the picnic. During that time, I've essentially buried myself in work. It's strange to say it, but I've seen Sean awake only three times.

That might be because I'm sleeping on the couch.

I don't know why I can't take that last step and pack up my suitcases and move back to Berkeley. It might be the drag of the commute, or the ghosts of my past that I know still live there—Mom and Dad are in every single particle of air in that house.

I've only been back for a total of seven days since I left for college. It would be like stepping into a time capsule.

Sabrina's face when I walk into the Wooly Pig tells me all I need to know about how successful I was at covering the dark circles under my eyes this morning.

"Jesus Christ," she mumbles as I sit down across from her. "You look like you've been raised from the pet cemetery."

I laugh, grabbing the water in front of me. "Thanks."

"If I'd known to expect this I would have had an espresso waiting for you."

"No coffee," I say, holding up my hand. "It's been the sole source of my calories this week and I need something . . . juicy. A smoothie or something."

I feel her inspection as I look down at the menu.

"Okay, tell me what's up," she says, leaning closer. "I saw you two weeks ago, but today you're like a different person."

"I've been working a ton. It's a busy time—flu season is starting." Without thinking, I glance at Viv, asleep in her stroller beside the table. "And things with Sean aren't great."

"Oh yeah?" Sabrina asks, and I don't look at her face after she says it because I'm not sure how I'll feel if her expression matches the giddy edge to her words. "What's going on?"

I meet her eyes, giving her the *spare me* face. "Sabrina."

"What?"

"Do we have to do this?" I feel like I'm going to break down in tears. "You *know* what's going on." Holding up a hand, I begin to count off the events on my fingers: "I barely know Sean. We get engaged after two months. I run into Elliot at Saul's and seeing him is like . . . I don't know, a kick to the soul. And then, what do you know? Elliot is back in my life and, surprise! I think things with Sean maybe aren't so great."

Sabrina nods but doesn't say anything.

"You're quiet *now*? I thought you'd be happy to hear this."

"The point is that I want *you* to be happy. I want to see that spark I saw the other day. I want to see you blush when someone just *looks* at you."

"Sabrina, I *have* been happy with Sean. Just because I feel *more* overall when Elliot is around doesn't mean that those feelings are more valid, or happier."

"Really? Do you even know what happy looks like? I was wondering this the other day, actually. Had I ever seen you happy before the picnic?"

This feels like a violent shove from someone who has known me for ten years. "You're joking."

She shakes her head. "When Elliot walked up to us . . . I swear that was the first time I'd seen you smile like that—with your entire body—and it made me question everything about your personality before then."

"Wow," I say slowly. That feels . . . enormous.

"You think you're happy, but you're barely living."

"Sabrina, that's residency and working eighty-plus hours a week."

"No," she says with a firm shake of her head. She leans

back in her chair, taking her mug of coffee with her. "Do you remember freshman year?"

I feel the cold shadow of that time creeping over me. "Barely."

"Ever since I met you, Elliot has been the third person with us, every second. I sometimes felt like the things you told me, you only told me because he wasn't there." She holds up a hand when I start to respond to this. "That's not a complaint, by the way. I had Dave, and I had you. You had me . . . but you also had *him*—in your thoughts, in every single thing you did. When you went out with guys, it was like . . . you were slinking out and sneaking back in at night, as if there was someone who might be mad that you'd been on a date."

Letting out a long breath, I study her, hating her for doing this, for putting these truths, which so far lived only in the dusty shadows of my memory, out into the public space.

"The first time you slept with Julian? You remember that?"

I let out a laugh-groan. I do remember. It was halfway through freshman year. Guitar-playing, long-haired Julian was a demigod on campus, and a junior. Beautiful, mildly vain, not as deep as he thought he was—or maybe that's just my take in hindsight. For whatever reason, he started pursuing me in October, much to the heated jealousy of his band's groupies. I finally agreed to go out with him; at the time I thought maybe diving into something with someone else would make everything back in California disappear.

We had sex at his place after our first date. I don't really remember much about it other than thinking, while it was happening, that there were at least fifteen other women who would want to be in this bed right now, and that he was probably doing a fairly capable job at the whole thing. But all I wanted was for him to be done so I could go home and curl into a ball.

I got back to the dorm room I shared with Sabrina, and before I could say a single word, I threw up on her favorite pair of purple Docs before breaking down into a hysterical puddle and telling her everything about Elliot.

"Poor Julian," I say.

"He was cute," she says. "And it worked for a while because you weren't invested. You're *never* invested, Macy. You only have a handful of people you'd actually call friends, and keep everyone else on the surface."

I move to object and she lifts a sassy hand to stop me.

"Let me get this out, I've been working on this speech since the picnic."

I smile in spite of my anger. "Okay."

"I'm sure Sean is a great guy, but it's another version of you and Julian; everything's on the surface. You never feel what you felt for Elliot, but it's convenient: you don't want to feel that again anyway."

I nod tightly. Sabrina can't really be blamed for saying aloud the things I've started to wonder, too.

"But, shit, Mace," she says gently, "doesn't it seem sort of selfish? You give only as much as you're willing. Luckily this time, Sean is happy with the scraps."

I sit back in my chair. "My goodness," I say. "Tell me what you really think."

She chews on her lower lip, studying me. "Are you saying I'm wrong?"

I scrub my hands over my face, feeling more tired than I've been all week. "It's not that simple, and you know it."

Sabrina closes her eyes, breathing slowly in and then out. Looking at me again, she says gently, "I know, honey. The thing is . . . you're pretending like you can just walk away from Elliot. Can you? And if not, what are you doing staying engaged to another man?"

"I know, I know," I say, feeling a simmering in my stomach.

Her expression softens. "Don't you just want to see where it could go with Elliot? The worst thing that could happen is it doesn't work and he's not in your life anymore." She leans back in, saying more quietly, "You know you can survive that. At least, minimally."

I spin my fork on the table.

"What's keeping you with Sean?"

I know she wants a serious answer, but I'm just done with the intensity of this conversation. "His place is so convenient."

She lets out a barking laugh that actually startles Viv in

her sleep. "They're fluffing your pillows in hell, Macy Lea Sorensen."

"I don't think one gets pillows in hell," I say, smiling back at her. "And I'm kidding. I'm just having a hard time trusting these new doubts, because a few weeks ago I was perfectly happy with Sean. What if this is a blip?"

She lets out a skeptical "Mm-hmm."

I blink up to her. "Come on."

"*You* come on. You know I'm right. Sean is easy, I get it. He's a cactus and Elliot is an orchid. I get that, too. Just . . ."

"Just what?"

"Just don't be a testicle about this," she says. Sabrina hates using *pussy* to mean *weak*, especially after birthing her ten-pound baby the old-fashioned way. "When you think about kissing Elliot, what does it make you feel?"

My entire body explodes in heat, and I know it shows immediately on my face. I *know* what it's like to kiss Elliot. I know how he sounds when he comes. I know how his hands become wild and roaming when he's hard. I know how he learned to touch, and kiss and give pleasure, because he learned with me.

I know how good it was, even for the short time I had it.

"I don't even need you to answer." She leans back when our waitress comes by to take our orders.

When she's left again, my phone vibrates in my bag and I pull it out, laughing. It's a message from Elliot, whom I haven't spoken to since the picnic.

> Have you talked to Sean about New Years?

> I'd love for you to come with me.

> Think of it as a chance to do research for the wedding you don't feel like planning.

I turn my phone around, showing it to Sabrina, and she laughs, shaking her head. "Intervention complete."

then

saturday, january 14

eleven years ago

Elliot sprawled on the floor, pulling a new, furry pillow off the futon and tucking it beneath his head. It was nearly two p.m., and Dad and I had barely made it up here due to some terrifying dry rattling under the hood of the Volvo. While Dad and Mr. Nick had worked on Dad's car, Elliot and I had devoured some cold leftover chicken on the front steps. Back in the warmth of the house, I was more likely to take a nap than read an entire chapter.

Elliot's voice seemed deeper than it had even the weekend before: "Favorite word?"

I closed my eyes, thinking. "*Excruciating.*"

"Wow." Elliot paused, and when I looked over at him, he was staring at me curiously. "That's a zinger. Update?"

I kicked off my shoes and one of them barely missed the side of his head. We'd spent the past hour together, but something about being back in the closet, with the blue walls, and stars, and the warm bulk of Elliot's body nearby, seemed to loosen everything inside me. Things had been hard in ninth and tenth grade, but eleventh? Definitely the worst.

"Girls suck. Girls gossip, and are petty, and suck," I said.

Elliot marked his place in his book and closed it, placing it at his side. "Elaborate."

"My friend Nikki?" I said. "She likes this guy Ravesh. But Ravesh asked me to spring formal and I said no because he's just a friend, but Nikki is mad at me anyway, as if I could help that Ravesh asked me and not her. So she told our friend—"

"Breathe."

I took a deep breath. "She told our friend Elyse that *I* told Ravesh's friend Astrid that I wanted to go with Ravesh just so he would ask me, and then I turned him down. Elyse believed her and now neither Nikki nor Elyse are speaking to me."

"Neither Nikki nor Elyse *is* speaking to you," he corrected, and then, at my glare, apologized under his breath before adding, "Clearly Elyse and Nikki *is* bitches."

I laughed, and then laughed harder. Everything felt so easy in the closet. Why couldn't it always feel this way?

He scratched his jaw, watching me. "You should take *me* to your spring formal."

"You would go? You hate that stuff."

Elliot nodded and licked his lips distractingly. "I would go."

"Everyone wants to meet you." I found myself unable to look away from his mouth, imagining being tasted.

"Well, that is perfectly lopsided. I have no desire to meet everyone." He grinned at me. "But I do want to see you in something other than pajamas, jeans, or shorts."

"You would really go to spring formal with me?"

He tilted his head, brows drawn. "Is it so hard to accept that I want to be the only person you'd consider taking to a stupid formal?"

"Why?"

"Because you're my best friend, Macy, and despite your ridiculous reticence—"

"Good alliteration."

"—you are the girl I want. I *want* to be together."

My stomach flipped in thrill and anxiety. "You kiss other girls."

"Rarely."

"Uh, *ever.*"

"Obviously I wouldn't if I could kiss you."

I sighed, chewed my lip, fidgeted. "Why can't everyone be like you?"

"I can be enough of your world that it feels like everyone is."

227

I smiled up at him, softly, pressing down the familiar bubble of need. It was getting harder and harder to ignore that I really, truly loved Elliot.

"What's *your* favorite word?" I asked him.

He sucked on his lower lip for a moment, thinking. "*Vex*," he said quietly.

now

wednesday, november 8

After that one text during lunch with Sabrina, things with Elliot snowball and we're doing something we didn't do even in high school: talking nearly every day. Maybe only for a few minutes. Sometimes it's just over text. But I feel his presence almost constantly, and no matter how much I want to talk myself out of it, I know the gentle hum of relief in my thoughts is because of him.

Perhaps relatedly, things with Sean are . . . weird, at best. We've had zero arguments. We've had zero conversations about what we're doing. When I happen to catch them awake, Phoebe seems happy to see me, Sean seems happy to see me. I'm sure if I planned a big wedding tomorrow, Sean would still happily show up. I'm sure if I put off planning it indefinitely, Sean would never ask about it.

I'm also sure I could leave and he would be fine with that, too.

It's the strangest thing I've ever been a part of, and yet, it could be so fucking *easy*. It requires nothing of me, requires no involvement from my heart, and I know without a doubt that he doesn't *need* me. We could have a relationship that gives us both sex, financial security, a roof over our heads, and stimulating conversation at the dinner table, but otherwise live entirely separate lives.

But the critical truths—that we aren't really in love, never have been, and its absence troubles me—don't seem to come in little drops of awareness. They're suddenly *there*, in stark black and white, shouting *This Relationship Is So Very Over* every time we smile politely as we shift around each other at the bathroom sink.

I'm sick over it. I'm desperate to find the best way out. Unfortunately, I worry that Sean's chief reaction will be disappointment. I am as convenient a lover to him as he is to me; but in his case he may not need more: he has the love of his life already, in the form of a six-year-old daughter.

A good start seems to be to make sure I can afford to live on my own in the city. I take a rare vacation day and drive to El Cerrito to do something I've been putting off for months: meeting with my financial adviser. Daisy Milligan is Dad's old finance whiz, and I kept her more out of sentimentality and laziness than any particular knowledge about her skill.

That said, though she's approaching seventy, she barely needs to refer to my file while lecturing me on what I have in my trust (enough to cover home repairs and taxes, but not much more) and why I should sell one of my houses (I need a retirement account more than I need two properties). I don't dare mention that I'm living in San Francisco and not even making rental income from the Berkeley house.

I hate talking about money. I hate even more seeing how badly I need to get organized financially. Afterward, I'm sort of high-strung and buzzy, and when Elliot texts asking how my day is going, and I tell him I'm on his side of the bay . . . meeting up seems like a pretty obvious choice.

He suggests Fatapple's in Berkeley, having no idea how close that is to my house. So instead I suggest we meet at the top of the Berkeley hills, in Tilden Park, at the entrance to the Wildcat Creek Trail.

I get there before he does, and outside my car I pull my fleece higher on my neck to battle the wind. The fog rolls in over the hills, making it look like the gray horizon is sinking down into the valley, an inch at a time.

I love Tilden, and have so many memories of coming up here with Mom, riding the ponies, feeding the cows at the Little Farm. Dad and I would come nearly every weekend after Mom died to feed the ducks at the pond. We'd sit in silence, tossing torn-off pieces of bread into the water, and watch the ducks snatch them up, quacking at one another competitively.

The nostalgia of Tilden seems to mix with the nostalgia of Elliot and forms a potent brew in my blood, tearing through me. Even though he and I have never been here together, it feels like we have. It feels like he's part of my nuclei, entwined with my DNA.

So seeing him emerge from the fog of the parking lot and move toward me with his long, loping stride and tight black jeans . . . it makes my anxiety just . . . evaporate.

In a pulse of Obvious Epiphany, I realize Sabrina was right: I haven't been *living* without him. I've been merely surviving.

I want to share this life with him somehow. I just . . . have no idea how that looks.

He seems to read my mood as he lowers himself onto the bench beside me, sliding his arm along the back. "Hey, you. Everything okay?"

The impulse to hug him is nearly debilitating. "Yeah, just . . . long day."

He laughs at this, reaching with his hand to wrap a gentle fist around my ponytail and tug. "And it's only noon."

"I met with Dad's old financial adviser."

With his other hand, he reaches up, scratching his eyebrow. "Yeah? How'd that go?"

"She wants me to sell one of the houses."

Elliot falls silent, digesting this. "How does that feel to you?"

"Not great." I look up at him. "But, I know she's right. I don't live in either of them. It's just that I don't want to get rid of either of them, either."

"They both carry a lot of memories. Good and bad."

Like that, he cuts right through everything. Even since the first time he asked about my mom, he's gently relentless.

I pull a leg up and turn to face him. We're so close, and even though we're outside, in a public park, there's no one around us and it feels so intimate. His eyes are more green than brown today; he's a little stubbly, like he didn't shave this morning. I slide my hand between my knees to keep from reaching out and cupping his jaw.

"Can I ask you a question?"

Elliot's eyes dip briefly to my mouth and then back again. "Always."

"Do you think I keep things bottled up?"

Straightening, he looks around, as if he needs a witness. "Is this a serious question?"

I push him playfully, and he feigns injury. "Sabrina suggested I have a habit of keeping people at arm's length."

"Well," he says, choosing his words carefully, "you always talked to me, but I had the sense you didn't really do that with anyone else. So maybe that's still true?"

A car drives past, and its diesel engine chugs loudly around the parking loop, pulling our attention momentarily away from each other and out to the grass-lined lot. The faint noises of animal life trickle to us from the Little Farm, just up the gravel road.

When I don't respond, he continues. "I mean, maybe I'm biased by our current circumstances, but I feel like maybe you don't really . . . talk about stuff. And I might be pushing my luck here, but I get the feeling that Sean is that way, too."

I choose to ignore that part, wanting to avoid the Sean conversation with Elliot entirely. I know now what I have to do, but I owe Sean enough to discuss it with him first. "I used to talk to Dad," I say, sidestepping like a pro. "Not like I did with you, maybe, but about school. And Mom."

"Yeah, but we're talking about *now*," he says. "You were always pretty insular, but do you have anyone? Other than Sabrina?"

"I have you." After an awkward beat, I add, "I mean . . . *now* I do." Another pause. "Again."

His expression straightens and Elliot picks up a twig from the ground, resting his elbows on his knees and spinning the stick between his fingers and thumb. Fidgeting.

I know—

I know—

I know what's coming.

"Macy?" He looks over his shoulder at me. "Do you love Sean?"

I knew it was coming, yeah, but the weight of his question still propels me up off the bench and two paces away.

"I've seen you in love," he says gently, not standing. "It doesn't look like you're in love with him."

I don't answer, but he reads me anyway.

"I don't get it," he growls. "Why are you *with* him?"

I turn back around to catch his expression, brow furrowed, mouth tight with emotion. It takes a few breaths for me to put the words together in a way that doesn't feel supremely melodramatic.

"Because," I tell him, "we have the totally fucked-up agreement of emotionally messed-up people—that was unspoken, I guess, until recently—that we only give each other a fraction of ourselves. Losing him would never wreck me." I shake my head and look down at my shoe, toeing the dirt. I feel my epiphany from earlier about a robust, shared life starting to fade as Elliot pokes at my self-preservation instincts. I hate that Sabrina was right. I hate that retreating to my cocoon is my first reflex. "I realize how cowardly that sounds, but I don't think I could take losing someone I love again."

"It hurt that much," he says quietly, not really a question. "What I did. When are we going to *talk*?"

"I didn't just lose *you*," I remind him.

I stop, needing a second to breathe. The memories of the last time I saw Elliot used to make me physically sick. Now they just send a wavy lurch through my body.

I can see he's processing this. He studies my face, turning the words around in his mind and looking at them from different angles, like he knows he's missing something.

Or maybe I'm just being paranoid.

"What's his story?" he asks.

"You mean Sean's?"

Elliot nods, picking up another twig. "He was married?"

"Yeah. She was in finance, and got addicted to cocaine on a work trip."

His head shoots up, eyes shocked. "Seriously?"

"Yeah. Terrible, right?" I look past him, out into the parking lot. "So, I think part of it for him is that he has his daughter, and he never really got to get over Ashley. It's been . . . really easy for both of us to just fall into something permanent without really *needing* each other."

Elliot leans forward. "Macy."

"Elliot."

"Are you *staying* because of Phoebe?"

I stare at him, genuinely confused. "What?"

"Phoebe."

"No, I heard the name. I just don't understand how— *Oh.*" I get what he's saying. "No."

"I mean, she's this sweet little girl without a mom . . ." He says it like it's obvious why I'd stick around, and okay, from the outside I can see why he'd think that. But he doesn't know them.

"She doesn't need me," I reassure him. "She's got an awesome, involved dad. I'm this . . ." I wave my hand around, unsure. "This *accessory*. I mean, let's be real: I don't really know how to . . . 'mom' anyway, so she doesn't seem to need anything from me."

He grunts a little, looking down at the twig he's slowly and methodically shredding. "Okay."

I glare. "What does 'okay' mean?"

"It means okay."

"You can't think that long before giving me an 'okay.' That's a condescending 'okay.'"

He laughs, and tosses the stick to the ground before looking up at me. "Okay."

A challenge. He wants to engage me, I can tell.

"Goddammit." I turn and stare up at the education center and the gray clouds rolling in behind it.

"She might need a mom when she gets her period," he says quietly. "Or when her friends are jerks."

"Maybe she'll have a friend in a closet who listens to her instead," I counter, and then turn to look up at him, suspicious. "Why does it feel like you're trying to talk me into staying with Sean? Are you reverse-psychologizing me?"

Grinning, he relents. "Come on, let's talk about something else. Favorite word?"

Heat ripples across my skin. I'm so unprepared for this that my mind stalls and suddenly, there are no words, anywhere. "I'd need to think . . . What about you?"

His laugh comes as a low rumble. "*Mellifluous*."

I scrunch my nose. "That's a mouthful."

"It most certainly is, ma'am," he growls, with a meaning-ful lean to his words.

He gets a pebble tossed at him for that.

"Your voice is *mellifluous*," he murmurs, pushing off the bench to stand and move toward me. "And come on. Your turn. You don't get to think too hard on this, cheater. You know the rules."

I watch his lips part as he looks at my mouth. Watch his tongue dart out.

"*Limerence*."

There's no other word like it: *The state of being infatuated with another person.*

Elliot's eyes shoot up to mine, pupils dilating like a drop of ink in a pond. "You're terrible."

"I'm not trying to be."

He nods to the trail marker, beckoning me to follow. We hike down the path, and it reminds me of walking with him through Armstrong Woods, or along the dry creek bed in summer. It's so weird how it feels like another lifetime, and also like it was two weeks ago. Slowly, our steps converge into the *crunch . . . crunch . . . crunch* of feet on gravel moving in tandem. He's shortened his strides to match mine.

"Are you happy?" I ask him.

The question is so abrupt, I expect him to balk a little, but he doesn't. "I've had moments of it, yeah."

I don't like this answer. I want him to be joyful, loved, adored, full of everything, all the time.

"I'll admit," he adds, "I feel more of it being near you."

It's heady, knowing I have the power to deliver that.

"Are *you* happy?" he asks.

"I haven't been," I tell him, and feel him turn to look at the side of my face. "And being near you again has made me realize it." We stop on a tiny, slippery bridge in the middle of the woods, looking at each other. "You make me feel so many things," I admit in a hush.

He reaches up, gently pulling my ponytail through his fist. "Me too. That was always true." Shifting his hand to smooth a palm over the front of my hair, he murmurs, "I wasn't trying to talk you into staying with Sean, by the way. I just think you're being too hard on yourself."

My eyes narrow in skepticism. "Me?"

Nodding, he says, "I think you're beating yourself up for being with Sean. It's why I asked about Phoebe and . . .'"

"Ashley?"

"Yeah. Ashley." He uses the tip of his index finger to push his glasses up, and stares out at the thick trees in front of us. "You act like you're with him only because it's easy. But in some ways, he's your dad in this scenario, and you're the woman who came after your mom. Sean doesn't have as much to give, but you understand why. After all, you wouldn't want to try to replace anyone."

I stare up at him in shock. In only a few sentences, Elliot has just explained why it makes sense for me to be with Sean, while simultaneously proving that he—Elliot—is the only person who truly understands a thing about me. *I didn't even see this truth until now.*

"Why are you so good to me? After everything?"

Elliot tilts his head as he looks back at me. Of course he doesn't see it skewed this way. He only knows his betrayal, not mine. "Because I love you?"

Emotion clogs my throat, and I have to swallow a few times to get the words out. "I don't think I really noticed before how numb I've been. Or cared, maybe."

I see the way this hits him, physically. "*Mace . . .*"

I laugh darkly at this, at how fucking horrible it sounds. "That's awful, isn't it?"

He steps forward abruptly, pulling me into his chest. One hand cups the back of my head, the other wraps around my shoulders, and it feels like I haven't really cried in ten years.

then

saturday, june 3
eleven years ago

D ad and I packed up our lives for a summer to be spent in Healdsburg. Nervous clawing took up residence in my stomach. Everything felt different this summer: We'd finished junior year and were on the cusp of being seniors. School seemed more interesting, friends seemed less dramatic. And although Elliot and I hadn't gone to my spring formal together—I hadn't gone at all, actually—summer always felt like when things between the two of us shifted monumentally.

I was seventeen. Elliot was nearly eighteen. Last summer, we had kissed. We'd admitted to feelings. And ever since, he'd looked at me differently, more like something to be devoured than something to be protected. As much as I tried to think we could stay the kind of friends we'd always been, I knew I also wanted more. He was already one of the two most important people in my life. Instead of worrying about losing him, I had to focus on how to keep him.

I was draped on the pillows in the corner when he stepped into the room the Saturday after our arrival.

"Hey, you," he said.

At the sound of his voice, I jumped up and ran to him, flinging my arms around his neck. It was a different sort of hug; instead of creating the careful triangle-embrace we'd always managed—shoulders touching, nothing else—I pressed my front all along his, from my chest to my stomach to my hips. Of course I knew he was the same Elliot from only a few weeks ago, the last time we'd been to the house, but after all my nervous obsessing over what the summer might be like, I suddenly didn't feel like the same Macy.

He froze for a moment and then reacted with this tiny, perfect grunt of relief. Bending, he wrapped his arms around me and exhaled a quiet "Hey" against the top of my head.

For a few breaths, everything went still, and my entire world was the feeling of Elliot's heart beating against mine, and the way his hand spread across my lower back.

"I'm so excited it's summer," I said into his neck.

He stepped back, still smiling. "Me too." There it was

again—the breathless silence between us. And then he broke it, brandishing two books in his hand. "I brought you something to read."

"Something for our library?"

He laughed dryly. "Not really. You may not want to leave these out."

His words confused me until I looked at the covers: *Delta of Venus* by Anaïs Nin and *Tropic of Cancer* by Henry Miller.

I was enough of a book nerd to know these were not books I would already find in my high school's library.

"What are these?" I asked, seeking confirmation.

He shrugged. "Erotic literature."

"When did you get them?"

"A couple of years ago. I read them in January."

I swallowed thickly. After my revelation that things were definitely changing between me and Elliot, these books felt like blistering rocks in my hands.

Elliot flopped down on the futon. "You're all curious about boys and sex, I thought you might want to read them."

I felt my entire face heat and handed the books back, avoiding his eyes. "Oh, that's okay."

I was ready for a step forward. But the idea of sex, and Elliot, sent me into light-headed territory.

"'That's okay'?" he asked, incredulous.

"I'm not sure I'd like them." My voice was thick; the lie didn't want to roll off my tongue.

He smirked. "Cool. Well, I'm done with them anyway. If it's okay, I'll leave them here."

A week into vacation and I caved. The nondescript book spines had been staring at me, daring. I'd put them on the shelf between *The Hitchhiker's Guide to the Galaxy* and *Zen and the Art of Motorcycle Maintenance*—in other words, squarely in Elliot territory, as a hint that he was welcome to take them home if he chose.

It's not like I wasn't curious. It's not like I didn't itch to pick them up. But with Elliot stretched out in front of me every day, absently reaching to scratch his stomach or crossing his legs at the ankle—the movement somehow redefining and emphasizing what existed beneath the buttons of his jeans . . . I wasn't sure what I really needed was more erotica.

Alas, *Delta of Venus* was first. I started it at daybreak, hours—I reasoned—before Elliot would show up.

But as usual, it was like he knew.

"Oooh. What are you reading?" he asked from the doorway. The barest daylight weakly lit my bedroom behind him; he blocked most of it with the width of his shoulders.

I ignored the rising heat in my cheeks and turned back to the cover as if I needed to remind myself. "Oh. Just one of the books you got me."

"Ah," he said, and I heard the satisfied grin in his voice. "You're up early, too. Which one?"

Unwilling to say the name, I simply held up the book and waved it at him, struggling to look casual even though I knew my face was a ripe, heated red.

"Mind if I join you in the closet?"

"Suit yourself." I rolled onto my stomach and continued reading.

Whoa.

The words were almost too much even for the privacy of my thoughts. I'd always thought of sexual things in such abstract ways, not with language but with visuals. And even more intense? I realized while reading this . . . I always imagined Elliot. I would imagine him coming closer and touching me, what he might say or how he might look. But never had I thought words like *quivering*, and *tormented with desire*, and *absorbed him until he came*.

I could feel him watching me but worked to keep my expression neutral. "Hm," I said thoughtfully. "Interesting."

Elliot exhaled a laugh.

"What did you just read?" he asked a while later, voice teasing. "Your eyes are going to fall out of your head."

"It's erotic literature," I said, shrugging. "Safe money says I read something *erotic*."

"Share."

"No."

"Yes."

"Not a chance."

"It's okay if you're embarrassed by it," he said, returning to his book. "I won't push."

I was *intensely* embarrassed by it. But, at the same time, I was thrilled by it, and vexed by it. It was sexual, but so impersonal. I wanted to infuse it with more feeling. His hands became Elliot's. Her hands became mine. I imagined emotion there that wasn't on the page. I wondered if it was the same for Elliot when he read it, and whether he noticed how . . . distant it all seemed.

I inhaled a shaky breath and read, "'So was Venus born of the sea with this little kernel of salty honey in her, which only caresses could bring out of the darker recesses of her body.'"

Elliot stared at his book, eyebrows knitted together as he nodded sagely. His voice came out a little hoarse: "That's a good line."

"'A good line'?" I repeated, incredulously. "It's . . ."

Actually, I didn't have an ending to the sentence. It was a level of thinking I didn't really have the capacity or experience to articulate, but something about it felt familiar, in an ancient kind of way.

"I know," he murmured. "Do you like the rest of it?"

"It's okay." I flipped back through the pages. "It's a little impersonal and . . . some of the stories are kind of sad."

Elliot laughed and I gaped at him. "What?" I asked.

"Did you read the foreword, Macy?"

I scowled. "Who reads the foreword to erotica?"

He laughed again and shook his head. "No, you should. The stories were commissioned by a wealthy man. He just wanted sex. No feelings, no emotion."

"Oh," I said, looking down at the book that suddenly made so much more sense. "Yeah, no. I don't like it. Not like that."

He nodded, adjusting the beanbag beneath him.

"You read this?" I asked.

He hummed an affirmative noise.

"Did *you* like it?"

"I had the same reaction you did, I think." With a tiny grunt, he stretched his legs out, putting his hands behind his head. I didn't look at the buttons on his jeans. Certainly not twice. "It's sexy, but distant, too."

"Why did you read it?"

"*Why?*" he repeated incredulously as he lifted his head to look at me. "I don't know. Because I love to read? I love that you can use words to convince people, or anger people, or entertain people. But you can use them to . . ." He shrugged, blushing a little. "Arouse people, too."

I looked back down to the book, unsure what else to say.

"I haven't seen you since April," he said. "Whatever happened with spring formal?"

Laughing, I told him, "Nikki went with Ravesh."

"Of course she did. Drama always settles with the dullest outcome possible. But I meant you."

"Oh." I dropped the book and lifted a hand to chew on my fingernail. "Yeah, I just stayed at home."

I could feel him watching me, and he pushed up onto an elbow. "I would have come, you know."

Looking at him, I tried to show him with my eyes that I really hadn't wanted to go. "I know."

"You don't want me to meet your friends?" he asked, and his tone was playful, but at the distant edge was a sincere worry.

Quickly, I shook my head. "It's not that." I looked at him—at his face that was nearly in perfect proportion now, his expressive eyes, full mouth, angled jaw. "Okay, I guess it's partly that. I want you to meet them, but I don't really want them to meet *you*."

He scrunched his nose. "Okay?"

"I mean," I said, wanting to diffuse the insult I saw on his face, "I didn't really trust Nikki and Elyse at the time, and I felt like if they met you they might flirt with you—especially at that dance—and I would have been a ball of rage."

His brows lifted skyward in understanding. "Oh."

"And also . . ." I glanced back down again, finding it easier to say these things to my lap. "This is sort of our little bubble." I gestured vaguely around the room. "And when I met Emma, it changed that for me. Before, she was just a name, and I could pretend that you didn't have more time with her every week than you had with me."

"But I don't, Mace—"

"I'm just using that example," I explained, looking back

up. "I wasn't sure that you would really want to have a face to put with these names I'm spending time with."

Some clarity washed over him. "Oh. I think I get it."

I think he did.

"There's a guy who likes you."

I nodded. "Yeah."

"There's a few guys. And they were at the dance. And you and I are a weird noncouple, and you weren't sure how to . . ." He let the words trail off before saying, "You didn't want me to end up feeling like the outsider."

I pulled my legs under me on the futon. "Yeah. I just think it could have been weird. You're not my outside, you're my *every* side. But in the moment, you might not have seen it that way, or believed me." I looked up at him, hastily adding, "Just . . . speaking from my experience with the Emma thing."

"Okay," he murmured.

"I want you in my whole life," I said carefully, stepping a toe out into the vast landscape of *More*. "I think all the time about how my real fear isn't other girls, it's losing you. I'm terrified of what it would feel like if you weren't in my life anymore."

His eyes grew tight, his voice reverent: "That won't *ever* happen."

"And if we started . . . and it somehow went wrong . . ." I had to swallow a few times after saying this, tamping down the storm that happened inside me at the prospect of this. "Anyway. I don't think the dance was the first place to do that. To bring this life into that one. It would have been too much off the bat."

"I get that." He stood, walking over to the futon and sitting down next to me. "I told you already, Mace. I want to be your boyfriend."

Reaching out, he coaxed me to him, until I was leaning against him, and finally laying my head in his lap. He picked his book back up, and I had mine, and I listened to the even rhythm of his breathing.

"You know," I said, staring up at the ceiling, while he had one hand slowly dragging again and again through my hair, "these books were sort of the perfect gift."

"How's that?"

"Number forty-seven on Mom's list is to tell me not to have sex until I can talk about sex."

Beneath me, Elliot went very still. "Yeah?"

"I just think that's good advice, I guess. Like, if you can't talk about it, you shouldn't be doing it."

A tiny, nervous laugh burst out of him. "Do you want to talk about sex *today*?"

Giggling, I gently punched him in the thigh, and he feigned pain.

I wanted him to be my boyfriend, too. But I knew even then that I needed baby steps. I wanted the slow transition. I didn't want to lose a single precious bit of him.

now

wednesday, november 8

Sean is on the couch waiting for me when I come home after midnight. Other than my hike with Elliot, I had a crap day. Knowing what I had to do but avoiding it anyway, I went into work around three in the afternoon—a terrible decision. I ended up delivering two terminal prognoses and halting chemo on a third because the little girl couldn't tolerate another dose (even though her cancer could). I'm in a mental place where I know I'm doing *Good* but it just doesn't feel like it, and seeing Sean on the couch intensifies the self-flagellation.

"Hey, babe." He pats the cushion next to where he sits.

I shuffle over, falling down beside him. Not really onto him, or in any sort of snuggly position. For one, I'm in scrubs and want to shower. And two, it just feels weird to lean into him. There's this invisible force field there, repelling me.

As if reading my mind, Sean says, "We probably need to talk."

"Yeah, probably do."

He takes my left hand in both of his, massaging my palm with his thumbs. The touch is distracting because it's wonderful and reminds me of all the other wonderfully distracting things Sean can do with the rest of his body.

"I'm pretty sure you're not happy," he says.

I turn and look at him. It takes a few seconds for his face to come into focus because he's so close, and I'm so tired, but when it does I can see how much this is actually wearing on him. Just because he didn't talk about it didn't mean he wasn't thinking about it.

Sean and I are exactly alike.

"Are *you*?" I ask.

Shrugging with one shoulder, he admits, "Not really."

"Can I ask you something?"

His smile is genuine. "Of course, babe."

His answer won't change how I feel, but I have to know. "Do you love me?"

The smile straightens, and he searches my expression for a few breaths. "What?"

"Do you love me?" I ask again. "Seriously."

I can tell he *is* taking it seriously. And I can tell that he's not so much surprised that I asked as he is surprised at his own instinctive answer.

"It's okay," I say quietly. "Just answer."

"I think I need the word between *like* and *love*, which means . . ."

"'I hold her in great esteem,'" I say with a smile.

Never, in the history of time, has a breakup been so gentle. There's barely a ripple in the water. So maybe we were barely together enough to even break.

"Do you love *me*?" he asks, brows pulled together.

"I'm not sure."

"Which means no," he says, smiling.

"I love you . . . as a friend," I say. "I love Phoebs. I love how easy this is, and how little it requires of me right now."

He's nodding. He gets it.

"But trying to imagine this"—I gesture between us—"for the rest of my life?" I say, kissing his forehead. "It's sort of depressing. It feels like we're both headed down the path of least resistance."

"Mace?"

"Hmm?"

"Isn't the path of least resistance for you the one with Elliot?" he asks.

I go still, thinking of the best answer here. In some ways, yeah, of course, falling into Elliot's bed would be the easiest route, and Sean knows it. There's no reason not to be honest there.

But there's a part of me that believes Elliot and I were always only meant to be best friends. I was so scared of taking that next step with him when we were teens, and as soon as we did, it fell apart.

"We have history," I say carefully. "Not *bad* history, for the most part. But he fucked up. And I fucked up. And we haven't really discussed that."

"Why not?"

God. The most simple, obvious question.

"Because . . ." I start. "Because, I don't know . . . that time in my life was really hard, and I made some bad decisions that I don't really know how to explain. Apparently I'm also mostly dead inside and not really great with expressing the emotions."

He sits up, looking at me earnestly. "You know what? If Ashley came home, and was totally clean, and said that to me—'Sean, I made some bad decisions. I don't know how to explain them'—I think that would be enough."

"Really?" I ask.

He nods. "I miss her."

I wrap my arms around him, holding him against my chest. I don't think Sean has ever cried about Ashley leaving, or about the very real possibility that she'll never come back. Or the even more horrible likelihood that the doorbell will ring someday and it will be her asking for money.

Or, even worse, that there will be a policeman there, tell-ing Sean that she's gone for good.

"Stay my friend?" I ask.

"Yeah," he whispers, pressing his face into my neck. "Yeah, I need that, too."

I move out a few days later. It really just entails me packing up the two suitcases I brought here a few months ago and moving about six blocks away. For less than seven hundred a month, I'm renting the spare bedroom at Nancy Eaton's place—she's a physician on the unit, and her daughter just left for col-lege back east. It's a temporary situation; not because Nancy hasn't offered the room indefinitely, but because it *feels* that way. I own a house in Berkeley and could easily sell it and buy a place in the city, but even the thought feels like a betrayal. I could rent out the house and afford to rent my own place in the city, but that would require me going through all of my parents' things, and I'm not ready for that, either.

"You're a mess," Elliot says on the other end of the line, after I've skimmed through the details of what to do with the Berkeley house.

He has no idea: I haven't even told him I ended things with Sean. If Elliot knew that Sean and I broke up, he would come to the city immediately and stare me down until I re-lented, stretching to kiss him. Sean is the only barrier. He's the buffer, giving me time to think. I don't want Elliot to swoon me into falling in love with him again, or to press me to make a decision. I need time.

I hear something crash in the background and he mumbles a frustrated "Shit."

"What was that?" I ask.

"I just knocked over a pot in the sink. I should do dishes."

"You should."

"How's Sean?" he asks.

The subject change is so abrupt, it catches me off guard. "Good," I say, adding without thought, "I think."

I feel the way Elliot goes still on the other end. "You think?"

"Yeah," I deflect. "I've been busy."

"Are you being evasive with me?"

"No," I say, wincing as I search for the best half-truth. I look around my new bedroom, like the right answer will materialize on the wall somewhere. "I just haven't seen him much the past few days."

"What are you guys doing for Thanksgiving?" he asks. "This will be your first one together, right?"

Fuck.

"I think I work."

"You *think*?" he asks again, and it sounds like he's eating. "Aren't residents' schedules mapped out years in advance?"

"Yeah," I say, pinching the bridge of my nose. I hate lying to him. "I was going to trade so I didn't have to work

Christmas, but I haven't gotten organized about it. I'll probably be off."

Elliot pauses—probably because he *knows* I'm lying and he's trying to figure out why. "Okay, so, you have plans or not?"

"Sean and Phoebe are going to his parents' place." I hesitate, holding my breath. "I'm not."

I expect him to poke at this, to make some sort of *What does that mean?* investigation, but he doesn't.

He just clears his throat, and says, "Okay, so you're coming here. I'd better do these dishes before then."

then

wednesday, july 12

eleven years ago

The Healdsburg summer had turned from the warm humid hum of bees, berries, and sunshine to the brittle creaking of drying up creeks and unremitting heat. As we passed through the days, it seemed like we started to move more slowly, too. Nowhere was cool enough, except for the river or the closet. But even our blue, starred sanctuary had started to feel claustrophobic. Elliot was so tall; he seemed to take up the entire length of it. And at nearly eighteen, he was vibrating with sexual intensity—I felt entirely too full of nervous energy trying not to touch him. We would spend the mornings roaming the woods near the houses, and the afternoons walking down the road or biking into town for ice cream . . . but we always ended up back in the closet anyway, lying on the floor, staring up at the painted stars.

"School's starting soon," I said, glancing over at him. "You excited?"

Elliot shrugged. "Sure."

"You like your classes at Santa Rosa?"

He looked up at me, brows furrowed. "Why are you asking about this now?"

I'd just been thinking about it. About school starting in the fall, and getting closer to finishing high school. About what he and I would do when we were done, and if we'd end up living closer to each other.

Living *with* each other.

"Just thinking about it, that's all," I said.

"Yeah, I guess I'm excited to be that much closer to finishing," he said. "And the classes at SRJC are fine. I wish I'd decided to come down to Cal for a few days a week instead."

"You had that option?" I asked, shocked.

He shrugged. An obvious *yes*.

"Are you going to your fall formal with Emma?" I asked, returning to doodling in my notebook.

"*Macy*. What?" He looked bewildered and then laughed sharply. "No."

"Good."

"Do *you* want to go with me?" he asked.

"You want me to go to a school dance with you?"

"No? Yes? After all our talk of the right way to blend our weekend lives with our weekday lives, I'm not sure what the right answer is," he said, wincing. "But if you don't go with me, I probably won't go."

"Really?" I asked, heart pounding. "Because I don't want to go and get the death glare from all the skanks who love you, but I don't want you to go and get ogled without me to glare at them, either."

He shook his head, laughing. "It's not like that."

"So Emma doesn't email you all the time anymore?"

"Not really."

"Lies."

"She doesn't." He held my gaze, steadily. "I'm not into her, she figured it out."

I gave him a coy flutter of my lashes. "It's not that I'm jealous."

"Of course not."

Just then his phone buzzed and he looked at it, read a text, and then shoved it back in his pocket. He looked very guilty.

"That was from Emma," I guessed.

"Yes." He picked at nonexistent lint on his pants. "It's like the universe wants me to look like a liar right now."

"What did she say?"

"Nothing interesting." He laughed at my skeptical expression. "I swear she never texts me."

"If it's not interesting, why won't you tell me?"

He eyed me. "She just asked to hang out."

"That's it?"

"Yep."

"Well, then hand me your phone. I'll tell her you're busy."

He smirked. "Will you include the part where you're acting insanely jealous?"

I rolled onto my back and closed my eyes. "Whatever."

"Or we could take some pictures of your boobs and 'accidentally' text them to her."

"Jesus Christ. Give me the phone."

I reached for it but his long monkey arm kept it easily away from me and I ended up falling on top of him instead, my boobs completely in his face. He made a muffled happy sound and laughed out a string of unintelligible words, totally pushing his face into my chest.

I screamed, scrambling back and pushing at his chest to get away. "Pervert!"

Elliot grabbed my waist and flipped me over as he sat up, pulling me backward into his lap and tickling me with his crazy long fingers, digging into my ribs.

I gasped and cackled, squirmed as he tickled, and laughed and held his arm around my waist until he rolled over onto me.

He pinned me gently; his hips fit perfectly between my legs.

We both froze, out of breath, staring at each other.

I was seventeen, but I'd never felt something like this before. He was hard, pressing right up against me.

The mood was suddenly completely different from the wrestle-ticklefest of one minute before.

Elliot glanced down at my mouth, and then back up to my face. I wanted to say something, to joke about the wood in his pants, anything. But my throat felt tight, my face burning.

With one elbow propped by my head, he whispered a quiet "Sorry" and began to climb off me.

I trapped him with my leg around his thigh, and his eyes flew back to mine.

"Stay," I whispered.

I think.

It might have been my subconscious saying it, because I really didn't want him to get up. I was obsessed with what was under those buttons on his jeans, and more than that, I wanted to know if . . . well, I wanted to know what could happen.

He swallowed audibly. "Okay."

I rolled my hips up, watching as his mouth fell open and his eyes fell closed.

Elliot shifted forward and back, pressing the solid length of himself against me, and did it again. And again. His breath was harder, puffing my hair off my neck, and then his hand gripped my leg and he held his breath and we started grinding in earnest . . . together. My body was all instinct, chasing something familiar, just in the distance.

Oh, my God, what were we *doing*?

I ran my hands down his back. If I overthought it, I would ruin it.

This was Elliot.

This was *my* Elliot.

I made fists around his T-shirt, thought about the weirdest things like how his weight felt over me, and that I wanted to kiss him but didn't want to turn my attention away even a little from the feeling building inside me . . . and then I spun into a strange loop of wondering whether I was imagining this.

We were having sex with our clothes on.

He was so quiet, although I guess I was quiet, too, because I was listening so intently for any clue as to what he was thinking.

I needed more. I needed *him*. I'd never felt that sort of weighted heat before, not even when I was thinking about him by myself. It was a rush all over my skin and that heavy need low in my belly. The warmth of his mouth landing on my neck pulled a tiny, helpless sound from me. He wasn't sucking or licking, just pressing his mouth there, putting his breath that much closer to my ear so I could hear his reaction in every sharp exhale.

He let out a low growling sound, and I pressed up into him, grinding, so close. I heard the sound I made—heard the tight plea for *faster* come tearing out of me.

With a strong grip, Elliot stopped me with a hand on my hip.

"Shit," he said. "Wait. *Shit*."

Suddenly he was pushing away, standing. I sat up, with fumbling words on my lips, but Elliot was already out the door.

What had just happened?

Did he . . . ? Or did he just realize what I'd started and freaked out? In the end, did Elliot really want to be my boy-friend, or was he wrong about it all?

I careened headlong into panic.

This is how it starts. This is how the friendship goes from perfect and best friend ever to nothing but weird, dirty looks across the yard.

I sat in the closet alone for an hour, staring at the pages of whatever book I'd slid from the big bookcase and not read-ing a single word.

I would count to one thousand, and then I would go to his house and apologize.

One . . . two . . . three . . .

Twenty-eight . . . twenty-nine . . .

Two hundred thirteen . . .

"What are you reading?" His voice came from the door-way, but instead of walking in and flopping down next to me, he lingered there, leaning against the frame.

"Hi!" I said too brightly, eyes looking anywhere but at his. I noticed he had changed his clothes. My face flamed hot and I looked down, staring at the book in my hands. The let-ters of the title slowly swam into a single word and I pointed at it lamely. "Um, I started *Ivanhoe*. No *d*."

When I looked up, confusion flickered across his face like a blink, and he stepped inside. "Really?"

"Yeah," I said slowly, watching him stalk into the room. His lip turned up in a half-teasing smile. "Why do you say it like that? *You've* read this about fifty times."

"It's just that it looks like you're already about halfway through it." Scratching his temple, he added quietly, "That's impressive."

I blinked down to the page I'd randomly opened. "Oh."

It was tense and thick between us and it made my chest hurt. I wanted to ask him if I embarrassed him or . . . crap. Did I *hurt* him?

"Macy . . ." he started, and I knew that voice. That voice was a let-me-down-easy voice.

I tried to laugh but it came out as a gasp, going for casual but missing by about a mile. "I am so mortified, Elliot, seriously. I'm so sorry. Let's not talk about it."

Elliot nodded, his eyes on the floor. "Sure."

"I'm sorry I did that, okay?" I whispered to my lap.

"What? Macy, no—"

"It will never happen again, I swear. I was just playing around. I know I've been all 'let's not be together because that could ruin things' and then I went and did that. I'm *so sorry*."

He pulled a book off the shelf and I returned to *Ivanhoe*—starting from the beginning now—and read for two hours, but hardly understood a word. I blamed it on my state of mind. The idea that I might have hurt him, or embarrassed him, or made him angry ate at me like a drop of acid in my gut. It grew and gnawed at me and eventually had me so twisted inside that I felt like I might be sick.

"Ell?"

He looked up, eyes softening immediately. "Yeah?"

"Did I hurt you?"

A corner of his lip pulled up in a smile as he fought a laugh. "No."

I exhaled for what felt like the first time in a few hours. "Okay, good." I opened my mouth and closed it again, not sure what else to say.

He put his book down and moved closer. "You didn't hurt me." He searched my eyes, waiting. "Do you get what I'm telling you?"

I watched as his eyebrows slowly lifted, and then he smiled that sneaky, sexy smile . . .

"You mean you . . ." I made a circular motion with my hand, and he laughed.

"Yeah. I . . ." He mimicked the motion, eyes teasing.

My heart became a victorious monster in my chest, thrashing to climb out.

I *had* made him come.

"I was trying to make sure you went first," he admitted in a low voice, "but the sound you made . . . when you asked me to move faster . . ." He swallowed, lifting a shoulder in a silent *Oh well*.

"Oh." I stared up at him, watching him fight the heated blush. "I'm sorry."

"Macy, don't be *sorry*. I'm telling you it was sexy." He looked at my lips, and his expression grew serious again. "It's hard for me sometimes that we aren't together. I never know where the lines are. I want to cross them all the time. We've kissed and touched, but then we'll go back to being just friends and it's confusing. What we did today? It didn't even feel like enough for me." He held his hands up, eyes wide. "I don't mean you *should* do more. Just that I want it all with you. I think about it all the time."

I thought about how much I wanted that, too. And how, earlier, I wanted so much more than his body over mine, our clothes between us. I would have given him everything today. And still, the words that came out were "But I would die without your friendship."

He smiled and leaned over to kiss my cheek. "I would, too."

now

thursday, november 23

Elliot's building is narrow, a faded turquoise stucco, and must have once been a beautiful Victorian before it was sloppily chopped up into four cramped apartments.

The front door opens to a narrow hall on the right and a steep flight of steps leading to the upstairs apartments. Elliot lives in number four. Upstairs and to the right, he said. Each stair squeaks beneath my boots.

His front door is flat brown, and before it is a thin door-mat with the Dickinson quote *The soul should always stand ajar.*

I lift my fist and knock.

Is it possible I recognize the weight of his footsteps and the rhythm of his walk? Or is it that I know he's the only one inside—because I'm early? Either way, my pulse accelerates so that by the time he turns the knob and swings the door open, I feel light-headed.

Sometime in the past decade, Elliot figured out how to manage his hair and dress himself. He wears black jeans and a well-loved—either honestly or artificially—dark denim shirt rolled to his elbows. His feet are bare.

Bare feet. Elliot's apartment. Inside there somewhere is Elliot's *bed*.

If I'm not careful, I won't even go home tonight.

Holy shit, I'm a mess.

"Macy," he says, pulling me into a hug and drawing me inside with one arm around my shoulders. When he moves away, shutting the door behind me, the smile I see on his face could power a small city. "You're here. You're in my apartment!"

Bending, he kisses my cheek, chastely. "Your face is so cold!"

"I walked from BART. It's chilly outside." Heat radiates from the point where his lips pressed against my skin, and I put down the pie I brought so I can shrug out of my jacket.

He pulls back a little, surprised. "You didn't drive?"

"I'm not a fan of cars," I say, smiling.

He takes my coat, quiet at this. "I could have picked you up."

Pressing a palm to his chest, I whisper, "You live six blocks from the station. I'm fine."

"I'm sorry, I'm nervous." He shakes his shoulders a little, as if loosening up. "I'm going to try to be cool about this— about tonight. I will probably fail."

I laugh, handing him the pecan pie I bought this morning. "It's not your mom's recipe, sadly. Are they coming down?"

He shakes his head and then tilts it, beckoning me deeper inside. I follow him through a tiny living room into an even tinier kitchen. "They're going over to Andreas's future in-laws' place up in Mendocino. We didn't want the entire Petropoulos clan to descend on them; his fiancée, Else, is an only child and I don't think they'd know what to do with all of us. It's just Mom, Dad, Andreas, and Alex headed up there."

"Who's coming today?" I ask, watching him slide the pie onto the counter. He's managed to set up everything he needs in the small space, and it's meticulous despite the size.

Elliot turns, leaning back against the counter, gripping it gently. The shirt stretches across his chest, spreading open at the collar, revealing the edge of his collarbone, the hint of chest hair. My heart punches me from the inside.

"My friend Desmond," he says, and reaches one hand to scratch his chin. "And Rachel."

I freeze, staring wide-eyed at him. Instinctively I look down to what I'm wearing and then back up at him.

"*Rachel* is coming?"

271

He nods, watching me carefully. "Will that make you uncomfortable?"

I'm trying not to react too much outwardly, but I feel my brows pulling down, setting a frown on my forehead. "I don't think so?"

"That sounds an awful lot like a question," he says quietly. Pushing off the counter, he takes two steps over to me. "I should have mentioned that. She doesn't have local family. Or . . . very many local friends."

I look around the room we're standing in. "Did she live here with you?"

"No," he says. "But she stayed here a fair amount."

Oh. I look at the stove and see images of this unknown Rachel standing there, scrambling eggs in her underwear while Elliot showered. I picture him pouring coffee for her after, kissing her bare, pale shoulder. I wonder if this burning jealousy is how he felt seeing me with Sean and knowing I slept in the same bed as he did, let him touch me in ways Elliot had only started to.

Looking up at him, I say, "I'm trying not to have a fit about your ex-girlfriend coming over today."

Elliot lifts one shoulder. "I understand. I might not have planned this so well."

"It wasn't intentional to have us both here to make me feel . . . jealous? Not even a little?"

"I swear it wasn't."

One look at his face, and I believe him. Elliot has occasionally been oblivious about how other girls in his life affected me, but he's not cruel. Nodding, I look down at the floor. "Does she know who I am?"

"Yes."

Another thought occurs to me. "Does she know I'll be here?"

He hesitates, and guilt spreads in a flush up his neck. "Yes."

"So she knew, but I didn't? Elliot, *seriously*?"

He lifts a hand, scratching the top of his head. "I wanted you to come." His eyes go warm and soft, the way they do when he feels urgent about something. "I really, really wanted you to come. And I didn't want her to be alone today. But I worried if I told you that you'd back out."

I probably would have. Nothing sounds more awkward than a holiday meal with Elliot's ex-girlfriend.

"Does she think we're . . . back together?"

"I don't know what she thinks," he says. "But it's sort of moot, isn't it?" He watches me carefully. "You're engaged."

Guilt slices sharply through me, sending a jolt of pain to my ribs. I'm not ready to tell Elliot that I'm single, but I'm not okay letting him think I'm being chronically emotionally unfaithful, either. "Things there are . . . complicated."

He seems to marinate in these words for a few beats before reaching for my hand, tugging it. "Come on. Let me give you the tour."

The living room is longer than it is wide, and at the narrow end is a tall leaded-glass window looking out onto a surprisingly beautiful backyard. There are fig trees, plum trees, and a tiny, lush lawn—a rarity in the Bay Area.

"The lawn is fake," he explains. "The owner is insistent that we keep this outdoor space."

I look around the living room, at the bookcases that span from the floor to the ceiling, with a sliding ladder connected to the upper lip. His couch is a vibrant blue, and clean, with bright multicolored throw pillows. On the other end of the room, closer to the front door, he has placed a folding card table and set it with a linen tablecloth, placemats, and a tiny centerpiece of gourds and cranberries. I must have walked right past it when I came in, so excited and nervous I didn't even notice.

"Your place is so nice," I whisper, tucking my hair behind my ear. Elliot watches it slide forward again anyway, and swallows. He probably knows I wore it down for him. "Tell me about your novel."

"High fantasy," he says, looking around at his bookshelves. Then he looks back at me and his eyes shine with restrained amusement. "There are dragons."

"So you're writing porn?" I joke, and he bursts out laughing.

"Not exactly."

"That's really all you'll give me?"

Smiling, he takes my hand again. "Let's finish the tour."

Through a door on the other side of the living room from

274

the kitchen is a tiny hallway. To the left is his bedroom. To the right is his bathroom.

The bathroom has a small tub and no shower, just a smooth hose attached to the faucet and hanging limply downward, a neck bent in defeat.

"You don't have a shower," I say, walking back out and feeling the sudden intimacy of being in his space. It's all so quintessentially *him*: sparse furniture other than floor-to-ceiling shelves packed with books.

Elliot watches me as I lean against the hallway wall. The space is tiny, and he seems to fill it with his height and the solid width of his chest.

"I don't know if I could handle only having a bathtub," I babble.

"I call it a shath," he says.

"That sounds dirty."

I'm staring at his chest but hear the smile in his voice: "I think that's why I call it that."

He takes another step closer. "It still feels surreal to have my own place. Like it's some small miracle that I live here alone. It's so different from how I grew up."

"Do you like living alone?" I ask.

He hesitates for the duration of three pounding heart-beats in my ear. "How honest do you want me to be here?"

I look up at him. *Oh.* I think what's coming will probably wreck me, but I ask for it anyway: "I always want you to be honest."

"Okay," he says. "In that case, I like living alone, but would rather live with you. I like sleeping alone, but would rather have you in my bed." He reaches up, running a finger over his lip, thinking about his next words, and his voice comes out lower, and quieter. "I like having friends over for Thanksgiving, but would rather it just be the two of us, doing our first Thanksgiving as a couple, eating turkey off the bone, cuddling on the floor together."

"In our underwear," I say without thinking.

His first reaction to this is quiet shock, but it slowly melts into a smile that heats my blood, sets something simmering beneath my skin. "You said things are 'complicated,' huh?"

I'm saved from my crumbling resolve to keep quiet about Sean when there's a knock on the door behind him. Elliot stares at me, some urgent light in his eyes, as if he knows I'm about to tell him something important.

I lift my chin to the door after we've stood there staring at each other for nearly ten silent seconds. "You should probably get that."

With a small growl of defeat, he turns and opens the door to let the other two guests in.

Desmond enters first. He's shorter than Elliot but thick with muscle, with smooth dark skin and a smile that seems permanently fixed in his eyes. He hands Elliot a bowl with a colorful salad inside and claps him on the back, thanking him for inviting him.

Rachel steps in next, but I'm distracted from her entrance by Desmond coming over to me, introducing himself in a thick Aussie accent. "I'm Des. Nice to meet you."

"Macy," I say, shaking his hand and adding awkwardly, "Yes, so glad we're finally meeting."

In truth, I have no idea how long Elliot's known him. My mouth feels dry, hands clammy.

I look up and find Rachel staring at me. She blinks away, smiling tightly at Elliot as she waits for an introduction.

"Rachel," Elliot says, guiding her forward. "This is Macy."

She has short dark hair, bright blue eyes, and a dusting of freckles across the bridge of her nose and cheeks. When she smiles this time, it looks at least partly genuine, and reveals a set of bright, even teeth. She's completely lovely.

"Hi, Rachel." I reach out and she returns the handshake, limply.

"It's really nice to meet you," she says, and smiles again.

The words are out before I realize what I'm doing: "Thanks for coming."

As if I've been here a million times. As if I live here, as if I'm *hosting*.

She turns to Elliot, her eyes tight again. He ducks, giving her a little reassuring smile.

My chest twists in jealousy and possessiveness. I don't like their silent exchange. I don't like the feeling that they have a past, a rhythm, an unspoken language.

"Where should I put this?" she asks, lifting a canvas grocery bag with a few bottles of wine inside.

"Fridge," Elliot says, squeezing her shoulder and giving her another lingering, encouraging look before releasing her and returning to my side.

Rachel disappears and Elliot glances at Des, who shakes his head a little when she's gone.

"She's all right, mate," Des says quietly. "Onward." And then he turns to me, unleashing the grin. "And you. Here you are. In the flesh."

I deflect this possible conversation with a question: "How do you two know each other?"

"Rugby," Des says.

My laugh comes out louder than I expect it to, and Des's eyes widen with thrill. "I don't know you, Macy, but I think we're going to be best friends."

"Hey!" Elliot protests, laughing.

Returning his attention to me, Des adds, "Actually, he's really quite good."

"No way," I say, biting back a grin as I look up at Elliot in all his bookish glory. "This guy? Rugby?"

"Come on," Elliot says, giving me a playfully wounded look.

"I just remember watching you learn to skate," I say.

Desmond's eyes narrow. "Ice skate?"

A loud cackle bursts from me, and Elliot pulls me into a gentle headlock, growling, "*Skateboard*, you menace," into my hair.

We wrestle for a second and then stop in unison, looking up at the sound of still silence. Rachel is standing just inside the door from the kitchen, holding an open bottle of wine. Des's eyes flicker between her and Elliot.

"Does anyone want some wine?" she asks. "Or . . . just me?"

Des lets out a delighted laugh at this, thinking she's being funny, but Rachel remains unsmiling, tilting the bottle to her lips and taking a few deep swallows. She pulls the bottle up, wiping her mouth with the back of her hand.

Elliot slowly releases me from the headlock, straightening his shirt while I smooth down my hair. I feel like we've just been busted for some mildly criminal behavior. Here we are, standing in his spartan living room with this stark truth laid out before us: We've never dealt with fallout before. The messiest parts of our lives have always been compartmentalized to the school week, or kept private for a decade. I have no idea how he'll react.

"Rach," he says quietly. "Come on."

It's a gentle chastisement I can't imagine him ever delivering to me, but still, there's a seduction there, a reassurance that feels a little slippery, too intimate.

"Come on *what*?" she says.

"I thought you wanted to do this," he says.

"Turns out, it's not as easy as I expected."

Why on earth would she think this would be easy?

"I don't need to stay," I start to say, but both Des and Elliot quickly jump in.

"No, no, no," Elliot says, turning to me.

"Don't be silly," Des says. "It's fine."

I look at Rachel, who is looking at me with such a flat fury, I know exactly what she's thinking: *I'm not fine at all.*

"You did such a number on him," she says quietly.

"Rachel," Elliot says, voice low in warning, "don't."

"Don't what?" Her eyes turn to his face. "Have you guys talked yet? Does she have any idea?"

Des seems to find a reason he needs to jog to the bathroom at this precise moment, and I'm immediately jealous that he can just split and I have to stand here while the awkward shrapnel rains down on us.

But at the same time, I want to know what she thinks I need to hear.

"Any idea about what?" I ask him.

Elliot shakes his head. "We aren't doing this now."

She answers, leaning against the doorway to the kitchen: "How much you fucked him up. How no one—"

"*Rachel.*" Elliot's voice is a blade, cutting through the room. I've never, ever heard him use that tone before, and it sends goose bumps down my arms.

I continue to look at him, and it takes monumental effort to not fall apart thinking about what I'm missing here. I know what my life looked like after we split, but I couldn't bear to think about his, too.

"I'm pretty sure we fucked each other up," I say. "I think

that's what we're trying to fix, isn't it?" I look back to Rachel. "None of this is your business, though."

"It was my business for five years," she says. *Five years*. That's how long I had, too. "And it was *really* my business for at least one."

What the fuck does that mean?

Elliot reaches up, scrubbing his face. "Do we have to do this?"

"No." Rachel looks at him, and then at me, and then moves across the room to pick up her purse, and walks out the door.

then

friday, august 25
eleven years ago

Summer vacation ended on a scorching day in August. Dad, Elliot, and I packed up the car, and then Elliot shuffled conspicuously to the side, waiting for our customary good-byes.

This was the fourth time we'd done this—the parting of ways after a summer of long afternoons together—but it was by far the hardest. Everything had changed.

As it had always been with us—two steps forward, two steps back—we hadn't kissed again, and we certainly hadn't spent any more time grinding on the floor. But there was a new tenderness there. His hand would find mine while we read. I would doze off on his shoulder and wake with his fingers tangled in my hair and his body loose with sleep beside me, my leg thrown over his hip. It felt, finally, like we were together.

Dad seemed to sense it, too, and after closing the hatch to his new Audi wagon with a firm click, he smiled tightly at us and walked back into the house.

"We should talk about it," Elliot said quietly. He didn't really have to explain what he meant.

"Okay."

He took my hand, leading me to the shade between our homes. There we sat, our backs to the side of the house and our hands interlocked, in a patch of grass beneath my dining room windows, out of view of anyone in either house.

"We fooled around," he whispered. "And . . . we touch like . . . we're more than friends."

"I know."

"We talk to each other and look at each other like we're more than friends, too . . ." He trailed off and I looked up, catching the tenderness in his expression. "I don't want you to go home and think I'm doing those things with anyone else."

My mouth twisted, and I pulled up a long blade of grass. "I don't want to think of you doing that with anyone else, either."

"What are we going to do?"

I knew he was asking about more than just the obvious

284

kissing-touching, boyfriend-girlfriend thing. He meant in a bigger sense, when our lives started existing more outside the closet or his roof, and when we had to satisfy ourselves with only one or two weekends a month together.

I traced the lines of the tendons on the back of his left hand. With his right, he ran a finger slowly up and down my leg, from my knee to the midpoint of my thigh.

"What's your favorite word?" I asked without looking up.

"*Ripe*," he answered, no hesitation, his voice low and hoarse.

My blush exploded across my skin, a scorching trail of red that I felt lingering on my cheeks long after he gave up trying to catch my eye.

"Yours?"

I looked up at him, his hazel eyes wide and curious, something wilder barely contained in the dark ring of black around his irises. Beneath the surface, layered under the word *Yours?* there was something hungrier: teeth on skin, fingernails, the sound of him growling my name. Elliot was *sexy*. What boy our age used the word *ripe*?

There was no one else in the world like him.

"*Epiphany*," I said quietly.

He licked his lips, smiled. The *something* beneath the surface grew darker, more insistent. "That's a good one, too."

I stared down at his hand, smoothing the back with my thumb, and said, "I think we should stop pretending we aren't together."

When I looked back up, his smile grew. "I agree."

"Good."

"I'm going to kiss you goodbye," he said.

I tilted my face to him, saying, "Good," again as I felt his breath on my mouth, his hand cupping my jaw. My lips parted against his, and like before it seemed natural to suck at his mouth, to let his tongue touch mine, to taste his sounds. His fingers slid into my hair, both hands now cupping my head, mouth urgent.

And why did we do this out here, where we couldn't lie back and kiss until our mouths were numb and our bodies on fire? Even with this tiny touch, I *ached*. I wanted him over me again, wanted that last reminder of his weight and the hard presence of his need for me pressing between my legs.

I let out a small, tight gasp and he pulled back, eyes flickering back and forth between mine.

"We'll take it slow," he said.

"I don't want to take it slow."

"That's the only way to make sure we do it right."

I nodded in his cupped hands, and he kissed me one more time. "I'll see you in two weeks."

now

thursday, november 23

Des emerges from the bathroom, wiping his hands on his jeans as if he went in there for the usual reasons, and not to hide from the battle of the exes in the living room. He looks up with a bright smile that slowly melts as he realizes that Rachel is no longer with us.

"Seriously?" he asks Elliot, who shrugs helplessly.

"I don't know what to tell her," Elliot says. "She said it would be fine. But clearly it wasn't."

Elliot turns and heads into the kitchen. I can tell that it bothers him that Rachel bolted, and I want to think that it's because he's a tenderhearted person, and not because he's worried he messed something up with her long-term.

But, Jesus—who couldn't have seen that coming a mile away?

He stands at the small range, bending to check on the turkey, and then leans with both hands on the sides of the stove, taking a few deep breaths.

I meet Des's eyes, and he lifts his chin, telling me to go in there. "He's terrible at this shit."

Which throws me. I'm sure Des is absolutely right here, but it's a rewiring I have to do to really believe it: between the two of us, Elliot was always better at managing complicated emotions.

Even though it's bright, with a huge window at one end, the kitchen feels tiny. I slide my hands up Elliot's back, feeling the muscles tense, and to his shoulders, kneading.

The touch is so intimate, I know I can't lie to him much longer about Sean without looking like a game-playing tease. He looks over his shoulder at me, questioning.

"I'm sorry," I say. "I feel like maybe I shouldn't have come."

He turns to face me, leaning back against the stove. "I really want you here. That you were invited wasn't up for debate. She had the choice whether to come or not."

"I know, but you've been friends with her a long time."

Turning to the side, he stares out the window, his jaw tense as he thinks. His profile is so . . . grown-up. My brain still has an overwhelming number of young Elliot images. Looking at him now is like looking through a telescope into the future. It's so weird to be so close to him and imagine all the moments he's had without me.

"We really do need to talk, at some point," he whispers.

"About Rachel?"

He scowls. "About *all* of it, Mace."

I know I need to hear what he has to say—and God, I owe him my story, too—but today is definitely not the day for another woman to melt down in his apartment.

"So," I say, just as quietly, mindful of Des in the next room, "let's find some time. Maybe . . . after Andreas's wedding?"

"What?" He turns back to me, brows low. "That's a month away."

"I think a month is good." A shrill timer goes off on the counter, but we both ignore it.

Elliot shakes his head a little. "We've already had *eleven years*."

"Timer," Des calls from the living room.

"Since I have today off, I have to work on Christmas." I look past him, at the fume hood above his stove. "I'm taking four days at New Year's for the wedding, so I'm working almost every day between now and then, and I need . . ." I need time away from work to think how to unpack everything I have to tell him. About Sean, and the last night I saw Elliot eleven years ago, and everything that came after.

Des leans into the kitchen and yells at us before ducking out again: "*Oi*, something's beeping!"

Elliot reaches over, roughly silencing the noise with a slap of his hand.

Returning to me, he ducks low, meeting my eyes, searching. "Macy, you know that I would make time *any day* for you. Any sliver of time I have is yours."

This truth so easily given paralyzes my instincts to pace myself, to take a breather between the end of my engagement and diving right back into Elliot. My first admission slips out: "Sean and I broke up."

I watch his pulse accelerate in his throat. "What?"

I've just dropped a bomb from a cloud. "It wasn't—ever— what I really want—"

"You left Sean?"

I swallow down my urge to cry at the hope I see in his eyes. "I moved out, yeah."

Elliot's hand comes up to the front of my jeans, his index finger hooking just inside, sliding against my navel, and he uses the leverage to pull me closer. "Where?"

"I'm renting a room in the city."

Blood rises to the surface of my skin, hungry for what I imagine is coming—his mouth lowering to mine, the over- whelming relief of it, the feel of his tongue sliding over my lip, the vibration of his sounds.

I close my eyes, and for a second I give in to the fantasy: the glide of his hands up my shirt along my waist, the way it would feel for him to lift me, put me on the counter, step between my legs and press closer.

So I move back, shaking with the restraint. "Remember what I said at Tilden," I begin, "about feeling so much with you?"

He nods, his gaze fixed on my mouth, breathing jagged.

"I don't want to rush into anything blindly." I swallow, wincing. "Especially not with you. We messed this up once."

Blinking up to my eyes, his expression clears a little. "We did."

There's an intensity between us that has always been there. It used to make me trust that he's my person, and I'm his. And now, he's left his girlfriend for it, I've left my fiancé, but in truth, we've been back in touch for a single month after eleven years in the wilderness. His best friend in the other room is a stranger to me, and the woman who just left knows more about Elliot's heartbreak than I do. We are still so messy.

"Let's eat some turkey," I say, gently prying his finger from my jeans. "It's going to take some work for me to put my words together, okay?"

Elliot slides his hand to my hip, murmuring, "Okay. Of course. Whatever you need."

I allow myself one intimate touch and use it to press my hand over his wildly beating heart.

then

eleven years ago

From: Macy Lea Sorensen <minlilleblomst@hotmail.com>
Date: September 1, 6:23 AM
To: Elliot P. <elliverstravels@yahoo.com>
Subject: Miss you

Like crazy.

————————————

From: Elliot P. <elliverstravels@yahoo.com>
Date: September 1, 6:52 AM
To: Macy Lea Sorensen <minlilleblomst@hotmail.com>
Subject: re: Miss you

It's only been a few days, but I'm already wondering when you're
coming back.

————————————

From: Macy Lea Sorensen <minlilleblomst@hotmail.com>
Date: September 1, 8:07 PM
To: Elliot P. <elliverstravels@yahoo.com>
Subject: re: Miss you

I think this weekend. I went over to Nikki's this afternoon, and Danny was there. They were playing video games, and were having so much fun, and all I could think was that I wanted you to be there.

From: Macy Lea Sorensen <minlilleblomst@hotmail.com>
Date: September 1, 8:12 PM
To: Elliot P. <elliverstravels@yahoo.com>
Subject: re: Miss you

Crap. Dad says we can't this weekend, but maybe the weekend after. School starts on Tuesday and he wants to get a few things done here this weekend.

From: Elliot P. <elliverstravels@yahoo.com>
Date: September 1, 9:18 PM
To: Macy Lea Sorensen <minlilleblomst@hotmail.com>
Subject: re: Miss you

I think it's probably a good idea if we just try to keep our heads down during the week. It's going to be too hard, otherwise. I'm going crazy.

From: Macy Lea Sorensen <minlilleblomst@hotmail.com>
Date: September 1, 9:22 PM
To: Elliot P. <elliverstravels@yahoo.com>
Subject: re: Miss you

Do you think this is a bad idea? Being together?

My phone rang in my hand, Elliot's picture popping up on the screen. I had taken it only a week prior, when he was standing on a mossy rock in the woods behind our houses and staring up at the trees, trying to identify a bird he'd seen. In the photo, the sun caught him in profile, accentuating his jaw and the definition of his chest beneath his shirt.

My heart was pounding so hard, and when I answered, my voice came out thick. "Hello?"

"Macy, no," he said immediately. "That's not what I mean."

I nodded, staring at my wall, and the glossy poster of a unicorn there, which I'd had since I was eight and never bothered to take down. "Okay."

"I just mean," he said quietly, "that we'll drive ourselves nuts emailing every ten minutes every day of the week."

I sat down on my bed, kicking off my sneakers. "You're right, of course. It just feels different now. Scarier to be apart."

"It's *not* different." He seemed out of breath, like he was jogging upstairs. "We've always felt this way. I'm here. You're there. Just like before, we still belong to each other."

"Okay."

"And when you come up," he said, and I heard a door close in the background, "we'll spend as much time together as we can."

I curled into my pillow, cupping the phone close. "I just want to kiss you tonight," I whispered. "I just want you here, beside me, kissing me."

He groaned and then went quiet, and my heart felt twisted inside my chest, aching.

"Mace," he said. "It's all I want to do, too."

We fell into silence then, and I wondered if he would let me fall asleep with him on the phone, later. My hand slid beneath my shirt, feeling the warmth of my stomach, imagining his palm there.

"It's only one more year that it has to be like this," he said, finally. "Think about that. We're graduating in the spring. Our lives won't be separate anymore. It will go by so fast, and then we can be together, for real."

now

sunday, december 31

I'm here.

I'll be right out.

I step out of my room at the modest L&M Motel and into the sharp glare of the winter sun on asphalt. Shielding my eyes with a hand, I manage to see Elliot only ten feet away, leaning against the driver's-side door and holding a small bouquet of scraggly wildflowers. I'm immediately reminded of every teen romance hero at the sight of him straightening, staring.

After thirty-seven days, my eyes are thirsty, too, chugging

down every inch of what he looks like in a tux, his hair neatly combed, face smooth with a close shave.

We've texted a few times since Thanksgiving, and talked on the phone a little bit here and there when I had a question about the attire for the wedding, or when he wanted to check to see where to pick me up today, but I haven't seen him since he bent to kiss my cheek at his front door, our bellies full of turkey and wine, and looked at me meaningfully for three quiet breaths.

"Give me a chance," he'd said.

I'd promised I would. The question was whether he'd still want one, once he heard what I had to say.

I celebrated my Christmas on December 22 with Sabrina, Dave, and Viv. Just watching them from a kitchen stool, sipping my wine, it was easy to see their rituals taking shape: the Canadian Brass Christmas album played on a loop; Dave baked up a store's worth of Christmas cookies; Sabrina went to the living room, stringing tiny white lights all around their enormous tree. It was just one more tiny stab of awareness like those I'd been having all month, listening to colleagues share what they'd planned to do in their off-hours: parties, reunions, baking, flights out of town.

After I lost Elliot, and—of course—after I lost Dad, I'd also lost every tether to tradition. I'm ravenous to get them back. I want to make blueberry muffins on Christmas morning and light the *kalenderlys* at night. I want aebleskivers and books on birthdays, and hot dogs on the beach on New

Year's. But I also want Thanksgiving to be the day Elliot and I sit on the floor, just the two of us in our underwear, eating turkey off the bone. I want to celebrate an anniversary in bed all day, having conversations with our mouths only an inch apart.

I'm ready.

So, I step out onto the cracked parking lot, unsteady in heels, trying to walk gracefully toward him. What I really want to do is jump into his arms, but I manage to keep it together, coming to a stop a foot away. He smells so good, and when he pushes his sunglasses up, his eyes seem nearly amber in the sun. The opening words I've been rehearsing over and over for the past month—*When I left Christian's house, I went to the cabin. I fell asleep on the floor, and that's where Dad found me*—fade away into a distant echo.

Elliot presses the flowers into my hand and bends, kissing me just below my jaw, right where my pulse is the wildest.

I bend and inhale the flowers—they don't actually smell like anything, but they are so brightly colored, they're nearly fluorescent. "Flowers. Aren't you the perfect wedding date?"

"I picked them over there," he admits, nodding to a small patch of unruly weeds at the edge of the property. When he turns back and grins, he looks eighteen again. "Mom wouldn't let me take a rose from the suite."

He looks me over, his gaze heated as it moves up my chest, my neck, my face. I'm wearing a new dress, and I admit I feel pretty awesome. It's fitted crushed silk—a blaze of orange and red with small, beaded spaghetti straps. It makes my brown skin seem golden.

Our eyes meet, and I feel my smile explode across my face. We're going to unload everything later. The anticipation of the burden being lifted makes me feel weightless.

"Ready?" he asks.

"Ready."

Elliot puts the car in park in front of the enormous Victorian estate, and the engine ticks in the resulting silence. Turning to me, he asks quietly, "You okay?"

It was a ten-minute drive; there's no chance he missed my death grip on the door handle the entire time.

"I'm good."

"Okay," he says now on an exhale, and stops me from getting out with a hand on my bare leg, just above my knee. The touch feels loaded, and he seems to realize it at the same time I do, dragging his fingers away. "Let me."

He hops out, jogs around the front of his beat-up Civic, and opens my door with a chivalrous flourish.

Behind him, Madrona Manor rises up like something from a fairy tale, with wide sweeping lawns framing the expansive estate. It's a distant cry from the L&M Motel. Obviously, I *could* have stayed in the Healdsburg house I actually *own*—there aren't any vacationers currently renting—but although we're unburdening ourselves later, the idea of staying there alone, without Dad, seemed mildly depressing.

Elliot stands, waiting for me to climb out and finally reaching a hand forward. "Are you stuck?"

No, just silently melting at the sight of you.

I push up, letting him take my hand once I'm standing. "I'm good. Just . . . it's beautiful here."

Because it's chilly out, I'm wearing a wrap around my shoulders, and Elliot takes one step forward, adjusting it where it's slipped down my arm.

"There." He runs a thumb over the curve of my shoulder beneath the wrap. His skin is lighter against mine, and the contrast in color looks perfect. "Are you going to be warm enough?"

I nod, hooking my arm through his as we make our way toward the main building. It's midday, and the sun shimmers over the tops of the trees, leaving the edges honeyed and gold. Nestled in the hills above Sonoma County, Madrona Manor is surrounded by acres and acres of wooded property and overlooks vast fields of grapevines. Garden grounds seem to spread in every direction. In truth, I should be more curious about this hallowed place, but being near Elliot after taking a month to think about everything, having his body pressed right up against mine and knowing at any second I could stop him, turn to him, kiss him . . . I feel like I'm peeking over the lip of a canyon and at the bottom is a giant ball pit; I just want to dive in and play.

Inside the manor, the hall extends straight forward, with rooms coming off the main entrance. Elliot plans to go upstairs and check on Andreas in the groom's room. I told Elliot I was driving up from Berkeley last night, when in fact I booked a town car, took a Xanax, and slept the entire ride. I arrived at the motel, stumbled into my room, and slept until my body's alarm clock roused me exactly at six this morning.

What all of this means, really, is I still haven't seen any of his family, and admittedly, I'm a little anxious about it. But although I'm happy to explore the grounds alone, leaving the Petropoulos clan to themselves before the ceremony, Elliot won't have it.

"Come with me," he says, heading toward the wide staircase. The holidays have yet to be banished to boxes and locked up until next December, and garlands remain wrapped festively around the banister. A small golden Christmas tree brightens the landing at the top. "They're up here."

"I don't want to interrupt the getting-ready process," I say, pulling back, hesitating.

"Stop it." He laughs. "You're joking, right? If I come up there without you, they'll just send me back down."

A swarm of birds explodes into motion in my chest as I hear Mr. Nick yelling at George to go grab a suitcase from the car, Nick Jr. teasing Alex about something. I can hear Miss

Dina's full, round laugh, and her voice—still the same—telling Andreas he should let someone else tie his bow tie because it looks like a "limp Peter" around his neck.

We push the door open, creaking inside, and the entire room falls silent in a hush. Andreas turns from where he'd been futzing with his tie in the mirror. Nick Jr. and Alex straighten from where they appear to have been wrestling near the couch.

Miss Dina freezes with her hand on a pin in her hair.

"Macy!" she gasps. Her eyes immediately fill. She drops the pin, cupping her hands over her mouth.

I lift my hand in a shaking wave. Seeing their faces tunnels me back a decade, like I'm home for the first time in so long. "Hi, everyone."

Elliot pulls me close to his side. "Doesn't she look beautiful?"

I look up at him in shock, but his lazy grin tells me he's not at all self-conscious under their scrutiny.

"Stunning," Mr. Nick agrees.

Alex runs over, throwing her arms around my shoulders. "Do you remember me?"

I haven't seen her since she was three, and couldn't possibly tell her I've thought about her every day since then. Laughing, I wrap my arms around her long, willowy frame, asking, "Do you remember *me*?"

"Don't," Miss Dina says, shaking her head. "I'm going to cry."

Nick Jr. glances at her and groans. "Ma, you're already crying."

Elliot lets me go but doesn't move away as everyone comes over to hug me. When Andreas reaches me, he whispers a quiet "Thanks for coming," and I answer with my own quiet "Congratulations, meathead."

The scene explodes back into noise as Alex launches into a debate with her dad about why she should be allowed to wear her hair up, and George argues with Miss Dina about where he can find the suitcase. Elliot helps Andreas with his tie, and Liz walks in, carrying a tray of snacks for the wedding party. She's wearing a shimmering blue dress—clearly she's one of the bridesmaids.

"Hey, Macy!" she says, coming over to me. At the confused stare of the rest of Elliot's family, she reminds them that we see each other every day at work, and the room explodes anew, as they all remember what this means—that little Macy is a *doctor* now!—and I'm hugged all over again.

Wine is poured, Alex's hair is brushed down, and then up again to her father and older brothers' dismay, and the whole time, Elliot is there, his arm pressed to my arm, my twin heartbeat, a comforting presence.

"Dad," Elliot finally says, with a quiet, rumbling laugh. "She's *fourteen*. She's wearing a floor-length gown with sleeves. She's not going to get pregnant if someone sees the back of her neck."

Mr. Nick glares at Elliot for a few seconds and then

shakes his head at his daughter and wife. "Put it up. I don't care. It's just a *lot* of skin."

"It's *my neck!*" Alex cries, frustrated. "Tell the guys not to look if it bothers them so much."

"Amen," I say, grinning at her. Her grateful smile is like a sunbeam cracking through the window.

As the argument picks up again, Elliot leans down and asks, quietly, right up against my ear, "Want to walk around the gardens?"

I nod, shivering at his proximity, and he guides me toward the door with his hand on my lower back before reaching for my fingers. I feel the attention of the entire room on our joined hands as we leave, and Alex's confused "I thought she had a boyfriend?" followed by Miss Dina's sharply hissed "Shhhh!" and Andreas's "They broke up, remember?" in our wake.

Elliot looks down at me, grinning. "Is it just like you re-membered?"

I lean into his shoulder. "Better."

then

saturday, september 9

eleven years ago

The first trip after the summer—after our declaration that we were together, after that sweet, aching kiss—was in mid-September. The air was thick with the relentless heat of Indian summer, and I used it as an excuse to spend the entire weekend in my bikini.

Elliot . . . noticed.

Unfortunately, Dad noticed, too, and outright required us to spend our time reading downstairs or outside, and *not* in the closet.

That Saturday, we spread a blanket out on Elliot's scraggly front lawn, beneath the enormous black oak, and gave our updates on friends, and school, and favorite words, but it had a different weight to it. We whispered it now, lying face-to-face on our sides, with Elliot's fingers playing with the ends of my hair or brushing against my neck, his gaze dancing across the swell of my breasts.

According to rule number twenty-nine—*When Macy is over sixteen and has her first serious boyfriend, make sure she is being safe*—Dad put me on the pill almost immediately after that visit. I was still several months away from turning eighteen, and Dad told me he planned to call my "female doctor," but only after giving me a stilted, awkward lecture that it wasn't permission to have sex with Elliot, per se, but that he was trying to protect our futures.

Not that he had to worry. Despite seeing each other every weekend throughout October, Elliot and I never came that close to sex. Not since that day on the floor of the closet, his body over mine, working on instinct. And *Elliot* was the one taking things slow, not me. He kept telling me it was because every tiny step was a first, everything we did together we would only do for the first time, with this one person, our whole lives.

It seemed a foregone conclusion that we'd be together forever. We hadn't said *love* yet. We hadn't made promises. But it was as impossible to imagine falling out of love with Elliot as it was to imagine holding my breath for an hour.

So, we were winding our way carefully through exploration. Kissing for hours. Swimming together in the river: my legs slippery and cold around his waist, my stomach covered in goose bumps, sensitive to the feel of his bare torso pressed against me.

Weekdays back at school became infused with this desperate anticipation. We agreed to Skype once a week—Wednesdays—which made it painful to sit through classes that day. Those nights, he would look at me through his camera, eyes wide. I'd think about kissing him. I'd even tell him what I was thinking, and he'd groan and change the subject. Afterward, I'd climb into bed and imagine my fingers were his, knowing he was doing the same.

And weekends, whenever we had the smallest window, were a blur of kisses on the floor, our mouths moving together until our lips felt raw, our breaths shallow from the exertion of wanting.

But that was it. We kissed. Clothes stayed on, hands stayed put.

Until they didn't.

Late October. It was pouring rain and miserable outside. Dad took the car into town to get groceries, leaving me and Elliot alone in the house. It wasn't premeditated. He didn't even spare a glance back at us, reading in the living room by the wood-burning stove. He simply called out that we were out of milk, and he was getting stuff for dinner.

The door closed with a quiet click.

The car tires crunched on the gravel until the sound disappeared.

I looked up at Elliot across the room, and my skin flushed hot.

He was already crawling across the floor to me, and then he was hovering over me in the shadows of the flickering fire.

I still remember the way he lifted my shirt, kissing a path from my belly button to my collarbone. I remember how—for the first time ever—he figured out the clasp of my bra, laughing into my mouth as his fingers fought with the elastic. I remember the reverence of his palm as it slid from the open fastening, around my ribs, beneath the underwire. His hand came over my bare breast, his thumb and finger closing over the peak. It seemed like light flowed out of me from every pore; the pleasure and need were nearly blinding. He followed with his tongue, wet, his lips closing over me, sucking, and I pulled his thigh between my legs, insane for the relief, rocking against him until I melted, coming in front of him for the first time.

He stared down at me, pupils huge and black, mouth slack.

"Did you . . . ?"

I nodded, smiling, drugged.

The car tires crunched back up the gravel driveway, and Elliot let out a sharp, frustrated laugh, pulling away.

"I should go home anyway." He nodded down.

I looked down, too, at the heel of his hand pressed to the front of his jeans, seeking relief.

He started to stand, but stopped, still kneeling between my legs but now staring down at my bare chest. It was the first time he'd really looked, and the intensity of his gaze was like a match to the fuel in my veins. I reached for his free hand.

The car door slammed shut.

"Macy," Elliot warned, but his eyes remained unblinking and his arm moved without resistance when I pulled his hand down to my skin.

"He still has to get the groceries." I put his fingers on my stomach, ran them up my body.

The trunk slammed, too. Elliot jerked his arm away.

Slowly, I sat up, fastening my bra and pulling my shirt down.

Dad's keys fit into the lock, and he let himself in, glancing at us in the living room. I was exactly where he'd left me. Elliot hovered near the other end of the sofa, hands deep in his pockets.

"Hey, Dad," I said.

He stopped, arms loaded with groceries. "Everything okay?"

Elliot nodded. "I was just waiting until you got back to head home."

I looked up at him, grinning. "That was sweet."

"Thanks, Elliot," Dad said, smiling at him. "You're welcome to join us for dinner."

Dad walked into the kitchen, and I looked down at Elliot's button fly with a nearly obsessive need to feel him beneath the denim.

He bent low, so that I had to look at his face. "I see where you're looking," he whispered. "You're trouble."

I stretched, kissing him. "Soon," I said quietly in return.

now

sunday, december 31

There are more than eight acres of grounds at Madrona Manor, and I swear we walked every single one of them. Two hours we spent strolling, catching up, talking idly about tiny things: our favorite delis, late-blooming obsessions with Castelvetrano olives, books we've loved and hated, political fears and hopes, dream vacation destinations.

And still, the last New Year's we knew each other feels like a chunk of radioactive meteor held in a jar in the palm of my hand. I feel it every second. I'm doing everything to avoid opening it until later.

The afternoon sun dips behind the trees and a chill descends. Car tires crunch on the gravelly driveway in the distance, luring us back to the great lawn, which is decorated with flowered garlands and dotted with heat lamps, cocktail tables, and waitstaff circulating hors d'oeuvres before the ceremony.

"I need to head upstairs to get ready. You okay?"

I nod, and Elliot bends as he cups my face, kissing my forehead and then my cheek seemingly out of instinct. He doesn't register what he's done as he pulls away, smiling down at me. Not once on his journey to the house to meet up with the groomsmen does he turn back, eyes wide in realization that he's just kissed me the way he did so many times when he was mine.

Once he's gone, I look around, realizing I don't know anyone here. The entire Petropoulos family is inside, and although I've seen the cousins, aunts, and uncles on occasion, I don't know any of them well enough to just walk up and break into conversation.

Maybe this is why your circle is so small, Sabrina's voice rings in my ear.

A small circle is a quality circle, I snark back, reaching for a bacon-wrapped shrimp as it passes on a tray.

I'm lifting it to my mouth when a hand comes around my elbow. Turning in surprise, I blurt, "Oh, sorry!" and begin to hand back the hors d'oeuvre until I realize it's only Alex, and I've just dropped the shrimp into her hand.

She stares down at it and then up at me before shrugging

and popping it in her mouth. "Come with me," she mumbles around the bite. "We're sitting up front."

"What?" I say, resisting when she tugs me forward. "No, I—"

"No argument," she says, marching forward. "I have strict instructions from Mom: you're family."

This catches in my throat—a ball of cottony emotion gets trapped in there. Pulling my wrap around my shoulders, I follow her to a seat on the groom's side, in the very front row.

Alex sits in the third seat in, pulling me down beside her in the fourth. "It's starting soon," she says. "Mom told me to go sit so people would make their way over. Are they?"

I look behind her and see that, yes, people are beginning to make their way toward the ushers waiting at the entrance to the aisle. Seats are filling, the sun is setting, and the scene is breathtaking.

"I've wanted to meet you for years," Alex says, staring ahead at the altar—a small wooden arch decorated with flowers so lush I want to reach out and pinch a petal to see if it's real. "Well—meet *again*."

"Me?" She was only three when Elliot and I had our falling-out.

Falling-out.

God, what a weird phrase. Other people have a falling-out. What we had felt like a rupture. But really, was it? A breach along the fault line, maybe. A mallet cracked against our weak spot. And fate went in with a jackhammer.

Alex nods, turning to me. She looks so much like Elliot at fourteen that my breath is paralyzed for a second, like I've been punched in the solar plexus. Her eyes are hazel, wide behind her glasses. Her hair is thick and dark, barely tamed into submission by the flowers pinned around her oval face. Her neck is long, swanlike, hands delicate and bony. On Alex it looks graceful somehow; probably because she dances and she's learned to use her slim build to her advantage. Elliot's body always just seemed a little like a box full of tools: sharp angles, long bones, dangerous when clumsily wielded.

"He loves you so much," she says. "I swear he didn't bring a girl home *forever*."

My heart slows.

She nods. "Seriously. My parents thought he was gay. They were like, 'Elliot, you know we love you no matter what. We just want you to be happy . . .' and he'd be like, 'I really appreciate that, guys,' and then we'd all just stare at him, like, 'So when are you going to bring your boyfriend home?'"

I laugh a little, not sure what to say. Haltingly, I murmur, "But he did eventually bring someone home. I'm sure they liked her?"

She shrugs. "Rachel was nice."

My heart slows. *Rachel* was the first girlfriend he brought home? That was—what, a year ago?

Alex looks back over her shoulder to check the progress of the seating. It's filled up a bit, so she leans in closer as the guitarist and vocalist begin preparing to play the processional.

"Mom called her 'Macy' like three times the first time she came for dinner."

"Oof," I say, "awkward." I'm additionally sympathetic now that I've met Rachel. A lot more things make sense about that first encounter.

"Anyway," Alex says, smiling at me, "he eventually admitted to us that he's been in love with you since high school. I'm glad you're back in his life." Quickly she holds up her hands, adding, "Even if you're just friends. Okay, I'll shut up now." She bites her lip and then adds in a rush, "And I'm really sorry about your dad, Macy. I don't remember him, but Mom said he was a really nice man."

"Thank you, sweetie." I reach around her shoulders, pulling her in for a hug. "I missed you all like crazy."

A hush overtakes the crowd as the guitarist begins, strumming a simple, aching prelude before the vocalist launches gently into Jeff Buckley's version of "Hallelujah." The first people down the aisle are an older couple, presumably Else's grandparents. They sit in the section opposite us as Miss Dina and Mr. Nick come down the aisle with Andreas between them. Miss Dina's smile is so brilliant, it traps my breath in my throat, and I feel the sting of tears across the surface of my eyes. It's not just that it's a wedding—though I always cry at weddings. It's the song, it's the setting, it's being back in the arms of the people I love most in the whole world. It's not feeling alone for the first time in as long as I can remember.

Andreas stands at the head of the aisle, watching in anticipation of his bride. Miss Dina sits beside Alex but reaches over her lap, taking my hand and holding it so tight I feel her love and her confusion and—above it all—her relief in that single, trembling touch.

Next is Nick Jr., with one of the bridesmaids. He's filled out, barrel-chested like his father, tall like both of his parents. With a full beard, he looks more lumberjack than district attorney. I can't really imagine him in sharkskin, if I'm being honest.

Then it's George and Liz, arm in arm, all easy smiles. They're such a perfect combination of happy faces and confident strides that I catch myself grinning, eyes brimming.

Alex hands me a tissue. "Two criers, on either side of me."

"Shh," Miss Dina whispers. "Just wait. It'll afflict you soon."

I'm not prepared for it, somehow—I'd forgotten that Elliot would be walking down the aisle—and the sight of him, with the petite blond maid of honor on his arm, his smile calm as he makes eye contact with the gathered guests, is a blow to the emotions wrapped tightly in my gut. Warmth bleeds free.

He looks so good.

Smiling, well over six feet tall now, easy in his skin. He looks at me after he leaves the maid of honor near the altar, and our eyes catch and hold.

It's been hours since I thought of my ex-fiancé, but seeing Elliot now—at the altar and in his tux—makes me realize how monumentally wrong everything felt with Sean. How wrong it would feel with *anyone* but Elliot.

Stepping back, he files into position at the head of the groomsmen and manages to pull his eyes away from me as the music changes, and the guitar begins strumming the opening notes to Elvis Costello's "She."

The crowd stands. I know I should be looking for the bride, but my head is the only one facing forward, unable to stop staring at Elliot.

He can feel my attention, I'm sure, because he blinks away, turning his head just the slightest bit, meeting my eyes. There's a question there in his, the playfully obvious *What the hell is wrong with you?*

I don't know what else to do, so I simply mouth the word *Yes*.

Yes, I'm yours.

Yes, I'm ready.

Yes, I love you.

then

"God, this book is amazing," Elliot whispered, turning the page.

Inwardly, I gloated. Finally Mr. Snobby McClassicspants was reading Wally Lamb.

I rolled to my stomach, looking up at him on the futon. "I told you you'd love him."

"You did," he said. "And I do."

We were finally allowed back in the closet together— door open—because it was too cold to send us outside, and Dad didn't want to listen to us whispering downstairs all day long.

Senior year was already completely insane, and most weekends in November had been spent at home in Berkeley, preparing for college applications, SATs, and honors theses. We were trying to apply to schools in the same cities, if not the exact same colleges, and the intensity in our need to co-ordinate had us checking in with each other, constantly. This was the first weekend I'd actually been with Elliot in five weeks, and there was a forceful undercurrent, pushing us closer, and closer, and closer together, even with the door open.

"You should worship me," I told him.

He looked at me over the rims of his glasses, brows raised. "I do."

I grinned. "Or be my slave."

"I would." He closed the book, leaning his elbows on his long thighs. "I *am*." I had his full attention now.

"Fan me with palm fronds and feed me tiny succulent grapes."

It felt like the air stopped moving between us.

"Say that word again," Elliot asked hoarsely.

"Fan."

"No."

"Tiny."

He sighed, exasperated. "Macy."

"Grapes."

He turned back to his book, releasing a weary growl. "Pain in the ass."

I grinned, licked my lips, and gave him what he wanted: "Succulent."

He looked up, eyes dark.

Door open.

"Succulent," I whispered again, and he crawled to the floor, leaning in to kiss up my neck, tickling. I squirmed, glancing at the door. "You are such a word nerd."

His tongue followed the path of my throat and I heard his smile when he said, "Put your hand down my pants."

I cackled, whispering sharply, "What? No. My dad is literally twenty feet away."

Our eyes went wide in unison as, just then, the car engine started in the driveway, tires crunched down, down, down and then disappeared.

"Okay. I guess he's more than twenty feet away," I mumbled.

Elliot pulled back and stared at me, eyes dark and carnivorous, and it felt like a switch, bubbling something up inside me. I reached out and

finally

finally

put my hand over the buttons on his jeans, felt what I'd really *really* wanted to feel there.

"Now what?" I asked. This was happening. *This was happening*. I was touching. It. Him—*it*.

Elliot's eyebrows shot up to his hairline. "You don't know?"

"I'm not sure?" I said, left with no more questions when he growled out a smile and covered my mouth with his.

We fell back to the floor, legs and arms entangled, lips bruising against teeth, messy and desperate and completely perfect. After all the forced physical distance and discussions about everything we wanted to do to each other, and never knowing when or how we would get time alone, this tiny window felt like the Hope Diamond, dropped into our palms.

I had never known this feeling, this ache that bloomed in my stomach and spread, lower and hot, driving me past my senses and pinpointing my entire universe down to this one sensation, and then the next. And then wanting what came after.

My shirt came off. My pants were unzipped and peeled away. I pushed closer, afraid that even naked we wouldn't be close enough to satisfy this new hunger.

He bent down, licking my neck, my breasts, and then returned to me, greedy lips sucking at mine and then back down over my chest. His hand pressed flat against my stomach and fingers teased at the hem of my underwear.

"Too fast?" he asked, breathing heavily, and I shook my head even though he couldn't see me from where his mouth explored my breasts.

"No," I said out loud. It was too slow. Not too fast—too *slow*. Fire crackled up and down every nerve ending and I wanted more, even if I didn't know exactly what that was.

"Shit, Macy, I'm . . . this is insane. *Good* insane. You feel insane under me."

I laughed because Elliot's rare incoherence was strangely reassuring, and then his lips were on my mouth, swallowing my laugh and making it his, his tongue slipping over mine as his hand cupped my breast, squeezed, our sounds muffled by the way we could barely bring ourselves up for air.

His fingers went lower again, slipping over my ribs, across my navel, below the cotton to exactly where I needed them, and he made a strangled sound at the same time that I ground out something unintelligible. His hips shifted over me, seeking the same rhythm as his fingertips gliding across my skin.

In a flash he was moving down, tugging my underwear off, and kissing my belly, hips, and then lower, almost wild with the want that mirrored mine. He shook below me, between my thighs, shoulders trembling under my grip, and I missed his weight on top but whatever he had decided to do with his mouth distracted me from any other coherent thought. It was warm soft suction, hands on my legs, resisting the way they seemed to want to close around his head and the mad sensation of tongue and lips and his gasps of air. He was doing that thing I'd barely let myself imagine.

He moved back up when I started gasping, biting and kissing along my skin, wilder than I would have ever imagined, but then, in the moment, I realized it could never be any other way with us.

"Sorry," he said. "I wanted to keep going but—" He

closed his eyes, biting his bottom lip and groaning as if he was trying to keep himself together.

"It's okay, come here." I wanted his weight on me. I wanted to see him hovering over my body and then burn the image into my brain.

"I seriously thought I was going to come," he added with a laugh against my lips, his mouth still wet from *me*, and with an urgency behind his touch that made me a little wild.

I pushed ineffectually at his belt and then my fingers remembered function, pulling through loops and undoing one fascinating button at a time, and then my hands felt the bare skin of his flat stomach, his narrow hips, the soft hair on the backs of his thighs as I worked his pants down around his knees.

He was heavy on me, hard and thick against my hip, and I arched to him, wanting to rub across him *there*.

"I want to," I began, reaching for him and finding it. My mind turned to mush at the sound he made, at the feeling of him, so warm and hard in my hand. "Do you want to?"

"Have sex?" he asked, head bobbing in a frantic nod, eyes rapt. "Yes. Yes. I do. I do, I do, I do, Macy, but *fuck*, but I don't have any protection."

"Pill," I gasped as he shifted and I felt him slide across my thigh. Smooth and soft skin over something not at all soft.

Elliot lifted his chin in surprise. "You're on the pill?"

"It was one of Mom's rules. Dad put me on in October."

He reached between us and when he rubbed himself

across me I was completely gone. I barely heard him ask, "You sure, Mace? Look at me."

At the soft pulse of his voice, I moved my gaze from the fascinating place where he was about to be *in* me to his eyes, which were almost black with hunger but patient and waiting, too.

"Please," I said. It felt so good. If he kept rubbing over me like that . . . "I'm sure."

He looked down and guided himself to the right place before leaning over me and resting his elbows near my shoulders. This felt like the most natural thing in the world: my legs slid up and over his hips, his lips found mine. He moved forward, an inch. Not yet inside but *there*.

"This is not going to be a marathon," he groaned. "I'm barely hanging on."

"I just want to feel you."

He pushed forward an inch more but stopped when I cried out at the commotion in my body, at the cohesion of sense and stimulation. His eyes were riveted to my face and then rolled back in his head as I used my leg curled around his thigh to pull him quickly—and roughly—all the way inside me.

I bit his shoulder at the sharp stab of pain, his body muffling my cry. Elliot's hips shifted carefully back, and then in again, and I felt the tearing pleasure/pain of him, over and over as he started moving in earnest, pushing in and pulling out of me again, again, faster.

"You're okay?" he gasped.

I managed a strangled "Yes."

"Oh, God, I'm—"

I held him to me, with arms and legs banded around him, my eyes clenched against the tight pinching of it, my heart wanting to keep him inside more than my body needed him out.

"I'm coming," he gasped, and then shook beneath my hands, his breath held high and tight in his shoulders as he fell.

I felt what it did to him. Felt every single shift inside me.

In an echo somewhere I heard sound, feet, a voice. Desire still echoed through me, ricocheting against the sharp pain between my legs.

Elliot's touch was suddenly gone, the entire front of my body was cool without him over me, and I felt oddly, immediately hollow. With a foggy head, I realized he was scrambling back and pulling me up.

"Macy?" Dad called from downstairs. Or underwater, I couldn't be sure.

Elliot's face swam into focus above me, his brow damp, eyes wide, lips bright red and still wet from my kisses. "Get up, Mace."

Jerked into realization, somehow I found my voice, pushing out a hoarse "Yeah, Dad?"

Elliot yanked his pants up and threw his shirt over his head as my own fumbling fingers struggled to jerk on my pants. I paused at the brilliant streak of blood on my thigh, blinking up to Elliot, whose eyes snared with mine as he buttoned his jeans.

"You okay?" he whispered. Footsteps echoed down the long upstairs hallway.

"Yeah." I stood on weak, shaky legs to find my shirt, tug it on, and shove my bra under a pillow with my foot just as Dad walked in.

He paused in the doorway, taking in the scene. Elliot, having launched himself onto the pillows in the corner, was reading my worn copy of *The Joy Luck Club* without his glasses on. His face was red, his breathing uneven. I stood near the door, and realized I had no idea what my hair looked like, but I imagined it could not be good. Elliot had dug his fingers into it, pulled apart my braid, and slid his hands over and into my hair again and again.

My body bucked with the memory.

Dad looked me over and smirked.

"Hey," I said.

And to his credit, he simply replied, "Hey, guys."

"What's up?" I asked, trying not to gasp for air.

"Mace, sweetheart, I'm sorry, but do you think you could be ready to go in an hour? I just had to run into town to get a *fax*, of all things. We need to get back tonight." He looked genuinely apologetic.

We have two more nights here, I thought, but even as crushing disappointment spread through me, I nodded brightly. "No problem, Dad."

He waved to Elliot, who waved back, and then left.

Slowly, I turned. Elliot's eyes were closed, his hands over his face as he finally gasped for air, no longer needing to appear relaxed.

I moved to him, crawling into his lap, desperately wanting the feel of him against me.

"Holy shit, that was close," he whispered.

I nodded. I didn't want to leave. Adrenaline crashed through me, making my limbs shake. I wanted to curl up with him and talk about what we'd just done.

He turned his head, kissing my temple. "You were bleeding. I know it's . . . normal, but I just want to be sure: Did I hurt you?"

I looked up at the ceiling, trying to find an answer that felt both true and reassuring. "Not more than I expected."

His lips found mine. Slow, careful kisses dotted over my mouth, my chin, my cheeks.

"You need to pack," he said reluctantly, pulling away.

"Yeah."

He stood, lifting me with him and then put me down. "Email me tonight?"

I nodded. I was still shaking. Because of what we'd done . . . and because we almost just got caught doing it.

He cupped my face in both hands, searching my eyes. "Was it . . . okay?"

"Yeah." I bit back a nervous laugh. "I mean . . . I definitely want to do it again." The adrenaline was making me feel speedy and wired.

"Okay." He nodded frantically. "Okay, so we'll talk? You're okay?"

"Yeah." I smiled. "You?"

He blew out a controlled breath. "I'm going to go home and take a long shower and relive all but the minute your dad was standing there and I was still sort of hard."

I leaned against him, my forehead to his chest. "I don't want to go."

His lips rested on the crown of my head. "I know."

"Did we just have sex?" I asked quietly.

With his thumbs, he tilted my face so I'd look up at him. "Yeah. We did."

He leaned forward, kissed me once, twice, softly on the lips and then a third, deep kiss. Finally he pulled away, kissed the tip of my nose, and ducked out of the closet.

And I thought, as I heard his footsteps jogging down the stairs, how strange and wonderful it was that we had never said *I love you*. And we hadn't needed to.

now

sunday, december 31

Despite being born to the same parents, and raised in the same house, Andreas and I could not have been more different," Elliot says, opening his wedding toast and sliding one hand into the pocket of his tuxedo pants. He stands at the front of the expanse of tables and flowers and candlelight, a tiny grin working at his mouth.

"I was studious, he was . . ." Elliot scratches his eyebrow. "Well, he was athletic."

The guests laugh knowingly.

"I was obsessive, he was slovenly." Another appreciative rumble. "I learned Latin; he primarily communicated in grunts and frowns." At this, I join in the genuine laughter. "But anyone who knows us knows we have one important thing in common." Elliot glances briefly down to me, side-long, almost as if he can't help himself, and then back over to Andreas. "When we love, we love for good."

An emotional murmur ripples across the room, and my heart dissolves into a puddle of warm honey.

"Andreas met Else when he was twenty-eight. Sure, he'd had girlfriends before, but nothing like this. He walked into Mom and Dad's house one Saturday and looked physically windblown. Eyes wide, mouth agape, Andreas had lost the ability to speak in his normal, very basic vocabulary." Laughter rises up again, jubilant. "He brought her home for dinner, and you would think he'd invited the queen of England." Elliot smiled at his mother. "He nagged Mom about what she'd cook. He nagged Dad about not having the Niners game on the whole time. He nagged me about not doing something weird like quoting Kafka or performing magic tricks with my green beans. For a man who'd never voluntarily cleaned his own bedroom, this meticulous behavior was notable."

My smile spreads wide across my face; a giddy, lovesick fault line.

"And he's been as attentive, and loyal, and devoted for each day since. For four years I've watched you fall more deeply in love. To say that Else is well-suited for Andreas is an understatement. Apparently she loves meatheads." Laughter. "And apparently she also liked us well enough."

Elliot lifts his glass, smiling warmly down at his brother and new sister-in-law. "Else, welcome to our family. I can't promise that it will ever be quiet, but I can promise that you will never be so loved as when you come home to us."

Cheers ring out, glasses clink. Elliot bends to hug them both, and then returns to his seat beside me.

Beneath the table, he takes my hand. His is shaking.

"That was awesome," I tell him.

He bends, smiling as he takes a bite of his salmon with his free hand. "Yeah?"

I lean over, press my lips to his cheek. His skin is warm and a little rough now, like the mildest sandpaper. It's all I can do to not bare my teeth and bite him the tiniest bit. "Yeah."

When my lips come away from him, they've left twin petals of lipstick. I reach up, reluctantly smearing it away with my thumb. I sort of liked it there. Elliot continues to eat, smiling at me as I fuss over him, and never in my entire life have I felt so blissfully like someone's wife.

The feeling is bubbly, like being drunk from a shot—the way it warms the path from throat to stomach. But here, *everything* feels warm. I pull his hand in mine closer, onto my lap, high on my thigh. He pauses with his fork en route to his mouth, sending me a sly smile, but then takes the bite and chews, leaning to his left to listen when Andreas taps his shoulder.

The music begins for the first dance, and Andreas and

Else stand, moving out into the center of the room, dancing solo for only a few bars before the DJ calls everyone out. And then Miss Dina and Mr. Nick are out there, and then Else's parents, too. Elliot looks over at me, eyebrow raised in obvious question . . . and here we go.

He leads me to a spot near the center of the dance floor, pulling me with an arm around my waist until I'm right up against him: chest to chest, stomach to stomach, hips to hips.

We sway. We're not even really dancing. But our proximity sets my body on fire, and I can feel what it does to him, too. Right up against me, he's half-hard, his posture exposing the hunger he feels.

I want closer, too. With one hand clasped in his, the other on his shoulder slides around his neck, then—slowly—into his hair. Elliot tucks our joined hands against his chest and then bends, pressing his cheek to mine.

"I love you," he says. "I'm sorry that I can't help my body's reaction to you."

"It's okay." I count out fifteen heartbeats before I'm able to add, "I love you, too."

He reacts to this with a tiny catch in his breath, a slight tremor in his shoulders—it's the first time he's ever heard me say it.

"You do?"

My cheek rubs along his when I nod. "I always have. You know that."

His lips are close enough to my ear that they brush against the shell when he asks, "Then why did you leave me?"

"I was hurt," I tell him. "And then I was broken."

Now he reacts. His feet come to a stop on the floor. "What *broke* you?"

"I don't want to talk about it here."

He pulls back, eyes flickering between mine as if there might be different messages communicated there. "Do you want to leave?"

I don't know. I do want to leave . . . but not to talk.

"Whenever you can," I say. "Later is fine."

"Where?"

Anywhere. All I know is that I need to be alone with him. Need to in this restless, straining way. I *want* to be alone with him.

I want *him*.

"I don't care where we go." I slide my other hand up his chest, around his neck and into his hair. Elliot's breath catches when he realizes what I'm doing: pulling him down to kiss me.

His lips come over mine in a fever, hands moving to cup my face, to hold me close as if my kiss is a delicate, fleeting thing.

His kiss is an aching prayer; devotion pours from him. He sucks my bottom lip, my top, tilting his head for more, and deeper, before I pull back, reminding him with a tiny flicker

337

of my eyes where we are and just how many people have noticed.

Elliot doesn't care about them. He takes my hand, leading me down the steps from the lit dance floor and into the gardens.

Our shoes swish through wet grass. I pull my dress up into my fist, jogging after him.

Deeper down the trail we go, into blackness, where all I hear is the buzzing of insects and the ripple of wind through the leaves. The voices disappear into the light behind us.

then

sunday, december 31

eleven years ago

Dad materialized at my side, holding a flute of champagne for him and a flute of what smelled suspiciously like ginger ale for me.

"Not even one glass of hooch?" I asked, pretending to scowl. "This party sucks."

Dad took this in stride with an impressed sweep of his attention around the room, because this party, quite obviously, did not suck. It was in the Garden Court at the Palace Hotel and was packed with beautiful people who were dripping jewelry and were—thankfully—surprisingly lively. The entire room had been decorated with thousands—maybe even a million tiny white lights. We were spending New Year's in the heart of a constellation. Even though I was away from Elliot, I couldn't exactly complain.

It was only a few minutes away from midnight, and the crowd was growing thick around us, pressing in closer to the bar so everyone could get a drink in hand before the New Year was rung in.

Tucked beneath my arm, my clutch began to vibrate. I looked up at Dad, who gave me the single nod of permission, and stepped out into the hall.

I glanced down at my phone. Eleven fifty-five. Elliot was calling me.

"Hey," I said, breathless.

"Hey, Mace." His voice was thick and happy.

I bit my lip to keep from laughing. "Have we had a couple of cocktails, Mr. Petropoulos?"

"One or two." He laughed. "Apparently I'm a light-weight."

"Because you're not a drinker." Moving deeper into the quiet hallway, I leaned against the wall there. The clamor from the party faded into an array of background noise: voices, glasses clinking, music. "Where are you?"

"Party." He fell quiet, and I heard shuffling in the background, the sound of a doorbell in the distance. "At, um . . . someone's house."

"'Someone'?"

He hesitated, and with the intake of air I could hear on the other line, the way he held it, I knew what was coming. "Christian's."

I was quiet for a beat. I knew only enough about Christian to feel faintly uneasy about his influence. Things always turned too wild when Christian was around, at least that's how Elliot spun it. "Ah."

"Don't 'Ah' me, missy," he said, voice low and slow. "It's a house party. It's a party with lots of people in a big house."

"I know," I said, taking a deep breath. "Just be careful. Are you having fun?"

"No."

Grinning at this, I asked, "Who else is there?"

"People," he mumbled. "Brandon. Christian." A pause. "Emma." My stomach clenched. "Other people from school," he quickly added.

I heard something fall and crash in the background, Elliot's quiet "Ow, stop," and a girl laughing his name before he seemed to move somewhere quieter. "And, I don't know, Mace. *You're* not here. So I don't really give a shit who is."

I laughed tightly. This call felt like a shove forward, into a life where we had beers together, and dorm rooms, and hours upon hours alone. I felt our future looming, teasing.

Tempting.

"Where are *you*?" he asked.

"I'm at the glitzy soiree."

"Right, right. Black tie. *Society*."

I looked back over my shoulder into the wide ballroom. "Everyone around me is hammered."

"Sounds awful."

"Sounds like your party," I shot back, watching Dad across the room, talking with a pretty blonde. "Dad seems to be having a decent time."

"Are you wearing something fancy?"

I looked down at my shimmering green dress. "Yeah. A green sequined dress. I look like a mermaid."

"Like, Disney princess?"

I laughed. "No." Running my hand down my stomach, I added, "But I think you'd like it."

"Is it short?"

"Not really. Knee length?"

"Tight?"

Biting my lip, I lowered my voice. Unnecessarily, for sure: the party was roaring. "Not *skin*-tight. Fitted . . . ish."

"Eh," he grunted. "Wouldn't you rather be wearing jeans and a sweatshirt with me? On my lap?"

I giggled at his missing filter. "Definitely."

"I love you."

I froze, closing my eyes at the sound of these words.

Say it again, I thought, and then immediately wondered if this was really how I wanted to hear him confess this: while he was drunk—for the first time, as far as I knew—and many miles away.

"I do," he growled. "I love you so fucking much. I *love* you, and I lust you and *want* you. I love you as the person I want to be with forever. I just . . . Macy? Will you marry me?"

Time stopped. Planets aligned and then shifted apart. Years passed. The voices and music and clinking of glasses all around me faded to nothing and all I could hear was the echo of his blurted proposal.

I stuttered through several sounds before I was able to speak.

Unfortunately, *"What?"* was the first thing to come out coherently.

"Shit," he groaned. "*Shit*, I just totally messed that up."

"Elliot . . . ?"

His voice came out muffled when he said, "Will you come see me? I want to ask you to marry me. In person."

I looked around the room, my heart a blazing thunderbolt in my chest. "I . . . Ell . . . I'm not sure I can come up tonight. This is huge."

"It *is* huge. But it's real."

"Okay. I hear you," I said, pinching my eyes closed. He told me he loved me and asked me to marry him in one conversation. Over the *phone*. "It's just . . . there is no way Dad would let me get on the road with all the drunk people."

He was silent for so long that I looked down at my phone to make sure I hadn't lost the call.

"Elliot?"

"Do you love *me*?"

I exhaled, blinked away tears. This wasn't how I wanted this conversation—how I wanted to discuss our *future*—but here it was, in my face, demanding to happen like this. "You know I do. I don't want to do this over the phone."

"I know you don't, but do you know what I mean? Do you *want* to marry me? Do you want to make this forever? At Goat Rock, and the library, and walking everywhere, and traveling. Do you want to touch me and be with me and wake up with my mouth on you and do you want me to be the one to give you orgasms or . . . fuck, watch you have them or whatever? Do you think about a life with me or marrying me?"

"Ell—"

"I do," he said in a breathless rush. "All the time I do, Macy."

I almost couldn't speak, my pulse was firing so heavily. "You know I do, too."

"Come to me tonight, please, Macy, please."

Noisemakers started blowing and confetti fell from invisible containers somewhere high above my head, but all I heard was the crackle of the line.

"I'll come next weekend, okay?"

He sighed: a universe of weight buried in the sound. "Do you promise?"

"Of course I promise." I looked across the room and saw Dad walking toward me, a rare wide smile lighting up his face. Noise filled the other end of the phone and I could hardly hear Elliot anymore.

"Macy? I can't hear you! It's super loud here."

"Ell, go have fun, but be careful, okay? You can give me my New Year's kiss next Saturday."

"'Kay." He paused and I knew what he was waiting for me to say, but I wasn't going to say it on the phone. Especially not when I would have to yell it and I wasn't even sure if he would remember it.

"Good night," I said. He went quiet, and I looked at the phone briefly before bringing it back to my ear. "Ell?"

"Night, Mace."

The line clicked dead.

I don't think I could have described a single thing about the party after that phone call. After a hug and a dance with my dad, I paced around the hall outside the event room for about a half hour.

I hated not being with Elliot for that conversation.

I hated that we'd crossed this enormous line, that we'd acknowledged a future for us—outside the closet, in the real world, with a real relationship—and he'd been miles and miles away from me, and drunk.

I hated how he'd sounded when he said good night.

"Macy, why are you out here?" Dad asked. His shoes

clicked on the marble as he made his way to me, and the roar of the party felt like cold water spilling across my skin. "You want to leave?"

I looked up at him, nodded, and burst into tears.

"I don't understand the problem," Dad said, maneuvering into a sharp turn. I eyed him to make sure he was really sober. I hadn't seen him drinking, but he seemed about as mentally collected as I felt. "You had a good conversation with Elliot, and you're upset about it?"

"I just don't like how the call ended," I admitted. "I felt like he really wanted me there."

"I realize you're home more than you're up there, but that's how you two have always done it. What's the stress?" Dad asked, always logical. To be fair, he didn't have all the details. I didn't tell him that Elliot said he loved me. I certainly didn't tell him that Elliot had proposed.

"It just felt . . . weird."

Unlike Elliot, my Dad rarely pressed.

After twenty minutes of silence, Dad pulled into our driveway and slowly shut off the car. Turning to me, he said quietly, "Help me understand."

"He's my best friend," I began, feeling the tightening of tears in my throat. "I think we're both nervous about what happens when we figure out what we're doing for college, and what we do after this—after our lives aren't just punctu-ated by weekend trips. It felt bad tonight, the way the call ended, and I don't know what I'd do if something bad hap-pened between us." I sat, staring at the dashboard in the qui-etly ticking car. "Sometimes I wonder if we should just be friends, so that I don't have to worry about ever losing him."

Dad pursed his lips, thinking. "So he's your Laís."

My eyes filled with tears again at the sound of my moth-er's name. I hadn't heard him say it in years.

"You're both young, but . . . if he *is* that person for you," Dad continued, "you won't be able to just be friends. You'll want to give him everything, to show him every way you love him."

Tears spilled, running down my cheeks.

"I'd take any amount of time with her," he whispered, turning to look at me. "I would have taken anything I could get. I don't regret one moment of loving her, even though it still hurts that she's gone."

I nodded, throat tight. "I already feel like I'm wasting so much time away from him."

"It won't always be that way."

"Can I drive up tonight?" I asked him.

He stared at me for a long, quiet beat. "You're serious?"

"Yeah."

Closing his eyes, he took a few deep breaths. "You'll be careful?"

Relief flooded my limbs. "I promise."

Dad looked forward, out the windshield at our driveway, to his old car parked just beside this new one. "I filled up the Volvo this morning. You can take it."

I leaned over the console, wrapping my arms around him. "You'll call me as soon as you get there?"

Nodding into his neck, I promised.

now

sunday, december 31

Elliot comes to a stop in a tight thicket of olive trees, turning to stare at me. This far out the sound of crickets is deafening; the wedding party is a distant buzz. I imagine we walked half a mile away, down a wide path that went from manicured, to dusty, to farmland.

Jesus Christ, where do we start?

I want to start with touching.

He might want to start with words, and explanations, and apologies—mine *and* his. There's still so much I need to tell him.

His chest rises and falls with the force of his breath, and

my own lungs seem to be flapping around inside me, struggling to pull in air.

I expect him to say something, but instead he just falls to his knees in front of me, wrapping his arms around my hips and pressing his face to my stomach. Frozen for a moment, I stare down at the top of his head, trying to translate the shaking of his shoulders.

He's crying.

"No, no," I whisper. My hands go into his hair, tilting his face to me, and I lower myself, push him back against a tree, crawl down to him, over him until his face is right up against mine, so close he's blurry. So close he's the only thing I can see. I slide his glasses up over his forehead and off his face, placing them carefully in the grass nearby.

"What are we doing?" he whispers.

"I missed you." I bend, kissing his neck, his jaw.

He pulls me back by my shoulders, and I watch two heavy tears roll over his cheekbone. "I thought I would never touch you again."

"I thought that, too."

He bites his lower lip, eyes wide. "I'll take anything you give me. Is that pathetic?"

I lean in, lips touching his, inhaling the clean smell of his aftershave, the sharp scent of grass, needing oxygen to stay conscious for all of this.

His mouth opens against mine, and he sits up with a sharp inhale, hands cupping my jaw again. Urgently, he comes back for more, tilting his head, biting and sucking, and I need deeper, more. I need all of him. His moans are muted by my lips and teeth and breath. His hands come up beneath my dress, pushing it to my waist while I tug his bow tie loose, unbuttoning his shirt.

Cold fingers slide up the inside of my thigh. His chest is so warm under my hands, though, and I dig in, sliding my palms over his collarbone and down to his stomach, wanting to feel every inch.

He grunts out some unintelligible words when he feels me through my underwear. And then his fingers slide up my navel, carefully digging down inside the lace, and I push up to my knees above him, helping give him access to the place I need his touch more than I need anything else in the galaxy.

"Are you wet like this for me?" he asks, pulling back to look up at my face. His fingers push into me, thumb stroking. "This is *me*?"

I nod and his disbelief is contagious; it's what makes every touch feel amplified, makes me move with him, biting him while he touches me. It's what sends my body up a tight spiral staircase, one destination, just there, just two strokes higher. Two more.

"Ell."

"Yeah."

"I'm going to come."

His smile curves the single word: "Good."

I fumble for him, his belt, his zipper.

"Wait," I tell my body. "Oh God, I'm close."

Wait.

Hold on. Wait.

He doesn't stop what he's doing when he pulls back and looks up at my face. "You want . . . ?"

His fingertips glide over me, tighter, faster.

Clumsily, I dig in, finding the heavy heat of him, closing my hand around it, shifting so I'm there, tilting him up, making him wet with me.

He groans as he sinks in, and the sound hits me somewhere ancient and savage.

The relief of it—of him thick and hungry, finally sliding deep in and out of me—is a melting star, spreading fire into my bloodstream. He gasps that he doesn't want to come, never wants to come, doesn't ever want to stop. I'm already on the sharp edge, and our instant, frantic fucking gets me there through a jagged set of thrusts. Him up, me over.

The crickets and Elliot go quiet at the sharp, aching cries tearing out of me.

In the silence that follows, I can feel the drum of his pulse where my lips meet his throat. But then his hands come to my jaw, cupping, tilting my face to his.

"Yeah?" he whispers. I nod in his hands, feeling the weight of him inside me. "Holy mother of God," he says into a kiss, "this is unreal."

Everything narrows down to the tiny shifts of my hips

over his, and the soft sucking kisses. I'm barely moving. Just rocking, squeezing. It means I'm not expecting the tight way he tells me he's close.

I press the question against his lips: "Do you want me to stop?"

"Only if you're not on something." His tongue meets mine and he groans. "Macy, honey, I'm so close."

I'm not sure why it's this moment that makes the reality sink in, that we're making love, still mostly dressed, somewhere in the gardens at his brother's wedding. But when Elliot comes, I want his hands and the cool, humid air on my skin, not on the crushed silk of my dress. Every time we've touched each other, we've been mostly dressed.

I reach back, unzipping, pushing the straps off my shoulders and quickly doing away with the tiny strapless bra. My dress falls to my waist.

His mouth is there, and his words of approval—for the heat and sweetness of me, for the feel of my breasts on his tongue. Against my belly is the scratch of his open, starched shirt, and inside I feel him climb, feel him need more than the gentle shifting he's getting, and his hands find my breasts, holding them for his open mouth.

We are a crescendo again, faster now, I'm bouncing on him three,

oh

four five six times

"Fuck."

He bites me,

wild.

"*Yes.*"

Elliot stills me when his iron grip drops to my hips, and he's jerking into me, his mouth open, teeth bared on my breast.

It will leave a mark.

But even after he's finished he grazes his teeth back and forth, tongue stroking the tight peak, soothing the site of his gentle attack. I feel the way he spasms still. His breaths are tight puffs of air against my breast.

My fingers make a tangle in his hair, holding him to me. Goose bumps spread across my skin as his hands slide around, cupping my backside, holding me tight against him.

He came inside me.

He's *still* inside me.

What did we just do?

And how have I gone this long without him?

Making love to him suddenly feels vital, like air and water and warmth.

He turns his face up to mine, expectantly, and it's only a tiny shift forward for my mouth to meet his in this new, lazy relief.

It's both familiar and foreign. His skin is coarser with stubble, his lips stronger. Inside me, I know, he's thicker.

I start to move off him—worried about making a mess of

his tuxedo—but he holds me steady, his hips to mine. "Not yet," he says against my mouth. "I want to stay here. I still don't believe this is happening."

"Me either." I am lost in the lazy sweep of his tongue, the tiny kisses that melt into deeper ones.

"I might want to do it again."

I smile. "Me too."

He moves his mouth to my neck, his left hand coming up to cup my breast.

"Is it weird," I begin, "that I felt like I was having sex with someone new and old at the same time?"

This makes him laugh, and he bends, kissing my chest. Leaning back, he whispers, "Want to know something even weirder?"

My eyes fall closed. "I want to know everything."

And for the first time in over a decade, I really do.

"It was years before I was with someone other than you. You were the only woman I was with until I was . . . well, for a long time."

His words hit the blank wall of my sex haze, and then dread falls over me like blackness.

"I've loved you my whole life," Elliot continues, his lips moving against my collarbone. Slowly, I open my eyes, and he looks up at me. "At least from the minute I ever thought about love, and sex, and women."

He's still inside me.

He smiles, and the moonlight catches the sharp angle of

his jaw. "I've never wanted anyone the way I want you. It took a long time before I wanted anyone else, physically, at all."

It's a little like being in the eye of a tornado. All around me, things are happening, but inside my head, it's so quiet.

At my silence, his eyes widen first, and then fall closed. "Oh, my God. I just realized what I've said."

then

Just off the Richmond Bridge, I called Elliot, listening through the speaker as the phone rang and rang, eventually going to voice mail. About ten minutes into my drive it had occurred to me that I didn't know where in town Christian lived, and I didn't know how long Elliot would be there. It was after one in the morning now—he might even just be home, in bed, and I wouldn't be able to get to him without waking up the rest of the house.

Highway 101 stretched out dark ahead of me, dotted with the occasional burning taillights of another car. It was otherwise empty, with clumps of drivers getting on and off the freeway around the dotted small towns: Novato, Peta-luma, Rohnert Park . . . In Santa Rosa, I tried calling again, and this time an unfamiliar male voice answered.

"Elliot's phone." Noise blared, drunken and raucous, in the background.

A sour combination of relief and irritation twisted in me. It was nearly two in the morning and he—or at least his phone—was still at the party?

"Is Elliot around?" I asked.

"Who's calling?"

I paused. "Who's answering?"

The guy inhaled, and his answer came out tight, like he had just taken a giant hit off something. "Christian."

"Christian," I said, "this is Macy."

He let out a long, controlled breath. "Elliot's Macy?"

Someone in the background let out a sharp "Dude."

"Yes," I confirmed, "his girlfriend, Macy."

"Oh, shit." The line went quiet, muffled, as if someone was holding a hand there. When he came back, he said sim-ply, "Elliot's not here."

"Did he go home without his phone?" I asked.

"Nah."

Confused, I pressed, "So how is he not there if you know he didn't go home?"

"Macy." A slow, drunken laugh, and then, "I am way too high to follow that."

"Okay," I said calmly, "can you just give me your address?"

He rattled off an address on Rosewood Drive, adding, "Second house on the left. You'll hear it."

"Chris," someone protested in the background, "*don't.*"

Christian let out another low laugh. "What the fuck do I care?"

And then he hung up.

Christian's house was new, and therefore large for the Craftsman-modest Healdsburg, set on a hill and overlooking a vineyard. He was right: I could hear it as soon as I turned onto his street. Cars jammed the long driveway, fanning out messily toward the curb. I parked in the first empty stretch of street, several houses down. Zipping my puffy jacket over my dress, I left my heels in the car, grabbed some flip-flops from the trunk, and trudged back up the hill.

It seemed silly to even bother knocking. The door was slightly ajar, noise pouring out, so I just pushed inside, stepping over a wide pile of shoes that seemed paradoxically thoughtful given the state of the rest of the house. There were cans, bottles, and stubbed-out joints on nearly every flat surface. Blaring music and television battled from down the hall. On the living room couch, two guys were passed out, and a third sat with a game controller in his hand, playing *Call of Duty*.

"Have you seen Elliot?" I asked, yelling above the hammering of fictional gunfire.

The guy looked up, glanced over to the kitchen, and then shrugged.

I headed to the kitchen.

The room was huge, and a complete disaster. Blender drinks had been attempted and abandoned. A pyramid of beer cans sat on a sturdy marble island, surrounded by a wreath of broken chips, smears of salsa, a trail of M&M's. The sink was full of smudged glassware and a tall bong.

"He's upstairs," someone said behind me. I turned, and recognized Christian from the photos on Elliot's desk. He was tall—not as tall as Elliot, but wider, with an ill-advised goatee, and a beer stain on his Chico State Wildcats T-shirt. His eyes were bloodshot and dilated nearly to black. At his side, another guy stared wide-eyed at me, looking like he was going to be sick. It was Brandon.

Elliot's two best friends.

"Upstairs?" I repeated. Christian lifted his chin in a nod, rolling a toothpick from one side of his mouth to the other.

"He's really wasted," Brandon said, following me when I turned to head out of the kitchen and upstairs. His voice grew increasingly desperate as my foot hit the first step. "Macy, I wouldn't. I think he's been sick."

"Then I'll take him home." Even to me, my voice sounded hollow, tinny, like it was being projected from speakers in the faraway corners of the vaulted staircase.

"We'll bring him home." Brandon wrapped a gentle hand around my elbow. "Let him sleep it off."

My pulse beat in my throat, in my temples. I wasn't sure what I would find . . . but no, that isn't quite right. I think I knew. I understood Christian's laconic smirk and Brandon's buzzing anxiety. Looking back, it's hard to know whether I was prescient to head up there, or whether it was just so *obvious*.

"I would just head home, Macy," Brandon pleaded. "When he wakes up, I'll have him call you."

His voice continued as a hum in the background, following me all the way up the stairs and to the only closed door, at the very end of the hall. I pushed inside and stopped.

A long leg hung over the side of the unmade bed. Elliot's shoes were still on, still *tied*, but his jeans and boxers were at his knees and his shirt was shoved up under his armpits, exposing the lines of his chest, the dark trail of hair on his navel.

Brandon was right: Elliot was passed out.

But so was Emma, lying naked across his torso.

I took a step back, right into Brandon's chest.

"Oh, my God," I whispered.

I'd known heartbreak before, but this was a different sensation, like a lit match held to the bloody organ inside, holding steady, waiting patiently for it to dry out, harden into coal, catch fire.

I love you so fucking much.

I love you, and I lust you and want you.

I love you as the person I want to be with forever.

Will you marry me?

"Oh, my God."

"Macy, it really isn't what you think," Brandon said, cupping his hands on my shoulders. "Please trust me."

"It looks like he had sex with her," I said numbly, shrugging him off. As much as the scene horrified me, I couldn't look away. Emma's mouth was open on his chest as she snored. Elliot's dick hung limp along his thigh.

I'd never really seen him naked before, never just . . . *looked*.

Brandon shifted anxiously. "It's her, Macy. Elliot wouldn't—"

"Oh, shit," Christian said, coming up beside me. "Not a good look, Ell."

I made some gasping, choking sound that he seemed to interpret as a question.

"Nah, they have a history. Just . . . let it go," Christian said, and then held in a rumbling belch and punched his chest with his fist. "It's not really a thing. They just fuck around sometimes."

I turned, bursting past them down the hall, my feet fumbling down the stairs, through the kitchen and then out the front door to the cold, stark air where I couldn't seem to breathe. I tried to pull in a breath, but it was like I'd been punched over and over in the diaphragm.

Two thirty in the morning on New Year's, and I was the most sober but least safe driver on the road. Through a wall of tears, I navigated clumsily down the winding road, zigzagging up the narrow hill and down the gravelly slope of the driveway. I screamed at the windshield, and nearly turned around a handful of times because I almost couldn't believe my own memory. The two of them lying there.

I didn't look at Elliot's house as I vaulted up the front steps, afraid I would pound on the door, demand that he come downstairs, even though I knew he wasn't there.

I didn't know much in that moment, but I knew I couldn't make it back to Berkeley in one piece.

Inside, the house was ice cold. Wood was neatly stacked in the back pallet—I could make a fire, have something to eat to settle the grinding in my gut—but I could barely make it to the couch. I pulled a blanket from the back of the easy chair and curled up on the floor.

Honestly, I don't remember anything else but the feel of the cold floor along the right side of my body. I think my brain must have shut down immediately. Some self-preservation instinct didn't want me to see his naked hips anymore, see the familiar press of her hand to his navel. Some protective piece of my mind didn't want to recall the thick smell of that room—the cloud of bodies, and sweat, and beer, and sex—or the casual way Christian referenced their intimate history.

But was he right? Had that been what it was like all week

long, and for most of their lives? Emma and Elliot, casually hooking up, filling the tedium of their days with each other? Texting each other to hang when there was nothing else to do. Hooking up at the park because—why not? I had no doubt that Elliot loved me—I knew he did, felt it in the marrow of my bones—but I was there barely a third of the time, and the other two-thirds, there was Emma. Every day at school, all year long: accessible, convenient, familiar.

I had no idea who Real-Life Elliot was. My Elliot existed only on certain days, only in the confines of our library closet.

I don't know him at all. I don't know him at all. That was the horrible thought that threaded through my dreams—dreams of running into him on a bus and not recognizing him, dreams of passing him in the hall and feeling the uncomfortable echo that I'd somehow missed something important but didn't know what it was.

now

sunday, december 31

I shift my hips up, feeling the clench in my chest when Elliot's body slips from mine. I feel him retreat beneath me, his eyes filled with an ache that seems to build the longer we're silent.

"You never let me explain what happened," he says.

I can't meet his eyes. It goes so much deeper than this, but even though these details seem tiny now, I know it's where we have to start. "You said you loved me that night," I remind him, "for the first time."

He nods eagerly. "I know."

"You asked me to *marry* you."

Elliot reaches for my arm, circling his fingers around my wrist. "I meant it. I had a ring."

I look at him in shock. "If I'd said yes, would you still have fucked Emma?"

"Okay." He stands, pulling his pants up, buckling his belt. "Okay." His shirt hangs loose, hair remains a mess from my fingers. Elliot looks down at me, backlit by the moon and the distant glow of the party. Bending to retrieve his glasses, he slides them on. "Do you know how many times I've told you this story in my head?"

"Probably about as many times as I've tried to pretend I didn't see what I saw."

He crouches. "I didn't know what happened until a few days later."

"What?"

"I mentioned to Christian that you hadn't called me back, and he said, 'Probably because she saw Emma naked on top of you.'"

I blink away. I still see the image, so clearly.

"And the worst bit of that," he says quietly, "is that until he said it, I didn't know I'd been with *Emma*. She wasn't there in the morning."

I need to digest this for two, three, four breaths. "You woke up with your pants at your knees, Ell. That didn't clue you in?"

"This is the part I can't figure out," he whispers. "In my head, it was you. In my head, *you* came up to the party, *you* found me passed out on Chris's bed. In my head, *you* went down on me, climbed on top of me. I don't remember having sex with Emma that night. I remember having sex with *you*."

"Can you hear yourself?" I stare at him, mouth agape. Inside my rib cage, my heart is a barreling thunder at the words *went down on me*. I never went down on him—but she did? "Do you hear the bullshit meter screaming in the background? You're telling me that the night you had sex with Emma, you thought it was *me*?"

Elliot groans, raking a hand through his hair. "I realize how insane it sounds. Even at the time, I couldn't piece the night together, and I've had eleven years to try to make sense of it. I was so drunk, Mace. I remember waking up to the feel of your mouth on me. I remember touching your hair, talking to you, encouraging. And when I look back, I still see *your* face when she climbed on me."

He shakes his head, squeezing his eyes closed, and when he says this, I remember what Brandon started to say, something about how *Elliot wouldn't*.

"I woke up," he continued, "and had a moment of blistering embarrassment because Chris's bedroom door was open and a few people were walking around cleaning shit up. I was all alone with my dick hanging out. I texted you asking where you'd gone. Two days I went along with things, thinking I'd had drunk sex with my girlfriend at a party. I thought you were embarrassed or angry at me for being so wasted, and that's why you hadn't called."

Is *this* his truth—some quiet, heartbreaking mistake? Part of me aches for this version of things, wanting to believe it so badly that it makes my teeth clench. The other part of me wants to scream that this tiny whimper of a drunken misunderstanding unraveled everything. It should have been something intentional, something *enormous*. Something worthy of what came after.

"If you'd have let me explain . . ." he says quietly, looking at me in bewilderment. "I called you over, and over—"

"I know you did."

I was aware that Elliot called several times a day, for months. I never checked my old email account afterward, but if I had, there would probably be scores of unread messages there, too.

I knew his regret was enormous.

But that wasn't ever the problem.

"I fucked up," he says, "but Macy, even as bad as that is—and I know it was bad—was it really worth this?" He gestures between us. "Was it really enough to make you just . . . drop me? After everything? To not talk to me—*ever* again?"

I stare at him, plucking words from the masses and arranging and rearranging them into sentences. The Emma thing feels so small now. It was just the first domino. "We had this deep, unbreakable trust, you know—and you broke that, you did—but it's not just that. It's . . . it's me. It's been me, too."

"You don't think I deserved the chance to explain?" he

asks, misunderstanding my incoherence, restrained emotion making his voice tight.

I can tell he's waiting for an answer. And the answer is yes, of course he deserved a chance to explain. Of course he did. In an alternate reality, he would have called me later that day, and I would have answered.

"I loved you," he says. "I have *always* loved you. There was never anyone but you for me, you knew that."

I fumble through my words: "It was a really bad . . . it was a bad night—"

"I *know* it was bad, Mace." His voice is growing harder, nearly disbelieving. "We were each other's first love, first sex, first *everything*. But come on. That's a knockdown, drag-out fight. That isn't . . . disappearing for a decade."

"It wasn't just that." My heart and mouth seem to agree that we cannot, in fact, do this right now.

Metal screeches against asphalt in my ears. I close my eyes, shaking my head to clear it.

"Do you have any idea what it's been like?" he asks, getting more frustrated now in the face of my inarticulate fluster. "Every day, I woke up and wondered if that would be the day I'd see you again. And if I did, how would it go? I missed you, so much. I'm twenty nine, and I've never loved another woman." He stares at me, unblinking. "And every woman I've been with knows it, unfortunately for them."

I open my mouth to speak, but nothing comes out. He stares at me, bewildered.

"You want to know what Rachel meant about how fucked-up I was? Well, here's one example: the first person to go down on me after you left had to sit there while I broke down like a fucking maniac," he says, "trying to explain why I didn't want her to give me *head*."

"I'm sorry." I cover my face, breathing in, breathing out. Item twenty-seven on Mom's list was to remind me to breathe. In and out, ten times, when I'm stressed.

One . . .

Two . . .

"I'm sorry, too. I want this," he whispers. "I want *you*."

Three . . .

I want you, too, I think. *But I don't even know how to tell you that Emma is the least of it. Another woman giving you head is the least of it.*

"Talk to me, Mace," he urges. "Please."

Four . . .

Five . . .

"I want you," he repeats, and his voice carries a strange distance. "But I'm realizing now that maybe I shouldn't."

Six . . .

Seven . . .

By the time I reach ten, my hands are no longer shaking when I lower them. But because I didn't expect Elliot to leave, I never heard him walk away.

In the dark night, the reception on the outdoor porch is a beacon of tiny lights and stars thrown from candlelight traveling through glasses of champagne. Heat lamps placed at regular intervals are warm enough in the night chill to make the humid air warp around the slow-dancing couples.

I find George to the left of the dance floor, near the wedding cake, which has already been cut and shared. His cheeks are red, smile wide, eyes watery with happy inebriation.

"Mace!" he yells, pulling me into a lumbering hug. "Where's my brother?"

"I was going to ask you the same thing."

He reaches up, pulling a small twig from my hair and *good God* it only occurs to me now that I have no idea what I look like coming out of the gardens after fucking Elliot.

George grins. "I suspect you have a better idea than I do."

Liz comes up beside him, grinning at her tipsy husband. "Macy! Whoa, you look . . ." Understanding comes into her eyes and she barks out a laugh. "Where's Elliot?"

"The question of the hour," George murmurs.

"I'm right here."

We turn, finding him standing just to the side, holding a half-finished glass of champagne. The warm flush I felt on his cheek, against my lips, is gone. In its place is a pale stare, a slash of a frown. His tie is missing, shirt unbuttoned at the collar and smudged with both dirt and lipstick. Looking at him now, it is doubly obvious what we've been doing.

I smile at him, trying to communicate with my eyes that there's more to discuss here, but he's not looking at me anymore. Tilting the flute to his lips, he downs the rest, places it on the tray of a passing waiter, and then says, "Macy, did you need me to drop you off at your motel?"

Shock causes a cold wave to pass through me. George and Liz go quiet and then shuffle away under a haze of secondhand mortification. My heart takes off, a snare drum leading into a cymbal crash as I realize I'm being asked to leave.

"It's fine," I tell him, "I can grab a Lyft."

He nods. "Cool."

I take a step forward, reaching for him, and he stares at my hand on his arm with a frown, as if it's caked in mud.

"Can we talk tomorrow?" I ask.

His face twists, and he picks up another glass of champagne, downing this one in the time it takes for the waiter to offer me one, and for me to decline. Elliot grabs another before the anxious waiter ducks away.

"Sure we can talk tomorrow," he says, waving the glass. "We can talk about the weather. Maybe our favorite type of pie? Or—oh—we haven't yet talked about the merits of a Crock-Pot versus a pressure cooker. We could do that?"

"I mean finish what we've started," I whisper, realizing we've drawn the attention of a few family members. "We weren't finished."

Alex watches us at a distance with wide, worried eyes.

"Weren't we? I thought we had the grand finale. You did what you're best at," he says, smiling grimly. "You shut down."

"You walked away," I retort.

He laughs harshly, shaking his head and echoing in a murmur, "*I* walked away."

Softening, I say, "Tomorrow . . . I'll come by."

Elliot lifts the glass, swallowing four gulps and wiping his mouth with the back of his hand. "Sure thing, Macy."

At one in the morning, the sky feels haunted in its darkness. I climb the porch to my old summer home, skipping over the predictably broken step. Using the long-ignored key on my ring, I let myself inside, where it's even colder than it is in the woods; the insulation keeps the chill stored within the dark plaster walls. I turn on lights as I go, and kneel to set a small fire in the wood-burning stove.

Obviously, if I've been here only once in the past ten years, I should remember the exact dates, but I don't. I only know it was a week, maybe two, before I left for my sophomore year at Tufts, and we drove up at night to sift through our possessions and move all the cherished things into closets we could lock, to keep curious vacation renters from taking anything. The memory of that night feels like a blur of watery color streaking through fog.

Upstairs, I sift through the other keys on my ring, finding

the smaller one, and slide it into the lock on Dad's closet door. It enters in jagged steps, sticking halfway through, requiring a tiny wiggle before it clicks and turns with a rusty protest.

His closet opens with a whiff of musty air, and my stomach drops when the scent and realization merge: I'll need to throw most of this out. He kept some shirts and pants up here. Hiking boots, a fly-fishing vest. There are photo albums on the shelf up top, a nativity diorama I made in fourth grade. Letters from Mom. And, at the back, the stack of questionable magazines.

My butt lands on the floor before I realize I've been sliding down the door frame. Beneath the smell of mildew, there is the unmistakable smell of *him*: the Danish cigarettes, his aftershave, the bright linen scent of laundry. I pull a shirt from a hanger—messily; the wire flies up off the rod and hits the door on the way down. Pressing the flannel to my face, I inhale, choking through a sob.

I haven't felt this way in so long. Or maybe I never felt this particular emotion: I *want* to cry. I want to positively sob. I give it full access, letting it tear through me into these awful howls that echo off the high ceilings and shake my torso, curling me forward. Snot, spit: I am a mess. I feel him right there behind me but I know he isn't. I want to call out to him, to ask him what's for breakfast. I want to hear the even cadence of his footsteps, the intermittent snap of the newspaper as he reads. All these instincts seem to live so close to the surface that they warp and weave through the fabric of possibility. Maybe he *is* downstairs, reading. Maybe he is just getting out of the shower.

It's these tiny reminders that hurt, the tiny moments where you think—let me just call out to him. *Ah, right. He's dead.* And you wonder how it happened, did it hurt, does he see me here in a sodden, sobbing puddle on his floor?

This is the only thing that interrupts the torrent, pulling a thick laugh from my throat. If Dad ever found me crying like this inside his closet, he would stare down—befuddled—before slowly lowering himself to a crouch, and reaching out, gently running his hand down my arm.

"What is it, Mace?"

"I miss you," I tell him. "I wasn't ready. I still needed you."

He would get it, now. "I miss you, too. I needed you, too."

"Are you hurt? Are you lonely?" I swipe an arm across my nose. "Are you with Mom?"

"Macy."

I close my eyes, feeling more tears slide across my temples and into my hair. "Does she remember me?"

"Macy."

"Do either of you remember you had a daughter?"

I'm not myself, I know I'm not, but I'm not embarrassed to be found like this, either, especially not by Dad. At least this way he'll see how loved he was.

Strong arms come beneath my legs, around my back, and

I'm lifted from the fog of mildew and Dad, and carried down the hall.

"I'm sorry," I say, again and again. "I'm sorry I didn't call. I'm sorry, Dad. It's my fault."

I'm still on his lap when he sits on my bed. He's so warm, so solid.

I haven't been this small in years.

"Mace, honey, look at me."

My vision is blurry, but it's easy to make out his features. Greenish-gold eyes, black hair.

Not Dad, Elliot. Still in his tux, eyes bloodshot behind his glasses.

"There you are," he says. "Come back to me. Where did you go?"

I slide my arms around his neck, jerking him closer, squeezing my eyes closed. I smell the grass on him, the bark of the olive tree. "It's you."

"It's me."

He needs my apology, too.

"I'm sorry, Ell. I ruined everything because I forgot to call."

"I saw the lights on," he whispers. "I came over and found you like this . . . Macy Lea, tell me what's going on."

"You needed me, and I wasn't there."

He goes quiet, kissing the top of my head. "Mace . . ."

"I needed you even more," I say, and begin sobbing again. "But I couldn't figure out how to forgive you."

Elliot pushes my hair out of my face, eyes searching. "Honey, you're scaring me. Talk to me."

"I knew it wasn't your fault," I choke out, "but for so long it felt like it was."

I see the confused tears fill his eyes. "I don't understand what you . . ." He pulls me into his chest, one hand in my hair as his voice breaks. "Please tell me what's going on."

And so I do.

then

monday, january 1
eleven years ago

I woke to the sharp slam of the door, the pounding of footsteps along the entryway tiles.

"Macy?"

I groaned, cupping my stiff neck and sitting up just as Dad rounded the corner into the living room. A father's first assumption rippled through him, and he rushed to my side, crouching.

"Did he hurt you?" His accent pushed the words together into a ball of anger.

"No." I winced, stretching. Remembering. My stomach melted away. "Actually, yes."

Dad's hands made a careful trek over my shoulders and down my arms, taking my hands in his. He turned my palms over, inspecting them, and then pressed the pads of his thumbs to the centers of my hands.

I remember that touch like it was yesterday.

We linked fingers.

Realization pushed through the fog, and I registered that I was at the cabin, and Dad was here, too—in the freezing cold morning, more than seventy miles away from home. "What are you doing here?"

He gave me a hard look with soft edges. "You never called to tell me you arrived here safely. You didn't answer your phone."

Slumping into him, I mumbled, "I'm sorry," against his broad chest. "I turned it off."

He sighed a concerned sound. "What happened, *min lille blomst?*"

"He made a mistake," I told him. "A big one."

Dad pulled back to meet my eyes. "Another girl."

I nodded, and a thick sob escaped at the memory of Elliot's body, bare, just . . . lying there. Sprawled.

Dad let out a slow breath. "Didn't see that coming."

"That makes two of us."

He helped me up, curling a protective arm around my shoulders. "We'll come get the Volvo this weekend."

We'll come get the Volvo this weekend.

I wonder what ever happened to it.

Dad kept one giant hand on the steering wheel and the other curled around my fingers.

He glanced at me every five seconds or so, no doubt wishing he had Mom's list right there on the dashboard, to reference the *The first time a boy breaks her heart . . .* advice. I knew where to find it. Number thirty-two.

His eyes were worried, brows drawn . . . As much as I hated what had happened with Elliot, I loved the warmth of Dad's attention on me, the reassuring contact of his hand, the quiet questions—what did I want for dinner? Did I want to go to a movie, or stay home?

But his attention on me meant it wasn't on the road.

I'm not even sure he ever saw the car. It was a blue Corvette, merging from the onramp and already going too fast. Sixty, maybe even seventy. It cut in front of us in the slow lane, screeching into the narrowing space between us and the eighteen-wheeler ahead. The Corvette's tires skittered, his back end jerked to the side, and his brake lights went a brilliant red, right there. Right in front of us.

Was there a point when it wasn't too late? This is what I always asked myself. Could I have communicated something more than a garbled "Dad!" and a pointed finger?

Witnesses told police they thought the whole thing happened in fewer than five seconds, but it would forever happen in slow motion in my memory: I still feel Dad's worried eyes on me, not the Corvette. This was why he didn't even touch his brakes. We came on it so fast, with a deafening clash of metal, and our bodies jerked forward, airbags burst out, and I thought for a fraction of a second that it was okay. The impact was over.

Except we hadn't landed yet. When we did, it was a bruising of the driver's side against asphalt, a screaming twenty feet of sparking metal. We came to a stop on our sides. My forehead ended up near the steering wheel. My seat had crushed Dad's, with him still in it.

Later, I'd find out that the other driver was a student from Santa Rosa Junior College. His name was Curt Anderssen, and he walked away with a slight abrasion to his neck. Not from the seat belt—he wasn't even wearing one—but from the fabric of the passenger seat, where he was launched when his car spun sideways through three lanes of traffic.

Curt was unconscious at first, I think, and most of the activity focused on the far more gruesome reality of our car. I was already on the stretcher with a broken arm when Curt emerged, stoned out of his mind and laughing at his survival, until he was shocked into sobriety by the scene before him and the police with their handcuffs.

I've heard people say that they don't remember what happened immediately after being told of the death of a loved one, but I remember everything. I remember, acutely, the way my broken arm hung like a sack of bones at my side. I remember the feeling of wanting to claw my skin off, of wanting to run, because running would somehow undo what the paramedics told me.

Yes, he's gone.

Sweetheart, I need you to calm down.

I'm so sorry. We're going to take you down to Sutter, honey. You need a doctor. You need to breathe.

I remember asking over and over for them to take it back, to do more CPR, to let me try to revive him.

"Wait."

"Macy, I need you to try to breathe. Can you breathe for me?"

"Stop talking!" I screamed. "Everyone stop talking!"

I have an idea: We can start over.

Let's get back in the car, go back to the house. I just need a second to think.

We'll stay there tonight.

Or, no, let's go back further.

I won't forget to call in the first place.

I want to go back to that other heartbreak, not this one.

Today wasn't a good day to drive. If we drive today, I lose everyone.

If we drive today, I won't be a daughter anymore.

One of the police officers caught up to me easily when I clumsily rolled off the stretcher, sprinting down the freeway—away from the lights and the noise and the horrible mess of my father in the car. I can still feel the way the policeman wrapped his arms around me from behind, mindful of my broken arm, curling his body over me as I crumpled. I still remember him saying over and over that he was sorry, he was so sorry, he lost his brother the same way, he was so sorry.

Afterward, there was the intrusive numbness. Uncle Kennet came to Berkeley from Minnesota. He looked sour as we went over Dad's will and estate. He patted my back and cleared his throat a lot. Aunt Britt cleaned the house while I sat on the couch and stared at her. She got on her hands and knees, dunking a sponge into a bucket bubbling with wood soap, and scrubbed the hardwood floors for hours. It didn't feel like a loving gesture. It felt like she'd wanted to clean the house for years, and finally had the chance.

My cousins didn't come, not even for the funeral. *They have school*, Britt said. *This will be too upsetting for them. They're staying with my parents in Edina.*

I remember wishing I could find the cop who chased me down and cried with me, and bring *him* to the funeral, because he seemed to understand me better than anyone in my tiny remaining family did. But even that request felt impossible. The effort it took to eat and dress myself was already so intense, remembering a name, calling the police station was beyond my ability.

Or calling Elliot.

I was numb, but beneath it was a blistering anger, too.

Even at the time, I knew it wasn't quite right, I couldn't quite connect the dots, but the tiny kernel of hurt over Elliot with Emma got all wrapped up in Dad and why he came to get me in the first place. I needed Elliot, wanted him there. I saw the first few of his frantic texts, his insistence that it was a mistake. But then I vacillated between wanting him to know that I'd been shattered, and wanting him to know that he'd been the one to lift the mallet. And then it felt better to think he wouldn't know. He could have every other bit of my heart, but not this.

Like I said, I remember how it felt, and it felt like insanity.

Kennet and Britt took me back with them to Minnesota for four months. I picked at my cuticles until they bled. I cut off my hair with kitchen shears. I woke up at noon and counted the minutes until I could go back to bed. I didn't argue when Kennet sent me to therapy, or when he and Britt sat at the dining room table, sifting through my college acceptance letters and weighing whether to send me to Tufts or Brown.

I remember everything up to Britt's decisive tapping of the papers, her double take when she saw me standing at the foot of the stairs, and her satisfied "We've got it all figured out, Macy."

After that, there is nothing. I don't remember how they managed to secure my diploma. I don't remember sleeping my way through the summer. I don't remember packing for college.

I have to believe the administration prepped Sabrina in some way, though she insists they didn't. For sure they hand-picked her: she'd lost her brother in a car accident two summers before.

I also have to believe that leaving Berkeley saved me. By December, I could go minutes without thinking about Dad. And then an hour. And then long enough to take an exam. My coping mechanism was to wrap my thoughts—when they came—into a scrap of paper, then discard them like a piece of gum. Sabrina would let the ache tear through her. I would curl up and sleep until I was sure the thought could be wrapped up tight.

Time. I knew well enough that time numbed certain things—even death.

now

monday, january 1

Elliot sits back, eyes glassy, and stares out my bedroom window.

I watch it all pass over him: the horror, the guilt, the confusion, the dawning realization that my dad died the day after Elliot cheated, that Dad was coming to get me because I'd been so upset and hadn't called, that the last day I saw my dad was eleven years ago today . . . and for many years, I've blamed Elliot for it.

His nostrils flare, and he blinks away, jaw tight. "Oh, my God."

"I know."

"This . . . explains." Elliot shakes his head, digging a hand into the front of his hair. "Why you didn't call me back."

Quietly, I tell him, "I wasn't thinking very clearly—after—I wasn't able to separate—you. And it."

I'm so bad at words.

"Holy shit, Macy." Catching himself, he turns and pulls me back into his arms, but it's different.

Stiffer.

I've had more than a decade to deal with this; Elliot has had two minutes.

"When you stopped me outside Saul's," I say into his shirt, "and asked how Duncan was?"

He nods against me. "I had no idea."

"I thought you knew," I told him. "I thought you would have heard . . . somehow."

"We didn't have anyone else in common," he says quietly. "It was like you disappeared."

I nod, and he tightens. Something seems to occur to him. "All this time you weren't out there thinking that I intentionally slept with Emma, knew your dad died, and was fine with it, were you?"

I try my best to explain the fogginess of my logic at the time. "I don't think I really thought about it like that—that you were fine with it. I knew you were trying to call me. I knew, rationally, that you did love me. But I thought that maybe you and Emma had more of a thing going on than you ever told me. I was embarrassed and heartbroken . . ."

"We didn't have a thing," he says urgently.

"I think it was Christian who said you two hooked up sometimes—"

"Macy," Elliot says quietly, cupping my face so I'll look at him. "Christian is an idiot. You knew everything that happened with me and Emma. There wasn't some other secret layer to it."

I want to tell him that, in truth, this is all moot now, but I can see that to him, it isn't. His intent means everything.

He squints, still struggling to put this all together. "Andreas said he saw you, the next summer. Coming in here with your dad."

I shake my head, until I realize what he means. "That was my uncle Kennet." I sniff, wiping my nose again. "We drove up to pack our things and put them away." I look around us, at the familiar, now-drab paint on the walls, remembering how I didn't actually want to move a single thing. I wanted it left exactly the way it was, a museum. "That was the last time I was here."

"I was home that summer," he whispers. "All summer. I spent every day looking for you. I wondered how I could have possibly missed the moment you came by."

"We went in late. We kept the lights off." Even now, it sounds utterly ridiculous how we snuck in like burglars, using flashlights to get what we needed. Kennet thought I'd lost it again. "I was worried I would see you."

Elliot pulls back, mouth turned down. I hate that this is opening old wounds, but I hate even more that it's making fresh ones.

"Maybe 'worried' is the wrong word," I correct, though I know even in hindsight it isn't—I had a panic attack the night before Kennet and I got in the car to drive here, and I couldn't stand the thought of Elliot seeing me that way. "In the first year after Dad died, at Tufts, I had found this sort of quiet, calm place." Humming, I say, "Maybe I would have run into your arms. But I worried I would be angry, or sad. It was just so much easier to feel nothing instead."

He bends, resting his elbows on his thighs, head in his hands. Reaching up, I rub his back, small circles between his shoulder blades.

"Are you okay?" I ask.

"No." He turns and looks over his shoulder at me, giving me a wan smile to take the bite out of his answer, and then his face pales as he stares at me. I can see the realization wash over him again.

"Mace." His face falls. "How do I say I'm sorry? How do I ever—"

"Elliot, no—"

In a flash, he bolts up, sprinting out of the room. I stand to follow, but the bathroom door slams and it's quickly followed by the sound of Elliot's knees landing on the floor and him vomiting.

I press my forehead to the door, hearing the flush, the tap running, his quiet groan.

"Elliot?" My heart feels like it's been squeezed inside a fist.

"I just need a minute, Mace, I'm sorry, just give me a minute?"

I slide down the wall, setting up vigil outside the bathroom, listening to him throwing up again.

I wake up under the covers, on my bed, without any memory of how I got here. The only answer is that I fell asleep on the floor in the hall, and Elliot carried me to the bedroom, but the other side of the bed looks untouched, and he's nowhere to be seen.

A muffled cough comes from the closet, and relief flushes hot in my limbs. He's still here. It's cold, and I drag the comforter with me out of bed, peeking inside. Elliot is stretched out on the floor, hands behind his head, legs crossed at the ankle, staring up at the cracked, faded stars. He still stretches across the entire room. I haven't been back in here in years, and it seems tiny. How it used to feel like an entire world, a planet inside, amazes me.

"Hey, you," he says, smiling over at me. His eyes are bloodshot, nose red.

"Hey. You feeling better?"

"I guess. Still reeling, though." He pats the floor beside him. "Come here." His voice is a quiet growl. "Come down here with me."

I lie down next to him, snuggling into his chest when he slides an arm around me, squeezing me close.

"How long was I asleep?" I ask.

"A couple hours."

I feel like I could sleep for another decade, but at the same time, I don't want to waste a single second with him.

"Is there anything else we need to cover?" I ask, looking up at him.

"I'm sure there is," he says, "but right now I'm just sort of . . . rewiring everything inside my head."

"I mean . . . that's understandable. I've had eleven years to process it, you've had just a moment. I want you to know—it's okay if you have some hurt here." I rub my hand over his breastbone. "I know it's not going to be this immediate clearing of the air."

He takes a few seconds before replying, and when he does, his voice is hoarse. "Losing you was the worst thing that's ever happened to me, and I still feel the echo of that—those were really hard years—but it helps, knowing. As terrible as it is, it helps to know." He looks at me, and his eyes fill again. "I'm so sorry I wasn't there when Duncan died."

"I'm so sorry I didn't tell you. I'm sorry I just vanished." I kiss his shoulder.

He reaches up with his free hand, wiping a palm down his face. "Honey, you lost your mom at ten, and your dad at eighteen. It sucks that you disappeared, but it's not like I don't get it. Holy shit, your life just . . . crumbled that day."

I move my hand under his shirt, up over his stomach, coming to rest above his heart. "It was terrible." I press my face to where his neck meets shoulder, trying to push away those memories and inhaling the familiar smell of him. "What were those years like for you?"

He hums, thinking. "I focused on school. If you mean romantically, I had so much guilt that I didn't really get involved with anyone until later."

My heart aches at this. "Alex said you didn't bring anyone home until Rachel."

"Can we be clear about one thing?" he says, kissing my hair. "Definitively, and without question?"

"What's that?" I love the solid feel of him next to me. I don't think I'll ever get enough.

"That I love you," he whispers, tilting my chin so I'll look up at him. "Okay?"

"I love you, too." Emotion fills my chest, making my words come out strangled. I will always miss my parents, but I have Elliot back. Together we were able to resurrect something.

His lips press to my forehead. "Do you think we can do

this?" he asks, keeping his lips there. "Do we get our chance now to be *together* together?"

"We've certainly earned it."

He pulls back, looking at me. "I've just been lying here, thinking. In some ways, I should have figured it out. I should have wondered why Duncan never came back. I just assumed you were both so angry at me."

"Over time I let myself trust my memories more." I reach up, brushing his hair out of his eyes. "I realized whether or not you had something casual and consistent with Emma, you did really love me."

"Of course I did." He stares, eyes tight. "I hate that Duncan died thinking otherwise."

There's not really anything I can say to this. I just squeeze him tighter, pressing my lips to the pulse point beneath his jaw.

"I still love this room," I whisper.

Beside me, Elliot goes still. "It's funny you say that . . . I love it, too. But I came in here to say goodbye."

My heart peeks over the cliff, falling off. "What does that mean?"

He pushes up on an elbow, looking down at me. "It means I don't think we belong in here anymore."

"Well, no, we won't be in here all the time. But why not keep the cabin, and—"

"I mean, look, obviously it's yours, and you should do with it what you want." He runs his fingertip below my lip and bends, kissing me once. When he pulls away, I chase his mouth, wanting more. "But I want us to move past this closet," he says gently. "The closet isn't why we fell in love. We made this room special, not the other way around."

I know my expression looks devastated, and I don't know how to reel it back in. I love being in here with him. The best years of my life were in here, and I've never felt safer than I do in the closet.

And that's when I know Elliot is already two steps ahead of me.

"I bet, the way you see it, everything fell apart when we tried to live outside," he says, and leans down, kissing me again. "But that's just shitty luck. It isn't going to be that way this time."

"No?" I ask, biting back a relieved smile and tugging at his shoulders so he hovers over me.

"No." He grins, settling between my legs, his eyes going a little unfocused.

"What *is* it going to be like this time?" I slide his glasses off, setting them on one of the empty shelves.

Elliot kisses a slow path up my neck. "It's going to be what we wanted before."

"Thanksgiving on the floor in our underwear?"

He growls out a little laugh, pressing his hips forward when I reach down, lowering his zipper. "And you in my bed, every night."

"Maybe you'll be in *my* bed."

When he pulls back, his eyes narrow. "Then you have to actually go to your damn house, woman."

I laugh, and he laughs, too, but the truth of this sits between us, making him go still. He watches me, and I can tell it's turned into a question during our silence; he's not letting me off the hook.

"Will you go with me? To clean it out?" I wince, admitting, "I haven't been back in a really long time."

Elliot kisses me once, and then ducks, kissing my chest over my heart. "I've been waiting for you to come home for eleven years. I'll go anywhere you go."

now

wednesday, january 10

'm hit with a powerful blast of nostalgia as soon as we open
the door. Inside, the Berkeley house smells just as it always
has—like home—but I don't think I realized before how *home*
smells like Mom's cedar trunk we used as a coffee table, and
Dad's Danish cigarettes—apparently he snuck them more
than I knew. A sunbeam bursting in through the living room
window captures a few tiny stars of dust, spinning. I have a
woman come and clean the house once a month, but even
though things look tidy, the place still feels abandoned.

It sends a guilty ache spearing through my middle.

Elliot comes up behind me, peeking over my shoulder

and into the living room. "Do you think we'll make it inside today?"

He softens his joke with a kiss to my shoulder, and I can't exactly blame him for the gentle jab: we've driven by the house twice now, late at night after my shifts at the hospital. I've been too mentally drained to feel up to rejoining my childhood home. But I don't work until tonight, and today I woke up feeling . . . ready.

Our plan for now is to sell the Healdsburg house and clean out the Berkeley place to make it ready for visiting Cal faculty who want a furnished rental. But cleaning it out for this means taking all the important memories with me— photo albums, artwork, letters, tiny mementos sprinkled everywhere.

I take a step in, and then another. The wood floor creaks where it always did. Elliot follows me in, looking around. "This house smells like Duncan."

"Doesn't it?"

He hums, passing me to walk over to the mantel, where there are photos of the three of us, of Kennet and Britt, of Mom's parents, who died when she was young.

"You know, I've only ever seen one photo of her. The one Duncan had next to his bed."

Her. My mother. Laís, to everyone else. Mãe, to me.

Elliot trails his fingers over a few frames and then picks one up, studying it, before looking over at me.

I know which one he's holding. It's a picture Dad took of

me and Mom at the beach. The wind is blowing her long black hair across her neck, and I'm leaning against her, sitting between her legs, with her arms wrapped around my chest. Her smile was so wide and bright; in it, you can see without having to be told that she was an absolute force of nature.

He blinks down to it again. "You look so much like her, it's uncanny."

"I know." I am so grateful for the passing of time, that I can see her face and be glad that I inherited it from her, rather than terrified that looking in the mirror would be a greater torture every day as I aged and began to look more like how I remembered her.

I kneel down by the cedar trunk, where all our photos, letters, and keepsakes live.

"This one should go in our apartment."

The lid to the trunk is halfway up when Elliot says this, and I lower it back down without looking. Warmth spreads so quickly through my limbs that I grow light-headed. "'Our apartment'?"

He looks up from the picture. "I was thinking we should move in somewhere together. In the city."

It's only been ten days since we got back together, but even in that time, the commute between us is a beast. Renting a room from Nancy means that having "company" stay over is awkward enough to be impossible. And Elliot is simply too far away from the hospital for me to stay with him, either.

Most nights, he meets me for a late dinner in the city and then drives home, and I fall into bed.

The one day off I had in that time—two days ago—we didn't ever leave his apartment. We made love in his bed, on the floor, in the kitchen. For a brief pulse I imagine having access to him—to his voice and hands and laugh and weight over me every time I come home—and the desire for it becomes a second pulse in my chest.

"You'd move to the city?" I ask.

Elliot sets the picture down and sits beside me on the worn Persian rug. "Do you really question that?" Behind his glasses, his eyes seem nearly amber in the sunlight coming in the window. His lashes are so long.

I want to kiss him so much right now my mouth waters. I know we have work to do, but I'm distracted by the stubble on his jaw, and how easy it would be to climb into his lap and make love to him right now.

"Macy?" he says, grinning under the force of my attention.

I blink up to his face. "It's a big commute for you."

"My hours are more flexible than yours," he says, and then a wicked light fills his eyes. "And having you in bed every night might help inspire ideas for my dragon porn."

I laugh. "I *knew* it."

We move in together on March 1. It's pouring rain, and our apartment is a tiny one-bedroom, but it has a huge bay window and is only a half block away from the bus line that takes me directly to work. Elliot and his three brothers build a wall of bookcases, and—maybe a little awkwardly—Mr. Nick and Miss Dina bring us a new bed. I would have protested, but it's a beautiful four-poster frame, handmade by one of Mr. Nick's longtime patients. Alex, Else, and Liz drive to Nest Bedding to buy all manner of bed dressings—because neither Elliot nor I care what our sheets look like—and Miss Dina makes dinner while we all unpack, crammed into the small space.

By seven, the whole apartment smells like bay leaves and roasting chicken, and the rain outside turns from a downpour into a rare, violent thunderstorm, lightning cracking in bright flashes of light outside. Alex dances as she slips books onto the shelves, and we all watch her covertly, awestruck that something so profoundly graceful could have emerged from this gene pool. Out of a moment of quiet, Liz and George announce that they're having a baby, and the room erupts into noise and motion. Else cranks the music—and the energy whips into a frenzy of laughter and dancing.

Elliot pulls me to the side, pressing against me. I've never seen him make this expression before. It's more than a smile; it's relieved delight.

"Hey," he says, and rests his smile on mine.

I stretch for another kiss when he pulls away. "Hey. You good?"

"Yeah, I'm good." He looks around the room as if to say, *Look at this awesome place.* "We just *moved in together.*"

"Finally, right?" I bite my lip, feeling the urge to scream, I'm so happy.

I've never felt this way before.

Tonight we're going to fall asleep together, in our apartment, in our bed. When everyone is gone, we'll forget about the boxes we still have to unpack. He'll follow me under the covers with that hungry tension in his eyes, his bare skin sliding over mine until we're a breathless, sweaty tumble. We'll fall asleep, entangled, without even realizing it.

And I'll wake up before it's light out, and want him again.

In the morning, he'll be here. His clothes will be here, and his books, and his toothbrush. I'll pour cereal while he showers. Maybe he'll come find me in the kitchen holding a cup of coffee and I won't know he's there until I feel the press of his lips to the top of my head. The anticipation I feel for this everyday life of moving around him is so enormous, it fills me with a heavy, shimmering heat.

We aren't even really dancing; we're just swaying in place again, like we did at the wedding. But tonight, we have no secrets remaining, and no scary conversations looming. The past decade seems like a foggy blur, like we took a long road trip from one point of the earth and back again, traveling in a wide circle, destined to end up here.

Elliot's hands slide lower on my back, his head bends close to mine. George cracks a joke about us needing to get a room. Andreas cracks back that George is the one with the knocked-up wife. And then Miss Dina is off on a tear in the kitchen about babies, and maybe more weddings, and I watch Elliot struggle to block it all out. He winces, shifting his glasses up his nose, and studies me the way he always did, as if he could read my mind one blink at a time.

Maybe he could.

"Favorite word?" he whispers.

I don't even hesitate: "*You.*"

acknowledgments

Some of our books have little pieces of our history, some have pieces of people we know, and some have little pieces of us. And then there are books like *Love and Other Words* that have big pieces of all three.

I (Lauren) was raised in Northern California and spent most of my weekends from age seven onward on the Russian River with my family, in one of three funky little cabins we owned throughout the years. They weren't fancy, they weren't fussy—they were small, occasionally damp, shaded by trees, and surrounded by the babbling of the Russian River, or a little creek outside. Much like Duncan did for Macy, my parents got a weekend retreat as a way to get us out of the stress of our lives for a couple days each week, and at a time when buying a modest home in a small town wasn't prohibitively expensive for a middle-income family.

The area—from Jenner to Guerneville to Healdsburg to Santa Rosa—has been a constant in my life. My sister and I were both married in Healdsburg. My parents spent some of their happiest times together in the Russian River valley. We go there for vacations, reunions, girls trips.

Sometimes I think about my childhood weekends now, and how lucky we were to have a place like that. I think, too, about how it is to be a mother with small children, who—even at seven and eleven—sometimes still seem so plugged into the digital world. I wonder what it will be like for them, and whether it will be hard for me to not give them the same kind of retreat, where they can read for hours in a closet, or make a friend like Elliot, or simply unplug for two solid days.

But mostly I'm sort of devastated, because much of this area has burned in the recent fires in and around Santa Rosa. A house I rented this summer while we were editing this book is now nothing but ash and rubble. But it makes me exponentially more grateful that we wrote this book, that the memories of those areas and spaces are still fresh in Elliot and Macy's story.

This is our first foray into women's fiction, and it really was a complete joy to write. We were encouraged by our two most influential book people: our editor, Adam Wilson, and our agent, Holly Root, who waited for the right idea to come along before urging us to try a different voice. Gallery Books / Simon & Schuster is an unbelievably supportive place and we are grateful to everyone there for reading and loving and helping promote this book as much as they have: Carolyn Reidy, who heads up S&S; Jen Bergstrom, who runs Gallery Books; our marketing loves, Liz Psaltis, Diana Velasquez, Abby Zidle, and Mackenzie Hickey. Thank you, Laura Waters, for keeping us all organized, on time, and for giving Adam crap regularly since we're not around to do it in person. Thank you to the publicity department and particularly Theresa Dooley and our own precious Kristin Dwyer who, most days, feels like the Third Musketeer. We adore the cover, John Vairo and Lisa Litwack. And to the S&S sales team: next time in NYC, your drinks are on us—pinkie promise.

Thank you, Erin Service, for not only reading this over and over, searching for every tiny error, but also—as Lo's sister—for living so many of those Cabin Moments. Thank you, Marcia and James Billings, for taking us there. We lost one house in a flood and kept the next for over a decade, but every inch of that world will be precious to me forever.

Thank you, Christina, for writing this book with me, for learning and caring about this place as much as I do, for tunneling back in time to figure out who these kids were. We came up with these characters seven years ago, and I'm so glad we found the best place to put them.

We are so lucky that we get to do this and marvel every time that when people ask us what we do in our free time, we get to say, "We think about what we're going to write next."

love
and
other words

CHRISTINA LAUREN

This readers group guide for *Love and Other Words* includes an introduction, discussion questions, and ideas for enhancing your book club. The suggested questions are intended to help your reading group find new and interesting angles and topics for your discussion. We hope that these ideas will enrich your conversation and increase your enjoyment of the book.

Introduction

When Macy and her dad move in to their weekend house in the wine country outside of San Francisco, little do they realize how dramatically this decision will impact the rest of their lives. It is in this house that Macy first falls in love with her neighbor Elliot and comes to understand the complexity of love and heartache. The novel is told in two timelines—in the past, when Macy's mom has just died and her father is searching for a weekend home to help heal their fractured family, and in the present, when Macy and Elliot run into each other suddenly after being estranged for almost eleven years. At once thrilling and heart-wrenching, *Love and Other Words* is a celebration of the fragility of love, the beauty of literature, and the strength of true friendship to overcome anything.

Topics and Questions
for Discussion

1. In the prologue, Macy thinks back on watching her parents interact as a child, noticing the way they would hug each other, noticing the totality of their love: "It never occurred to me that love could be anything other than all-consuming. Even as a child, I knew I never wanted anything less" (p. 2). In what ways do you think Macy's parents' marriage is a sort of paradigm for Macy's future relationships? Does this desire for an "all-consuming" love color her decision to take things slow with Elliot initially? Do you think it impacts her decision to marry Sean? How so?

2. When Macy and Elliot run into each other in the coffee shop, Macy feels excitement and dread simultaneously, claiming "I've wanted to see him every day. But also, I never wanted to see him again" (p. 26). How does the contradiction of this statement relate to the novel's theme of love? Do you think falling in love might also be described as both wonderful and terrible?

3. Discuss the structure of the novel. How does the movement from past to present impact your understanding of Macy and Elliot? Do you feel more sympathetic to Macy's decision in light of seeing her both as a child at the start of a relationship and as an adult in its aftermath? Why or why not?

4. In an early email exchange, Macy writes to Elliot the following postscript: "No one here understands that I just want to be another girl at school not the kid whose mom died and who needs to be treated like she can break. Thanks for just saying stuff and not acting like it's all taboo" (p. 82). Connect this notion to the title. How do words shape Elliot and Macy's relationship? Do you agree that it is through the power of words that the two discover what it means to love?

5. Despite the fact that Macy's mother is deceased for the entirety of the novel, her presence looms large. It is her

list that inspired the purchase of the Healdsburg house to begin with, the catalyst that sets Macy and Elliot on their journey. Discuss Macy's mother as a character. In what ways do you find her haunting the pages of the novel? Can you find other instances when she impacts the choices the characters make?

6. Discuss Macy's career choice. Do you think her decision to care for sick children is a result of losing her parents so young? Of losing the love of her life?

7. When Macy first gets her period, she reads a letter from her mother, who writes, "You are my masterpiece" (p. 121). In what ways does Macy heed her mother's advice and care for her body? In what ways does she disregard her mother's wish that she care for herself?

8. Macy muses on page 136 that her dad "made a good living . . . but what we could never buy was chaos and bustle." Why do you think Macy is so attracted to the Petropoulos family? Is it that opposites attract, or is it something more?

9. A possible definition of love emerges on page 205 after Macy begins to reconsider her life with Sean. "I'm terrified of what I'm feeling," she says. "I feel like I've just woken up." As someone who loves words, why do

you think Macy finds it so difficult to articulate how she feels?

10. Loss plays a central role in *Love and Other Words*. Discuss the different kinds of loss that occur in the novel. Do all the characters handle loss similarly, or does "pressing down the familiar bubble of need" (p. 228) seem unique to Macy's character?

11. Answer Elliot's question to Macy on page 236: "Are you *staying* because of Phoebe?" If not, why does Macy stay in a relationship with Sean for so long?

12. The scene Macy walks into on that fateful New Year's Eve stands in stark contrast to the scene years later at Elliot's brother's wedding when the two friends say "I love you" face-to-face for the first time (p. 336). What other examples of contrasts can you think of in the novel? Consider Macy's family, Elliot's family, Sean, Elliot, and the past versus the present in your response.

13. Revisit the scene where Macy reveals what happened in the hours after she found Elliot passed out with Emma. Why do you think it took her so long to find the words to tell Elliot this story, the story he so desperately needed to hear?

14. Why does Elliot want "to move past this closet" (p. 395)? Do you agree with Elliot that you can't go backward and that the key to happiness is moving forward?

Enhance Your Book Club

1. Macy and Elliot's love affair begins over an innocent love of literature. The pair spends hours in Macy's closet, devouring books and sharing that contented silence of reading together. With your book club, read *Pay It Forward*, the first book the pair bonded over as children and a book that encourages hope. Share with your reading group why you think both Macy and Elliot liked this novel. What reasons do Macy and Elliot have to find hope in the world? Do they find it, eventually? Do you see yourself as more inherently hopeful, like Elliot, or more hopeless, like Macy?

2. Arguably the moment Macy admits to herself that she is in love with Elliot is at his brother's wedding when the musician plays a rendition of Jeff Buckley's "Hallelujah." Host a dinner party with your book club. Over dinner and drinks, listen to this song and imagine you are there with Macy. Why do you think this particular song made her feel like she wasn't alone? Can you point to a specific moment in the song that might have contributed to Macy's feelings? As you listen, consider if it is the words or the music—or the combination—that creates a feeling of comfort. Share your experience listening to the song with your group. Do you have a song that reminds you of a moment you fell in love?

3. Host a game night with your book club. As part of the fun, play Elliot and Macy's favorite word game. Be sure to mimic the rules by which the couple played the game. That is, no overthinking! Just say whatever word comes to mind first. After a few rounds, discuss the results. How do the kinds of words that popped into your head reflect who you are? Do you agree that letting someone into your subconscious in this way is an intimate act?

praise for the novels of
Christina Lauren

"At turns hilarious and gut-wrenching, this is a tremendously fun slow burn."

—*The Washington Post* on *Dating You / Hating You*
(A Best Romance of 2017 selection)

"Delightful."

—*People* on *Roomies*

"A passionate and bittersweet tale of love in all of its wonderfully terrifying reality . . . Lauren successfully tackles a weighty subject with both ferocity and compassion."

—*Booklist* on *Autoboyography*

"Christina Lauren hilariously depicts modern dating."

—*Us Weekly* on *Dating You / Hating You*

"Perfectly captures the hunger, thrill, and doubt of young, modern love."

—*Kirkus Reviews* on *Wicked Sexy Liar*

"Christina Lauren's books have a place of honor on my bookshelf."

—Sarah J. Maas, bestselling author of *Throne of Glass*

"Truly a romance for the twenty-first century. [*Dating You / Hating You* is] a smart, sexy romance for readers who thrive on girl power."

—*Kirkus Reviews* (starred review)